James Terry grew up in New Mexico. He has a BA in English from the University of California, Berkeley, and worked in film and television production in the San Francisco Bay Area before moving to Dublin, Ireland, where he lived for six years, teaching English. His short stories have appeared in numerous literary journals and have been nominated for the Pushcart and O. Henry prizes. Since leaving Dublin he has lived and worked in New Delhi, India and Edmonton, Canada. He currently lives in Liverpool, England, with his wife and son.

By the same author
Kingdom of the Sun

The
Solitary Woman
of
SHAKESPEARE

JAMES TERRY

SANDSTONEPRESS
HIGHLAND | SCOTLAND

Published in Great Britain by
Sandstone Press Ltd
Dochcarty Road
Dingwall
Ross-shire
IV15 9UG
Scotland.

www.sandstonepress.com

Copyright (c) James Terry 2016

author   copyright,

The publi   rds publica-

ISBN: 978-1-910985-19-9
ISBNe: 978-1-910985-20-5

Cover design by Mark Ecob
Typeset by Iolaire Typesetting, Newtonmore
Printed and bound by TOTEM.COM.PL

For Deana

Leading his burro through a grassy clearing in the woods, the last old prospector of those parts came upon a mattress, the ticking here and there a little foxed but otherwise in excellent condition.

'Don't mind if I do,' he told himself, lowering his weary bones onto the mattress. It was the softest thing he had ever felt. Too soft by far for a man like him, the earth his only bed. Eyes closed, he wondered how it was that such a mattress came to be there, so high in these mountains once prowled by savages, and it seemed to him he once heard a tale, told by a Mexican somewhere, a tale of a town called Shakespeare. It was a vague recollection, of a woman and a mattress and a play and a hanging, a strange eventful history. He doubted that this could be the same mattress, for that was many years ago, and even in country as dry as this a mattress would show its age, if so aged it was.

Night was falling, the air grown cold. In time he labored up from the mattress and went to his burro for a blanket. Looking back at the mattress, bright as the moon against the dead brown grass, he felt a stab of loneliness the likes of which he had never experienced in all his years of solitary wandering.

'Come on, old gal,' he said, guiding his burro to the mattress. He wrestled her down and wrapped a leg around her haunches and an arm around her neck, and there despite her braying he snuggled up against her warm, hairy bulk. Soon all was quiet save the burro's steady breaths and the sound of the wind in the trees.

I

ONE

They set out from Bird in the blue light of dawn, Brent at the reins, Troy beside him, both boys hunched against the high mountain chill. Low in the west three stars and half a tissue-thin moon still clung to the vault of heaven. Junipers and cedars, black and silent as sleeping bears, hunkered low on the grassy foothills of the Bird Range, southern prong of the Aguja wilderness. Barring a few lamplit windows on the outskirts of town, all was dark, all was blue. On the bed of the buckboard, softly luminous in the moonlight, lay a queen-size mattress filled with the choicest quality white hair, bound in superior ticking, two large goose-down pillows at the head of it echoing in their gentle undulations the contours of the road.

Brent snapped the reins, and the mules broke into a reluctant half-trot, wending their way across the fertile plain, drawing ever nearer the long, lonely road to Shakespeare.

For the nourishment of her sons, Mrs. Copes had packed into a potato sack a loaf of coarse bread, a quarter-wheel of asedero cheese, half a dozen sticks of Ibex jerky, an eight-ounce tin of Meyer's Potted Pork, a jar of her own prickly pear preserves, and a small tin of salted pecans. Feeling peckish as they rolled through the deep sand of Pheasant Canyon, the Copes boys pulled out of the road and halted the mules beside a walnut tree, and there beneath the low lattice of branches and leaves they sat and ate, the only sounds their own and the sleepy synaphea of cicadas. All around their island of shade throbbed a sea of light and heat.

The brothers ate without much talk, each boy easy in his private thoughts.

At length Brent yawned and said, 'Think I'll have me a little rest.'

He took off his boots and climbed over the box onto the mattress. Pillow beneath his head, he sighed such that Troy, hearing in his brother's voice the essence of contentment, took off his boots and followed suit.

There in the sun-dappled shade they lay, hats over faces, bellies full, heads cushioned by the cloudlike softness of down.

'Funny to think what'll be goin on on this here mattress fore long,' Troy said. 'And here's me and you havin a snoozy noon on it.'

'That all you can think about?' Brent said.

Troy smiled. 'It's like I got a little picture of the future keeps flittin fore my eyes. Right on this here mattress. The things a man and a woman'll get up to, particular when she's the only one they is.'

'Uh-hm,' Brent said without much interest.

'Won't know a thing about you and me lyin here under this tree thinkin on em in all kinds of funny ways.'

'That what we're doin, is it?'

Troy picked a piece of jerky from his teeth and licked it from his finger.

'Sure wouldn't want to be that woman,' he said. 'Only

2

woman in a place like that. Nothin but lowlife miners and gamblers. Town like that's no place for a woman. No, sir, I wouldn't want to be that woman. That man neither. Puttin on airs with a rich man's mattress.'

'Hell,' Brent said. 'He got himself a deal.'

'More trouble than it's worth if you ask me,' Troy said. 'Ten percent off and no freight. What's that? $16.50. That's a dollar sixty-five, makes fifteen, fifty minus sixty-five makes fifteen cents. Fifteen, eighty-five cents. $15.85.'

'$14.85.'

'And the ten dollars' freight, and the pillows thrown in to boot. Pop's practically givin it away.'

'Aint about the money, is it?' Brent said. 'No lady from the East intends on livin behind a saloon the rest of her life. Sooner or later she'll be clamorin for a house of her own. Rugs. Drapes. Sofa. Chairs. Settles. Bureaus.'

'If I was him,' Troy said, 'I woulda ordered it fore she got there. Lord knows what he's had her sleepin on all this time. Stinkin bag a cobs most likely. Probably never thought about it till she said,you expect me to sleep on that thing?'

'It's mighty big of you stickin up for the lady,' Brent said. 'Now how about you can it for a spell and let me get a little rest. We got a long way yet.'

Troy rolled onto his side, facing away from his brother. It was a while before he spoke again.

'Seems to me marryin's more trouble than it's worth when five dollars gets you more'n enough whore for a night. Seems to me it aint nothin but greed, a man not happy havin it once a week, once a month in the lean times, got to have it ever night. That's where we gone wrong as a civilization, I reckon. You think them Indians

3

saddle up to one woman and never look to another? Hell no. They screw any damn thing they feel like, they own daughters and sisters. No, sir, they aint as dumb as people make em out.'

To these observations Brent made no response.

'I wish they was somethin we could leave on this mattress so one day they'd know we was thinkin on em. A little message or somethin. Hey there, from the Copes boys. We was thinkin on you all them times you was doin it.'

Troy continued to share his thoughts with his brother until, hearing him snoring, he adjusted his pillow and likewise drifted off.

They awoke abake in the sun, glazed in the odors of denim and mulehide. A red-tailed hawk glided down from the sky while they were putting on their boots and, wings rowing backwards, landed on a branch of a walnut tree fifty yards up the road. Facing right, it sat motionless, the sun beating hard against its dark brown feathers.

Brent saw it first and nudged his brother and pointed. From the side of the mattress Troy quietly picked up the rifle and brought it to his shoulder.

'You hit him,' Brent said, 'and I'll forget what Ma said about not lettin you near that saloon.'

A small smile cracked the edges of Troy's chapped lips. He squinted his left eye, pursed his lips, and gently pulled the trigger.

Abigail stands in the front doorway of the saloon, watching Shakespeare come awake. In that soft morning light she sometimes finds beauty in the very wretchedness of the town. Heaps of junk — broken and spare wagon parts, empty crates, whiskey bottles, bull skulls, dismantled stoves, tin cans, sledgehammer handles, piles of rock, horseshoes, lumber, lanterns, all tangled in dead and living weeds — skirt the front and sides of every building. There are no awnings or sidewalks to speak of, and the shoddy wooden buildings with their false upper stories do little to inspire the sense of permanency the name would seem to suggest. Weeds and grasses grow freely here and there in the wide dusty street, fertilized by scattered clods of horse and mule shit. All these things, viewed against the desolation of the dull brown hills of mesquite and prickly pear and yucca and creosote, bitten through by jagged gray and blue mountains, strike Abigail at this milder time of day as worthy somehow of forgiveness. This feeling seldom lasts.

Three weeks have passed since she arrived in Shakespeare, and still she hasn't become accustomed to the monotony. Sometimes she wishes she were down in the mine with the miners, swinging a hammer against the rock. The hours between one and five in the afternoon, when she is alone, are the worst. Shakespeare is utterly still. She has tried many things to make her afternoons more bearable. She made a new dress for herself. She started reading the Bible from the beginning. She baked five different cakes. But the hours in Shakespeare are immense. Sometimes she rereads Henry's letters and feels she was deceived.

'Go then,' her mother said. 'Go and leave me to die alone.' The same mother who called her a whore. The youngest sister of four, Abigail had witnessed three times how women sold themselves to the highest bidder. In the case of the homely, dowerless Walker girls, to men who would spend the rest of their days under the double yoke of labor and drink. Wanting to see for herself what all

5

the fuss about putting a man in one's belly was, Abigail, sixteen at the time, tested her curiosity on her eldest sister's husband, which he repaid in kind one sleepy Sunday afternoon in the kitchen pantry, and, to Abigail's amusement in her power over this thoroughly uninteresting man, every Sunday afternoon thenceforth until Abigail's mother, seeking only a tin of stewed tomatoes, found something altogether different. That same year Abigail went to work at the button factory, sorting bad from good, boiling in the summer, freezing in the winter. She was still there when one day, four years later, a small ad at the back of the newspaper caught her eye. *Man in Territory seeks correspondence with adventurous gal.*

All spring she eagerly awaited each new letter from the man who wrote such lovely things about Shakespeare and the life that would be hers if she chose to come, all expenses paid, and be his wife. 'Don't listen to what any fool man in the Territory says in a letter,' her mother warned her. 'Saloonkeeper. That's the last place a girl as smart as you wants to end up.' But she had already made up her mind. She would start over, somewhere new, where no one knew who she was. In her sixth letter she accepted his proposition. Four weeks later his reply arrived with a draft for forty dollars and detailed instructions on which trains to take, which stagecoaches, what to do and not to do as a woman traveling alone in the Territory, and reading these things set her heart racing with excitement. She had always considered herself a practical person, and she conceived of her journey to the Territory in those terms. If this was the price of starting over, she told herself, then so be it.

All through that long, arduous journey from the East, through all the discomforts and ignominies for a woman traveling alone, it was Henry's words that helped her through. Whenever she was feeling low and afraid, she would take out and reread the letters, and to know that he was out there, waiting for her, gave her strength. Even when she stepped down from the stage into a throng of men seemingly gone mad with jubilation and he stepped forward to say, 'Miss Walker?' she had not faltered, for he had never said he was young, and it was her own fault if she had pictured him as such, and she knew in her heart she would have come anyway even had she known. Only when she discovered on her second day in Shakespeare that she was the only woman there did Abigail begin to feel, with an awful, sinking sensation, that she had been deceived.

The following Saturday they were married in the saloon. Crawford performed the brief ceremony. Vows were exchanged, a tentative kiss, then off popped the cork from a bottle of champagne and drinks all around. The first dance went to the groom, then every miner got his turn. The fiddler played and the dancers danced and all drinks were on the house, all night, and not a man left the establishment sober, and many did not leave at all, until morning, their eyes smiling, hungry for Abigail, their own sweet Abigails. Mrs. Abigail Jonson. Overnight, she was no longer herself.

'I'll wager you a glass a whiskey she aint on that stage,' a miner at the bar pronounced to Abigail one dull Friday afternoon. His face was badly sunburned, bits of dead skin flaking from his nose and forehead, and there were grains of black powder tattooed into his cheeks.

'I'm not the gambling sort,' Abigail replied as she tipped the barrel, pouring whiskey through the funnel into an empty bottle. Apart from a handful of miners, a few gamblers, and two of Shakespeare's stray dogs, the Ore was dead.

The Ore Saloon and Gaming House was the oldest building in Shakespeare. It was a squat adobe with a flat roof, a narrow white door, and one small square window to the right of the door. Legend had it that it was the station keeper's house for the Overland Mail when Shakespeare was known as Mexican Springs and there was nothing there but it and the well, and before that, before the Territory had come into being, it had belonged to an old Mexican man who lived there with his dog and a small flock of sheep. Little of the building had changed in the intervening years. The sign had gone up and the bar installed, but the gaps between the original piñon floor planks were still wide enough in places for a snake to slither through. Half a dozen crude tables and an assortment of chairs, crates, and trunks, no two alike, were strewn haphazard across the room. Against one wall stood a pianola that refused to perform no matter how hard or how often it was kicked. The ceiling was so low that Daryl Henderson, the tallest man in town at five feet eleven inches, routinely smacked his head against the vigas. With the exception of the smeared remains of dead flies and other winged insects, the whitewashed walls were wholly bare of adornment.

Dim in the daytime, a cave at night, the Ore was an unlikely place for a woman, and it took some time for the miners to get used to seeing one behind the bar. It took much longer for Abigail to get used to being there, to feeling their eyes undressing her, her body a source of limitless diversion from their private travails. They stumbled in after a night in the mines, stinking of their exertions, covered with sweat and dust and candledrip,

8

gashes and welts showing through grimy flesh, and collapsed in the chairs, silent and morose. Only after their second whiskeys did their shoulders begin to relax, the sharp creases in their faces soften. Out came the soiled decks of cards, the letters for third readings, pocketknives to jab between splayed fingers.

Abigail took some empty glasses from the bar and dunked them in the bucket of water.

The miner smiled to himself and took another sip of his whiskey.

'She won't come,' he said, peering pensively into his glass. After a while he leaned over and said to Abigail in a conspiratorial whisper: 'You want to hear what I think it is? I think either God or the devil is behind it. They put some kinda fence around this town, a fence you caint see, just to keep women out. It's some kinda test of us. And I can tell you exactly where the borders of this fence is because I been keepin track.'

Two miners on either side of the orator rolled their eyes and ordered more whiskeys.

He pulled a wrinkled, filthy piece of paper from his pocket, carefully unfolded it and set it on the bar. It was a crude, hand-drawn map of the Mendrugo Valley, boxes representing the town, cone-shaped mountains all around. Clusters of dots made a rough circle around Shakespeare, a woman's name and a date scrawled beside each. He pointed with a mashed fingernail at one of the dots and said: 'That one there's mine. Louise. All these others is where ladies changed their minds on the rest of us. There's Jenkins there. There's Kinney. There's Holt. All round Shakespeare. Now why are all them dots the same distance from Shakespeare? Darn good question, Mrs. Jonson. It took me a long time myself to realize what

9

was goin on. It wadn't till after it happened to Taggart out near Lizard Wells, which I jest happened to know is ten miles due south a town, and thinkin that was about how far I'd been when Louise turned on me, I went back there and lo and behold, ten miles. So I went and asked all the others where their ladies turned back on em and sure enough ever last one of em was ten miles outside Shakespeare in one direction or another. I've checked em all. Ever last one is ten miles from town. Now you tell me the hand of a higher power aint behind this.'

'Hobbs!' one of the miners barked from a table. 'You gonna bring me that goddamn whiskey any time this year?'

Hobbs folded up his map and slid it back into his pocket. He ordered a whiskey and after Abigail had poured it he took it to the table from which he had been summoned.

'Don't pay him no heed,' one of the miners at the bar told Abigail with a wink. 'He's got lead poisnin. Kelly caught him the other day out on a boulder, starin at the sun.'

Just then the stagecoach pulled into town. Buddy, the white-bearded driver who knowing Abigail was fond of cashews often brought a small bag of them for her from Bird, jumped from the boot before the wheels had stopped rolling and ran splay-legged into the Ore.

'They're dead!' he hollered. 'I seen em with my own eyes up in Pheasant Canyon. Naked! Scalped! Mutilated! Sweet Jesus! I known them since they was kids. They was Copes' only boys.'

At the sound of these words Abigail felt a strange nervous elation sweep through her. The few miners in the saloon sober enough to think took in Buddy's news with no more animation than if they had heard none at all. The gamblers in the back corner flicked the ash from their cigars and without so much as turning their eyes from their cards carried on with their hand.

Henry, hearing a panicked voice coming from the saloon, opened the door that separated their living quarters from the saloon proper. He glanced at Abigail and glanced away.

'For Christ's sake!' Buddy staggered. He looked at Abigail, as if seeking from that lone female face the outrage his news demanded.

'What's happened?' Henry asked.

'Indians got the Copes boys.'

'What about the mattress?'

'Mattress?' Buddy scowled at the word. 'There weren't no mattress.'

'No pillows neither?'

'No! No pillows, no mattress. What's gotten into you people? The Indians are on the warpath. We got to get out to the mines and warn the miners. Out to the ranches.'

Henry pulled his watch from his trouser pocket and looked at the time.

'No point goin out to the mines now,' he said. 'They'll be on their way in soon enough.'

Buddy shook his head in disgust.

'I don't know what's wrong with you people.'

He looked at Abigail and shook his head. She didn't know what to say. Henry poured a glass of whiskey and pushed it to the edge of the bar.

'Here,' he said. 'Have a drink.'

Two

If it had been up to Henry, he would have built a house for her long before she arrived. The problem, he explained to her that first night, was money. He needed at least five hundred dollars for the plot. Taking into account the monthly burdens of rent, fire insurance, liquor and gaming taxes, whiskey, food and other small but cumulatively substantial personal needs, not to mention the considerable moneys owed to the Ore by miners and gamblers whom Henry had allowed to drink on credit, it was easy to see why it was a rare month that the Ore cleared more than seventy-five dollars profit. Fifty was more common. At that rate it could take as long as another eight months before he had enough money for the plot. The price of land in a town like Shakespeare, on the verge of a boom, was liable to shoot up at a moment's notice to levels far beyond Henry's humble reach. More reason to buy the plot as soon as possible.

This was the thought on Henry's mind as he stood in the doorway between the parlor and the bedroom, waiting for Abigail to finish getting dressed. Every now and then another garment slid from the screen he had made for her from yucca shafts and cow hides. Hose. Skirt. Corset. Shirt. Other things he had no names for.

The length of this process was a revelation to Henry, for whom, apart from the matter-of-fact dressing of whores, for which he had seldom lingered around long enough to witness, the experience of waiting for a woman to put on her clothes was a rare event in his life.

'Do you want me to save the water?' she asked.

'No,' Henry answered, adding a thank you a few moments later.

A man of regular habits, Henry bathed only on Sundays. The rest of the week it sufficed to slick back his scant gray hair with perfumed jelly and keep his sideburns trimmed to the lean line of his jaw. Nor did his regularity of habit extend to drink or smoke. If it could be said that Henry Jonson had any vice at all it was his belief in the promise of patent medicines to deliver to mankind a prelapsarian state of health and vigor. In a polished mahogany case atop his chest of drawers he kept a diverse assortment of cures for everything from catarrh to St. Vitus dance, which nostrums he was forever recommending to his clientele. He liked to boast that he could spot a distemper from across the saloon. Seeing how pale Abigail was upon her arrival, Henry recommended to her — they were nearly his first words — Dr. Beaumont's Pennyroyal Pills, taken three times a day with a dram of sarsaparilla. It took Abigail a while to realize he actually had a sense of humor, so subtle was it. One day shortly after her arrival he had handed her the stalk of a yucca, about three feet long, sharpened to a point at one end. 'What's this for?' she had asked him. '*Snake*speare,' Henry had said with a wink.

'Who's watching the saloon?' Abigail asked, coming around at last from behind the screen, her hair still pinned up.

13

'Crawford's in there with some investor,' Henry said with a crooked little grin. 'I gave him the whole bottle.'

Abigail looked at him as if to say, *Are we going to do this or not?*

Henry's first impression of her had been that he had gambled and lost. She had a plain, boyish face that reminded him of one of his male cousins, and rather than make any effort to soften her features with feminine touches she did nothing at all. Her hair was the same light brown as her eyes and didn't so much drape or hang from her head as cling to it like a damp rag. Nor did her body curve or swell in the places Henry would have liked it to. But as the weeks had passed and still no other women came to Shakespeare, Henry became grateful for her lack of feminine allure. It cut down on his worry. The plainness of her person, coupled with her quiet strength, was gradually becoming, in his own mind, the most attractive thing about her.

He walked over and scooped her up into his arms as if she were nothing and carried her into the bedroom, setting her gently on the mattress on the floor. He yanked off his boots, pulled aside his braces and dropped his pants and drawers. Abigail was longer in removing the undergarments she had just put on, during which time Henry stood, eyes closed, muttering little obscenities to himself. When Abigail was ready she said so. Henry joined her on the mattress, kneeling before the tent of her dress, hem in hand the better to see what lay in the shadows beneath.

'Do you want me to do anything?' Abigail asked after a while.

Henry raised a silencing finger.

He continued to stare. Finally, having reached a state

14

of preparedness satisfactory to himself, he took her hand and brought it to his flaccid member.

It felt to her like the slack teat of the one cow she ever tried to milk. No matter how hard she had tugged and pulled, not a single drop squirted into the pail.

The first time it happened, the morning after the wedding, not yet knowing what fragile threads tethered man's organ to his heart, Abigail made a joke, only to be met with icy silence. Since then she had learned well the boundaries of acceptable behavior in the face of Henry's debility. To comfort was just as bad. To get up in a huff only slightly better. All she could do, she well knew, was wait, and then change the subject.

Henry, groaning, pulled her hand away and, red in the face, stood up and started to dress.

Abigail reached around and rubbed the small of her back where a corncob had been jabbing her through the mattress. She waited until he was nearly dressed before she spoke.

'That's promising news about the new vein in the Lear,' she said a little too cheerfully.

Henry grunted and rolled up his sleeves.

'Maybe that boom's coming sooner than we think.'

Henry straightened his collar and looked down at Abigail with unconcealed frustration.

'I never had this problem before,' he muttered.

Abigail sat up abruptly and pulled her dress over her knees, her face going pink and hot. She looked at him and thought of a number of things she could say to set the record straight. She wasn't the one who had failed to mention that the lovely little town of his letters possessed no church, no sheriff, no theater, and, oh yes, no women, and that he himself was old enough to be her grandfather.

But she said nothing. She only sat and fumed until he had left.

Standing at the back door, looking out across the barren wasteland of South Soda Flat, Abigail wondered if those boys had been alive when they were scalped.

It wasn't so much the debility, she had come to realize, that made things so difficult for her and Henry, but his own response to it, how he made it permeate and sour everything. She didn't know how to talk to him, this hard old man who was her husband. In some ways he reminded her of her father, who had died when she was six, killed when a stack of steel beams he was working near collapsed and crushed him, leaving her mother and sisters, and the small charity they could get from the church, to support the family. Not since then had Abigail lived under the same roof with a man. It was almost as if the intervening years had changed nothing; she was still that six-year-old girl, awkward and timid in the presence of this brooding being she was somehow united to. Because they worked at different times they didn't see each other much. He slept during the day, she at night. On the rare occasion that they ate supper together — normally she brought Henry's supper out to the saloon, where he ate standing at the bar — Abigail would find herself on the verge of asking him about his past, only to shrink at the prospect of learning something she would rather not know.

A cockroach fooled by the stillness ventured up from a gap in the floorboards and reconnoitered the nearby terrain. Abigail tapped her foot, and the roach described a frantic loop back into the dark. From the saloon came muffled sounds of drunken men. Laughter. Hollering. The rumble of the male voice box. Abigail thought to herself between the words of the Psalm she was reading that no such revelry enlivened her shift. Be it the fault of morning or the false propriety of men in the presence of a woman, she could not say.

She closed the Bible and sat long with it in her lap, as if sitting for a portrait of the eternity referred to therein.

An hour later she was still on the sofa, a bare pine box two feet square on her lap in place of the Bible. The lid of the box was open and she was handling one by one, as if not her own but some other woman's, the objects of sentiment and memory within. A small bundle of letters tied together by a piece of white lace. Bunches of dried flowers similarly tied. A tarnished silver locket in the shape of a heart. A small book of sonnets.

She took a cardstock stereograph titled *Sweet Southern Belle* from the box and bringing the tin mask of the stereoscope to her eyes she set it in the slot.

She had found it on the floor of the saloon one slow noon when she was sweeping, no one there but the oblivious gamblers, and it touched something in her, this tiny naked woman with the mellifluous name. She picked it up without hesitation and hid it behind the waist of her skirt. That night she took Henry's stereoscope down from the shelf, and by the time she had put it back there was a mauve-colored ring around her eye sockets. She had looked through stereoscopes before, thrilled to the sight of tree branches threatening to pierce her eyes, boulevards ablur with ghosts of moving people, colonnades of ancient temples receding far back in space and time, but never had the image before her pulsed with such life. Leaning back against the head of an ornate iron bed, a small Oriental fan in one hand doing little to conceal the contours of her pale naked body, the Sweet Southern

17

Belle peered out of her world through dark, taunting eyes. She was a young woman slender of build, with wavy black hair down to her waist. Her feet, protruding across the bed into the foreground, seemed close enough to touch, the pad of each toe a perfect little globe. A soft blur clouded the place where her pubes should have been.

Abigail knew every inch of the scene by heart, for not a night had passed since she found her that she had not taken the Sweet Southern Belle out of her keepsake box and shared her inmost feelings with her.

From the desert came the cry of a coyote, a mournful note pitched perfectly to the dull ache in Abigail's throat. The coyote was still crying when Abigail returned the stereoscope to its shelf and opened the back door. It was a moonless night, the air hotter outside than in. She could see nothing out there save patches of greater and lesser dark, as if the very darkness were a furnace giving heat but no light. Overhead the stars twinkled with almost nauseating clarity. Abigail thought she saw a lamp burning somewhere in the desert, miles and miles away. She remembered something a man had told her in the stagecoach. The Territory was full of men who had lost their minds trying to get rich. Reduced to the rags on their backs they either turned to crime or wandered off into the desert and became hermits, living like savages on mesquite beans and beetles. At night they burned cow patties to keep warm. Any given night you could look out across the desert and see their fires burning. But who would need fire to keep warm on a night such as this?

Abigail had been standing there for several minutes, lost in contemplation, when suddenly the door of the jakes swung open on its squeaky hinges and a figure stepped out and stood motionless. It was too dark to judge which way he was facing. Abigail stepped back into the room and, heart pounding, closed and bolted the door. Her back against the door, she listened, hearing only the noise of the saloon. At length she went to the window and looked out but saw no man there, saw nothing save her own ghostly reflection in the glass.

THREE

Their faces rouged by the sinking sun, A.W. Crawford and his young nephew sat eating their supper at the heavy oak table in the dining room. Points of rose-tinted light sparkled from the crystal glassware in the china cabinet against the west-facing wall. The sunlight warmed the somber hues of drapes, cushions, wallpaper and tassel. It pooled in every fret, every chase, every nameless touch of the lathe. All the tarnished silver was slowly turning to bronze.

Andy cut his piece of beef with a serrated knife and dipped it in his beans.

'Your beans always come out better than mine,' he said with an air of indignation, as if the true object of his complaint were not his own talents or lack thereof but some league of mischievous forces forever conspiring against him.

'I quite like your beans,' Crawford said, gingerly wiping the corners of his handlebar mustache with his cloth napkin.

He took a swig of wine, dark as ink in that ruby light, and swished it about his mouth. Andy nodded and went on eating, the sunset etching a golden nimbus around his slender forearms.

'You think I put too much salt?'

Crawford took a bite of beef and turned the question over in his mouth and mind. He swallowed.

'No. Salt isn't the problem. You don't scorch it enough. My dear old aunt, your great Aunt Vivian, taught me that. You want the outside to be a little burnt, she would say. Gives it that extra flavor.'

Andy nodded in agreement.

'It seems like maybe I don't get the stove hot enough.'

'Could be,' Crawford said.

Toward the end of their meal a salvo of deep booms sounded from the direction of Watt Mountain, stirring the flies from the windowpanes. Crawford stroked his mustache with satisfaction and silently counted the shots. After supper Andy cleared the plates and put them in the pail of water in the kitchen.

Out on the front porch, in the yellow velvet wingback chair to the right of the door, Crawford sat smoking his pipe, the top button of his shirt undone, his legs crossed at the knee. Frayed rags of tender pink and rose still smoldered across the western sky amidst shreds of brilliant blue-green. *The blessed sun himself a fair hot wench in flame-color'd taffeta*, Crawford mused contentedly.

In the young mulberry tree just inside the fence, small gray swifts were heralding the coming of night with frantic cheeps. Crawford, unwilling to wait for a seedling to reach maturity, had bought the adolescent tree from a prominent Bird businessman and had it shipped by ore wagon down from the mountains and planted in his front yard. Every evening before supper he made three trips to and from the well out back, pouring the life-giving water around the base of the trunk.

Andy came out and sat down on the stool to the left of the door.

21

'You think they'll catch them?' he asked.

Crawford took the pipe from his mouth and held it a few inches from his face.

'Not likely. Not in this heat.'

'It seems kind of silly, calling themselves Knights.'

'Makes them feel chivalrous, I suppose,' Crawford said. 'Defending the honor of maidens, that sort of thing.'

The ivory stem of the pipe clicked gently against Crawford's teeth. His cheeks scalloped twice and a pale wisp of smoke curled upward out of the bowl before dispersing, leaving a sweet, woody smell in the air.

'You think she's pretty?' Andy asked.

Crawford weighed his thoughts.

'I wouldn't say she is an especially remarkable exemplar of female beauty,' he said. 'A trifle spare in the bosom but otherwise agreeable. More handsome than pretty perhaps?'

Andy picked up a pebble and tossed it back and forth between his hands.

'I think she's perfect,' he said.

'Well,' Crawford said. 'She couldn't be as perfect as all that, coming all the way out here to marry a man she never met before. Rest assured, she had a compelling reason of one sort or another.'

'She's bound to be wondering why he doesn't talk like his letters,' Andy offered.

Crawford smiled, two embers of tobacco flaring briefly in his eyes.

'If you had seen the way her face fell when she stepped off of that stage and saw that her young Casanova was in fact a grizzled old outlaw, you would probably gather that Henry Jonson's lack of refinement in matters of speech is the least of her concerns.'

Andy tossed the pebble back and forth.

'You don't really think he killed all those people, do you?'

'I don't know,' Crawford said. 'And I'm not about to ask him. As long as he pays his rent on time, he's a model citizen as far as I'm concerned.'

Night was falling fast. The swifts were quiet. Andy tossed the pebble out into the pale blue dust and stood at the edge of the porch looking townward.

They rode in around sunset, covered head to toe in dust, nearly dead of thirst, their shirts and pants caked in dried blood. Some of their arms were pink and blistered where sleeves had been torn away to stanch the flow of blood. One man was missing altogether the lobe of an ear. They dropped from their horses and staggered into the saloon and called out in cracked voices for whiskey.

Every man in Shakespeare not in the mines was soon standing shoulder to shoulder in the Ore, asking where the others were. Adams, leader of the Knights, raised his hands to quiet the crowd.

By his account they had found the Indians, forty strong, two days' ride east of the Aguja River, camped in the rocky foothills of the Pesadumbres. They were a raiding party, no women or children in evidence. The terrain being marred by hidden arroyos and protrusions of rock, surveys through the telescope were insufficient to confirm the presence or absence of Mrs. Jonson's mattress. The Knights held council. All agreed that attacking such a large band of warriors by main force was folly. Someone suggested sending a man to Chloride, a day's ride north, for reinforcements, but, their water running low, they feared they wouldn't be able to hold out for two days more. If they were to attack, it had to be that very day. Davis came up with the idea of dividing the Knights and hitting the Indians from two flanks, creating the illusion of a much larger force.

At three o'clock the two regiments parted ways, Adams taking six men and circling around to the north, Davis taking the remainder and heading south. As soon as they were in their positions Adams made the signal, three flashes from his shaving mirror, and both units opened fire, killing six Indians in the first volley. But the Indians did not panic as planned. Instead they mounted and charged in both directions, forcing the Knights into defensive positions behind rocks and in arroyos wherever they could find them. All afternoon the battle raged, the Indians charging the positions only to be turned back by the sure aim of the thirteen Knights. Over the course of a dozen such exchanges, which according to Adams claimed the lives of ten more Indians, five Knights met their deaths. Rickman, Pacheco, Sullivan, Lopez, and Stroud. It was Rickman who, moments before taking a bullet through the eye, called out to Davis that he could see the mattress, though none of the surviving Knights, once they had regrouped back at Prospector's Farewell, could corroborate his claim.

A moment of silence for the fallen Knights, whose bodies the survivors had been forced to abandon to the ravages of the Indians, followed Adams' account of the battle.

Adams turned to Abigail, who had joined Henry behind the bar when she heard the commotion.

'We did our best, Mrs. Jonson,' he said. 'I'm sorry we couldnta done better.'

Abigail thanked him. She felt the gazes of the Knights

and the miners on her, seeing in her perhaps their own mothers and sisters and wives, happy to read in letters home that their valiant sons and brothers and husbands were still alive. These weren't the usual furtive leers, the drunken eyes undressing her. Tonight there was reverence, pride even, in their eyes, as if they understood better now, thanks to her, what they were capable of. If there was any sign of desire in them it was only that they should go on being the men that their service on her behalf had made of them. To Abigail, unaccustomed to attention of this nature, there was something compelling, something at once deeply satisfying and unnerving in being seen as the embodiment of more than she could ever hope to be. She straightened up and allowed herself to be looked at, admitting to herself some pleasure in it. As the night wore on and still this look persisted, it struck her that this was what it must feel like to be a queen, her minions subject to her every command. His eyes flitting back and forth between Abigail and the Knights, Henry seemed none too pleased with this attention.

Adams took off his hat and sent it around the saloon for contributions to the Knights of Shakespeare Fund, and every man dropped into it whatever he could.

Adams held up his hands again.

'Go on and show em,' he said to Davis.

Davis pulled from his satchel a gleaming chunk of native silver float the size of a goat's skull.

'It was lyin there right next to me where I was hidin,' he said. 'Right up against a porphyry dyke at the south end of the ridge.'

All bodies surged toward the ore, and Davis held it high for everyone to see.

'I done put my claim on that spot,' he said over the

excited rabble, 'but I reckon they's a whole lot more where she come from.'

Three cheers went up for Davis and the returning Knights, and everyone fell to drinking.

Behind the bar Abigail and Henry were in constant motion pouring whiskey. No sooner was a glass filled than an empty one was held up or nudged forward, and the drunker the men got the bolder became their vows of revenge.

The whiskey ran out around midnight, at which point Abigail retired. The sober helped Henry drag the drunk out into the street. Even the gamblers were made to leave the premises.

Henry bolted the front door and stood there in his empty saloon, hands against the bar. From the deep sill of the window and the far end of the bar the lamps burned softly. All was quiet. He stood for some time, seeing in his mind a ghostly mattress somewhere in the wilderness. Then, with odd grace, he pushed off from the bar and went and extinguished the lamps.

FOUR

The Bank of Shakespeare, sandwiched between the Stratford Hotel and the Shakespeare Assay Office, was the only brick building in town, the bricks having been freighted by mule from the kiln outside Bird. In keeping with the promise of security inspired by the masonry, hanging above the safe was an oil portrait of His Excellency H.L. Warren, Governor of the Territory, standing with one hand on the Scales of Justice, a sylvan landscape yielding its infinite glories behind him. The interior of the bank otherwise retained a humble aspect, much of the furnishings having not yet arrived. An L-shaped counter of lightly varnished scrub oak separated the lobby from the money, but as of yet no bars had been erected. This was a point of pride not only for Crawford but for every merchant in town, for it was true that in the five months of Shakespeare's existence, without even one officer of the peace on hand to enforce the laws, not a single dollar had been lost to theft. Crawford's desk, a wide curtain rolltop strewn with bonds and deeds and bills of lading, doubled as the office for his other enterprise, the Shakespeare Mining & Milling Co., which the tomes on geology and law interspersed amongst the ten-volume *Chamber's Cyclopedia* on the shelves beside the desk could rightly be said to belong to.

Dipping the nib into the inkwell in the counter, Andy drew on the back of a blank quitclaim deed a short straight line with a bulb at one end beside a long curvy squiggle. This seemed to please him, for he drew another identical. Eleven distinct species of squiggles were crowding the deed by the time the sound of light footfalls drew their creator's attention to Mrs. Jonson. She was standing at the counter, holding the canvas deposit bag, swollen beyond its normal dimensions. Her face was flushed, the tips of her fringe dark with sweat.

Even from a distance Andy could smell the scented soap on her, and that smell, of lavender and honey, filled him with a sort of gratifying despair, for in his heart he knew that he would never have a woman like Mrs. Jonson, if ever a woman at all, for he was no man, no real man like Henry Jonson, hale and hardy, sure of himself, easy with a lady, nor could he foresee ever becoming one, cursed as he was from birth with gangliness and frailness and sickliness and shyness and awkwardness and paleness and meekness and stupidity and a good many other things which his recently departed father had so relished pointing out to him. He was lucky to have an uncle like Crawford, generous enough to pay his fare to Shakespeare, convinced that the bracing air and unfiltered sunshine of the Territory would effect a miraculous change in his bilious young nephew. Maybe he did feel better about himself in the early days, when Shakespeare was still a womanless town, for in those days he was free from the panic and lust and private challenges and vainglorious dreams and intense self-loathing that women by their presence alone never failed to evoke in him. All that had changed with Mrs. Jonson's arrival. Had she been the prudish type, thick with religion and manners, things would have been easy. But no, Mrs. Jonson was exactly the sort of woman he most desired — a woman who would never in a sober state of mind want anything to do with a person like him. Anyone could see just by looking at her, forget the fact that she had braved the wilds unchaperoned to reach the Territory, that she was no docile schoolmarm. She walked with purpose and held her head high, and when she smiled it was as if to say, *There are so many things you will never understand.*

Mrs. Jonson set the bag on the counter with a somewhat exaggerated sigh of fatigue, and while she waited for him to count the money she picked up from a short stack at her elbow a thin booklet whose title was: *A Sketch of Shakespeare and Its Surroundings: The Mining Center of the Famous True Fissure District: Its Resources and Advantages Truthfully Presented to the Attention of Business Men and Capitalists*, by A.W. Crawford. She skimmed its pages, nodding to herself at certain phrases.

When Andy had finished he wrote the total on the receipt and transferred the figure to the register.

'What do you think?' Abigail asked with a mildly conspiratorial air, returning the booklet to the stack. 'Is there an invisible fence out there keeping women from reaching Shakespeare?'

Andy smiled bashfully.

'Well, if there was, you wouldn't be here, would you?'

Abigail made no reply but seemed to accept this reasoning. A miner stepped out of the Ore and, straightening his hat, squinted against the sun and walked with a slight limp north up Avon. Abigail gave Andy a curious look, pointing as she did so at the left corner of her mouth.

'You've got some ink there,' she said.

Andy licked his fingertips and rubbed his face.

29

'Wrong side,' she said. 'Here, hand me your handkerchief.'

With some reluctance, given the uses it had been put to, Andy pulled his yellow silk handkerchief from his back pocket and handed it to Mrs. Jonson. She took hold of his chin and wiped away the ink, stretching the soft skin of his cheek downward while he stared with a dazed expression into her light brown eyes.

'She must miss you,' she said, returning the handkerchief.

'Who?'

'Your mother.'

'You know my mother?'

Abigail gave him an indulgent smile.

'Everybody has a mother,' she said, and picked up the deposit receipt, saying, 'Good day, Mr. Selgren,' as she turned and exited the bank.

Leaning out over the counter so as not to lose sight of her, Andy watched Mrs. Jonson walk back across the street. The moment her figure faded into the dark doorway of the Ore, he unbuttoned his trousers and reached down inside them and gave vent all over his doodling to the growing warmth therein.

She came in each day to make the deposit, setting the bag on the counter and waiting for Andy to finish counting before she started in with her questions. At first it was only where was he from and why was he there and who were his sweethearts back home. Then she wanted to know what the miners and merchants he transacted with said about her in her absence. He was honest and told her that they rarely spoke of her at all, their minds preoccupied with matters monetary whilst in the bank, but when they did speak it was in the most respectful of terms. That she was a good pal and knew how to pour a whiskey as well as a man. To these declarations she could only voice suspicion.

When Crawford was there he (Crawford) fawned over her, coming around the counter, kissing her hand, asking her if there was anything he could do for her, and Andy was certain that he saw behind Abigail's smile a measure of contempt for his uncle. This amused him, for as much as he was grateful to his uncle for bringing him out to the Territory, he found it difficult to countenance some of his more obsequious and self-serving mannerisms. Nor did he care for the insinuations about Mrs. Jonson that Crawford sometimes made over supper, to the effect that of late she seemed to be the one in the family wearing the trousers.

Eventually Abigail stopped coming to the bank altogether when Crawford was there. Andy knew not to what good fortune he owed her favor, only that the days when she did not come were monotonous beyond compare. Which only made him all the more elated on the days when, Crawford having stepped out to get more tobacco or collect a debt, she would emerge from the doorway of the Ore and cross Avon with the canvas bag in her hands.

'I haven't told it to anyone else,' he said on such a day when she asked him in a forthright manner what he was intending to do with his life. 'Not because I don't want to tell it — I do — but because I'm afraid someone will steal my idea. I've never been in a place so full of people just waiting for an opportunity to take someone else's idea and claim it's their own. That's the only reason I've been reluctant to tell it to anyone.' He looked at her. 'Do you really want to hear it?'

'I do,' she said, and as she said this a cloud passed across the sun, softening the glare through the windows.

31

Andy looked down and gave a small, almost apologetic smile, then told her: 'Well, it would be a kind of restaurant, a small one, more like a canteen than a restaurant. A little shack even, but painted up real nice with bright happy colors. Like yellow maybe. And green. So you can see it from a distance and it makes you remember how happy you were the last time you ate there so you want to eat there again. And in this little shack, which I would call Andy's, you'd have one cook, and what he cooks is two things: beefsteaks and fried potatoes. If you want more than that then Andy's isn't the place for you. What makes Andy's special is two things: its price and its convenience. For one thick, juicy beefsteak and a plate of hot, salty fried potatoes you pay only ten cents. How is this possible? you ask. Easy. You know all that beef the government buys for the Indian reservations, something like a billion pounds a year? Well, the Indians don't pay anything for it, do they? They get it for free because we want them to stay on their reservation and not go out raiding and massacring. Well, an Indian can't live on beef alone. He needs his tobacco and his whiskey. And he can't buy tobacco and whiskey from the agents without money, so what I aim to do is buy some of this Indian cattle.

'I admit I haven't figured it all out yet, but the thing is just to get me started I need to get a load of cattle for at least half their true market value. That covers price. Now for the best part, convenience. I see an Andy's in every town in the Territory, especially wherever there's miners. You set it up not too far from the mines so when the miners come up for lunch they look out and see the colorful little shack where they know they can satisfy their ravenous appetites for ten cents without having to go all the way back into town or having to make their lunch ahead of time and carry it down into the mine with them and keep an eye on it all day so it won't get stolen or eaten by rats or mules.

'Once we've got enough of these little Andy's established it will be easy to attract capital to establish even more, and once that happens we'll be in a better position to get our beef at legitimate volume discounts. Eventually we should be able to expand outside the Territory, into the States, and when that happens it's not just beefsteaks and potatoes we're selling anymore but the romance and adventure of the Territory itself. I can see the ads already. GET A TASTE OF THE TERRITORY AT ANDY'S.'

Andy's eyes were ablaze with his vision, and as if on cue the cloud passed. Three rectangles of light, two broad, one long, blazed bright against the floor and wall, their edges straight and sharp. Andy looked at Abigail. All through his narration her smile had been growing wider, and now that he was through she couldn't help but burst out laughing.

'Oh, Andy,' she said. 'You do have an imagination.'

Andy smiled and laughed along with her while in his heart he felt the oddly gratifying despair which every night he felt as he lay on his bed, hands clasped behind his neck, thinking of the things he would do with her if only she was his.

Riding west through the dense creosote of Shakespeare Draw, it seemed to Henry that the weather was starting to change. The air was no cooler but in the miles-high cumulus clouds white and globous as bolls of cotton there churned the promise of storm. When the rain did come, he thought, it would be Shakespeare's first and there would be much scrambling to patch leaky roofs. He wondered if the Ore would hold, old as it was.

Up the bajada skirting the north face of Watt Mountain, Whiskey's shoes clattered over loose plates of shale and mica schist, the creosote giving way to ground wholly barren but for sparse tufts of browned burrograss. Here and there among the granite dykes the piled stones of claim markers stood like homage to gods of private fortune. He raised his hat to the miners up the grade sorting the ore from the gangue, and they bent up and waved and stood watching him go until he sank out of sight.

The country before him was bolson. Aeons of runoff from the surrounding mountains had washed down in centripetal swirls gravel and silt and volcanic ash in which a diverse array of shrubs and cacti took root, which when viewed as a whole appeared as one dense thicket light brownish-green in color, picketed at irregular intervals by the bonelike shafts of soaptree yuccas. Arroyos deep enough to hide a horse wove mazelike through the basin, awaiting the deluge that would make of them, if only for a day, a subtropical Venice.

The papery rustle of small creatures in retreat preceded him as he rode at an easy pace, humming every now and then the bars of a tune known only to himself.

He had seen worse days, that was for sure, out in the bleak wastelands running for his life, one step ahead of posses' bullets, hiding out in godforsaken caverns, Indians on one side, vigilantes on the other, days without food or water, living on the mercy of settlers too far from the world to know any better, stealing, killing when he had to, but only them that deserved it, and if there was a God above maybe He was saying, Henry you done some bad things in your day and it's come time to pay up, and if this was how he had to do it, it could have been a whole lot worse.

Nearing the southern ridges of the Gables he skirted a stand of magueys in the midst of which stood a roadrunner with a bloody lizard sagging from either side of its pointed beak. He coaxed Whiskey into a trot, breasting the escarpment on the east face and entering into shadow. On his left the mountain rose six hundred feet almost sheer. He rode along beside it, the air against the stone a ceaseless exhale recalling to his mind someone telling him once that this was the sound of the sea. Locust trees and prickly pears grew here amidst rust-colored boulders stained with lime. All at once the cicadas, stilled to silence by his approach, unleashed their racket, which echoed bright and shrill against the surrounding rock. He steered into the sandy creek bed and followed its meandering course up between walls of flesh-colored feldspar at the base of which grew sprays of bright yellow jackass clover and creamy zinnias, Whiskey's hooves unearthing with every step the darker sand beneath the surface, and the deeper he rode up the gorge the stronger grew the unmistakable stink of sulfur.

He dismounted on the platform of welded tuff surrounding the bubbling pools and proceeded to take off his clothes, Whiskey looking on with drowsy indifference. Standing there lean and wiry and, but for his face and neck and hands, pale as gypsum, he looked like some overgrown amphibian never touched by the light of day. Just below his lower right rib the flesh of a small pinkish scar, oblong in shape, dimpled when he bent. Stepping with almost dainty care over the hot, coarse stone, his legs still bowed from the ride, he walked naked to the edge of the main pool and tested the waters with a toe, then winced and pulled back cursing.

In time and by degrees glacial in slowness he did succeed in lowering himself up to his neck into the scalding water. There he stewed for nearly an hour, eyes closed, head tilted back, the healing powers of the earth's own gases roiling and bubbling around him.

He had tried Dr. Hammond's Virility Salve, generously applied twice a day to the affected area, had guzzled entire pints of Beef Iron Wine and Celery Malt, had even worn for a week, with much discomfort, a Himrod Magnetized Ring, all to little effect. In his darkest hours he castigated himself for the excesses of his youth, for it was true that between the ages of eleven and nineteen hardly a day had passed that Henry had not given in to the soul-destroying temptation of self-pollution.

It was not as though the member was entirely devoid of life. He was visited, at unnecessary times, by mild erections, often when he least expected them, at three or four in the morning, when Abigail was fast asleep. In the dead of night, the Ore empty but for the gamblers in the back corner and a few prospectors in from the mountains, hope would return. An image of Abigail naked, sprawled out on a white hair mattress bound in superior ticking, beckoning Henry with a smile, would form unbidden in his mind's eye and he would feel a kick in his pants. At that moment all of life's possibilities, of late so clouded over by this curse, would shine down on him again. More than once he had made the mistake of rushing back to the bedroom to arouse Abigail from her sleep, but her agitation at being yanked back to consciousness was more than enough to dampen his ardor.

Riding back across the bolson, a bouquet of sky-blue morning glories in his hand, Henry couldn't help thinking that if only the mattress had arrived he and Abigail might have gotten off to a better start. He had no doubt that Copes would make good on the bill. Under different circumstances Henry might not have felt compelled to wait so long, but given he was the one who, by ordering the mattress and requisitioning its delivery, had set into motion the massacre of the man's sons, Henry felt obliged to demonstrate his sympathy for Copes by letting him finish mourning before approaching him about the unsettled business of the mattress. Abigail understood. Or so she said. But the ways of women were mysterious to Henry. For all he knew, Abigail cared nothing for the reasons why the one thing she had asked of him, a proper mattress, had after all this time still not arrived.

It was past three by the time he returned Whiskey to the stables and walked up Avon with the bouquet behind his back. Six dogs lay asleep in the narrow shade against the front of the buildings on the west side of the street. They and he the only living creatures in evidence.

Upon entering the saloon Henry was surprised to see Abigail not there, no one there at all. He set the flowers on the bar and leaned over to check the till. It was there and had money in it, which first relieved him then brought his blood to a boil. He marched back to the rooms only to find her not there either. He went out back and called toward the jakes but Abigail did not answer.

After locking the till in the bedroom he went across the street to the bank to see if she was in there talking to the kid, but the bank was already closed. He took a stroll north up the west side of the street, glancing casually through every window he passed. Coming back down the other side he stopped in at Muldoon's.

'Afternoon, Henry,' Muldoon said from behind the counter.

'Afternoon,' Henry said. 'How's business?'

'Slow.' He stood up from his stool and grabbed a bottle of Sweet Spirits of Nitre from the shelf behind him. Tapping it with a fingernail he set it on the counter, saying, 'Sposed to be purer than the last batch.'

'Oh?' said Henry, picking up the bottle.

He studied it from all four sides before setting it down and casually asking if Mrs. Jonson hadn't stopped by.

'Not since last time,' Muldoon said, returning the bottle to the shelf.

Henry looked over the assortment of goods on display across the counter.

'Give me some of them pecans, wouldya.'

He stood for a while out front of the drugstore, cracking the shells with his molars and tapping the meat of the nuts into his palms, then he walked on. He made small talk with Floyd in the bakery, mentioning Abigail in passing, to no avail. He tried the same with Blaine in the General Store, Henderson in the Meat Market, Stovall in the Stratford, but none of them spoke the words Henry hoped to hear.

Heading back to the Ore he wondered if maybe it wasn't such an honor after all being the only man in Shakespeare with a woman. It didn't help matters that he had her working in the saloon, for if anyone knew what filth riddled the shafts of a miner's heart it was Henry. Nothing but veins of ore to take their frustrations out on. He saw the way they looked at her when she bent over to wash the glasses or when she walked across the room, skirts swishing and swaying. He knew there wasn't a man in town who given half a chance wouldn't...

A cold sweat broke out across Henry's forehead at the thought of Abigail down in one of the miner's tents.

The stench of unwashed feet and whiskey breath pervaded the air around the tents, every tent speckled with flies, the din of their buzzing nearly as loud as the snoring inside. Henry irately shooed a fly from his face and wiped his forehead with his sleeve. Pulling aside the flap of a tent he peeked in. Seeing only miners sprawled over each other in attitudes of deathlike repose, he moved on to the next tent, listening as he made his way from tent to tent for anything unseemly. At the fourth tent he reckoned he was behaving like a fool. He started back for the Ore only to stop dead in his tracks again when it occurred to him that she might have left town. Had enough and gone.

'Haven't seen her,' Miles at the stables replied to Henry's question with a questioning look of his own.

Henry thanked him and left, a knot rising in his gorge. He found himself at the well, peering down into it, but no woman, dead or alive, was afloat on the shiny black water.

He had been looking for Abigail for half an hour when he returned to the saloon to find her on the sofa in the parlor, knitting, as if she had been there all along.

She looked up at Henry and seeing him drenched with sweat, looking puzzled and irate, said, 'Where have you been? It's gone past four.'

'Where have I been?' Henry crowed. 'Lookin all over creation for you, that's where.'

'What are you talking about? You said you'd be back by two. I've been waiting here for over two hours. You expect me to stand on my feet in that saloon all day?'

'I came in here. You weren't here.'

'I told you I've been here the whole time. I went to the privy but that couldn't have taken more than a minute. What are you getting so het up about?'

'I called at the jakes,' Henry said. 'You didn't answer. I thought something had happened to you.'

'Don't be ridiculous, Henry.'

These words seemed to have a sobering effect on Henry. He ran his fingers through his hair, still sticky with the salts of the springs, then, as though he had suddenly decided such petty matters were beneath him, he walked over to the window and leaned against the sill and stood there looking out. If not for the air rippling on the horizon, the bleached alkali dust of South Soda Flat might have been mistaken for an endless field of snow beneath a cold blue sky, frigid and barren of life.

'Someone put some flowers on the bar,' Abigail said.

Henry nodded.

'Must be a secret admirer,' he murmured.

FIVE

Andy rode toward town by the light of the moon, everything liquid blue, as if the plain were once again an ancient sea, the brush so many coral reefs. Ahead in lamplit Shakespeare the trail he rode widened to Avon, and beyond Shakespeare to the road to Bird, a milky blue scar across the belly of the earth.

Passing the miners' tents, lit from within like magic lanterns, the burro ferried him with mincing steps into town. There were men about but they were few and seemed to him in the watery light like spectral beings from the moon. The blacksmith was working late, his hammer blows giving rhythm to the otherwise transitory sounds of night. The snuffle of horses. The barking of dogs. The strike and flare of a match, followed by a long easy exhale. The welcoming chandelier of the Stratford Hotel seemed to him of a piece with the laughter spilling from the Ore, the dark figures loitering around shop fronts, all of a piece with the warm blue night, all things in it lacquered by the moon, and he was struck as never before by a feeling of profound happiness, so much so that he halted the burro and dismounted and stood there in the middle of Avon with a smile on his face, allowing the feeling to suffuse his every sense. Struck by and aware of being struck by this happiness. Happiness upon happiness. An infinity of happinesses resounding from the walls of his soul. And he told himself that as soon as he got back home tonight he would write to his mother and thank her from the bottom of his heart for sending him to Shakespeare.

He took his time walking up the street. When he reached the bank he hitched the burro to the post and took the satchel from the horn of the saddle.

'Don't get into any trouble,' he said, patting the head of the scrubby little burro.

The Ore was doing brisk business, miners crammed into the squat building like anchovies in a tin, guzzling whiskey as fast as Mr. Jonson could pour it. He was almost tempted to go over and have a drink, but he knew that they would ask him where he was going dressed up so fancy in his cheviot suit and bow tie, yellow silk handkerchief blooming from his coat pocket, hair slicked back and smelling of his uncle's dandy water. *You best watch him, Henry*, they would say and laugh, and they would want to see what he had in his satchel. And he certainly couldn't have that.

He walked into the darkness beyond the hotel, then he crossed Avon, making sure no one was watching him, and angled toward the back of the saloon, careful not to catch his pants on anything in the thorny brush.

Shoulder to shoulder, elbow to elbow along the bar and in every chair at every table men were drinking, talking, laughing, boasting, the convection of their bodies and the whiskey burning within making an oven of the Ore.

Taggart's cowhands were back from a two-month drive and bent on raising hell. Spurred into town by rumors that women had arrived, they had come only to be told there was but one, and she married. So they turned to gambling and were presently in the process of losing to the professionals in the back corner all that they had earned in the saddle. The full moon as much as the whiskey seemed to be making everyone wild. Already Henry had had to coax a jigging miner down from a table, and if the continual bursts of howling and hollering were any indication he guessed there would be a brawl before the night was through.

Henry took his watch from his right front trouser pocket and wound it almost tight. He should be there by now, he thought. 'Why don't you do something for him,' he had told her. 'Bake him a cake. Have him over.' To prove to her, to himself, he wasn't jealous.

He dropped his watch back into his pocket. Taking the bottle, he went down the bar filling glasses, taking money.

There wasn't any harm in her having a friend. She seemed happier since she had started making the deposit. That was what mattered. Her happiness. So what if she liked to stay a little longer talking to the kid? Where was the harm in that?

'Hey, Henry, another round.'

Henry filled the glasses then casually came around to the other side of the bar. Wouldn't mind a little birthday cake myself, he thought, making his way through the bodies to the door at the back. Wish him a happy birthday.

Finding the door locked he returned to the bar, a little charge of something stirring at his joints. He poured more whiskey, glancing now and then toward the door at the back of the saloon.

It was good she kept it locked, he told himself. For her own safety.

43

He set a clean glass on the bar and poured a little whiskey into it. He sipped, looking at the door, a tiny ball of fire rolling down his gullet and spreading through his stomach.

'Well, I'll have to thank him on my way out,' Andy was saying.

They were seated side by side on the sofa, a foot or so apart, facing the wall. The warm smell of chocolate cake was thick and sweet in the air.

Andy took the silk handkerchief from his coat pocket and wiped the corners of his mouth then held the handkerchief in his hands, bunching and unbunching it. Abigail brushed some crumbs from her skirt.

'You'd never know this was the back of a saloon,' Andy said, glancing around the room, at which point a man began to howl on the other side of the wall.

'You were saying?' Abigail said.

They sat, speaking little, saying less, then Andy stood up and said he'd best be shoving off and that he sure was grateful for the wonderful birthday she — and Henry — had given him.

'So soon?' she said with a wounded look. 'Aren't you going to show me what's in your satchel?'

Andy scratched the back of his head. 'All right,' he said mock-begrudgingly. 'I'll show you, but you have to promise you'll laugh.'

'I promise.'

Sitting back down and placing the leather satchel on his lap, Andy unfastened the latches with a kind of solemn deliberation meant to prolong Abigail's curiosity, then he eased back the flap, and reaching in, took out a ventriloquist's dummy.

The sight of this little man made Abigail smile. She reached out and patted his head and touched his face and clothes.

'He's so like a man!'

The dummy was indeed proportional to but only a quarter the size of a man. He was blessed with a healthy complexion and a thick shock of black hair and sideburns and whiskers that, along with his wide-open, unblinking eyes, gave him an air of wildness, all the more comical given what he was wearing: a tiny pinstriped suit of real worsted wool, a black bow tie, and shiny black brogans.

Andy seated the dummy on his knee and slipped his hand into the slot at the base of its back.

'Theodore,' he said with an air of paternal sufferance, 'I'd like you to meet my good friend, Mrs. Jonson.'

'Pleased to meet you,' Theodore said in a high-pitched voice, his little nutcracker jaw opening and closing four times then snapping shut with a wooden knock.

'He talks!'

'Of course I talk,' Theodore replied.

'How do you do that?' Abigail cried in delight. 'Your lips aren't even moving.'

'Why should his lips move when I talk?' Theodore said with affront. 'Who's to say who's the dummy, who the man?'

Andy glowered at Theodore.

'All right, Theodore. Be nice. Tell Mrs. Jonson about your day today.'

'Well,' Theodore said, 'like most days it began in a hot and stuffy trunk and pretty well stayed that way until Andy came and got me and stuffed me into a satchel and threw me over a burro and rode me into town where I stayed in the satchel smelling chocolate cake until he

45

pulled me out and I met you, and here we are, you and me, me and you, and Andy.'

'Bravo! Bravo!' Abigail clapped.

Andy hung his head in mock shame.

'He's usually better behaved. It must be nerves.'

Abigail patted Theodore's head.

'Are you nervous, Theodore?'

'I've heard a lot about you, Mrs. Jonson,' Theodore said brightly.

'Theodore!' Andy snapped. 'What did I tell you about repeating private conversations?'

'No,' Abigail said, leaning her ear toward Theodore the better to receive the gossip. 'Please, do tell.'

'Go on then,' Andy said.

'All good things,' Theodore said.

'Such as?'

'Shakespeare is a much nicer town since you've come.'

Abigail smiled at Theodore. 'And I take it you helped Andy write all those pretty letters to me?'

A long silence followed this remark. No answer was forthcoming, from dummy or from master. Andy blushed deep red and looked past Theodore to the floor. Abigail could almost feel his thumping heartbeat.

The noise of carousal came pouring through the wall. Andy set Theodore on the sofa and gave Abigail a sheepish look.

'You have lovely handwriting,' Abigail said in answer to his unasked question.

It wasn't until Andy had shared with her his vision of his grub stands that Abigail, discerning in his voice the same quality of hope and joy that had won her in the letters, had begun to suspect that he was the one who had written them. The next time she made the deposit she asked him if he would mind giving her his mother's address — 'I know how mothers worry' — and Andy had gladly complied. A low-slung *g* was enough to confirm her suspicions.

Andy leaned forward, forearms on thighs, fingers interlaced, and stared at the floor.

'It wasn't my idea,' he said plaintively.

'It's kind of touching if you think about it,' Abigail said when the embarrassment on Andy's face showed no sign of abating.

'He went to my uncle first,' Andy confided. 'His letter was terrible. My uncle's, I mean. *How to Write Love Letters*. That was the book he copied it from, changing the particulars but nothing else. I didn't have the heart to tell him it was no good. All I said was, "Why don't I try my hand at one too, and we'll give them both to Mr. Jonson and let him decide." That's all I did. I just wrote what was in my heart, as if I were really writing to someone I loved. I didn't try to make things out to be any different than they were.'

'And Henry chose yours.'

'Yes. And when he got your letter and saw how much you'd liked his first one, he had me write the rest of them.'

Andy looked at her with imploring eyes.

'Please don't think he tried to deceive you. It's my fault if things aren't exactly the same here as I made them out in the letters. The truth is, I really didn't think you'd come. None of us did. When Mr. Jonson got that first letter from you, he read it to everyone in the saloon. It was the first sign of hope we'd had in a long time. You should have seen how everyone's faces lit up. It was something. After he chose my letter I got to thinking, maybe I can do this, maybe I'm the one who can finally get a woman out

47

here. And it hit me that there was more than myself to think about. I had a responsibility to the others to do my darnedest to keep you writing, and maybe, with a little luck, I could, we could, all of us together, could get you out here.'

'It's all right,' Abigail assured him, touched by his embarrassment.

Andy shook his head.

'What you've got to understand,' he said, 'is — maybe you already do now that you've been here a while — well. I think you know what I'm saying. Maybe every word wasn't Mr. Jonson's, but those feelings in those letters, they sure are his, Abigail. I'd hate for you to think he set out to deceive you.'

Andy searched her eyes for some sign of forgiveness.

Abigail took hold of his hand and gave it a squeeze. She continued to hold it despite his deepening blush.

'Do you forgive me?' he asked.

Abigail leaned over and gave him a small kiss on the lips. To the remark Theodore had earlier made — who is the dummy, who the man? — Andy seemed to have arrived at the answer, for all he could do was sit there, as if on a knee, wide-eyed and wooden, while Abigail looked into his eyes and said, 'No, I do not.'

'Hey, Curtis,' Henry said. 'Cover me for a spell, wouldya? I need some fresh air. Have yourself a drink.'

The air outside felt almost cool. It was a beautiful night, the moon bright as magnesium, the clouds like great effusions of silver-coated pewter. From the direction of the miners' tents came the soft strumming of a guitar, some old trail song, a peaceful sound to Henry's roaring ears.

He leaned against the front wall for a while, wiping the

back of his neck with the bar rag, then he straightened up and walked over to the south corner of the saloon where it gave way to the desert. Seeing no one pissing there, he casually walked down the side of the saloon, whistling as he went. From the back corner he could see the rectangle of lamplight from the parlor window where it lay across the ground like a dull yellow rug. The other windows were dark. He stood there for a while then walked out to the jakes. He gave the door a soft knock and opened it and looked in and closed it. He couldn't see anything from there but the top of the bath screen. Not even their shadows on the walls. Then again his eyes weren't what they used to be. Got to make some curtains, he thought.

Making sure no one was coming around to use the jakes, Henry stole across to the back of the saloon again and sidled like a thief over to the parlor window, a thief come to steal his own possessions. He tilted his head and peeked around the window frame. No one there. Both lamps burning. A satchel open on the floor. A bolt of jealousy shot down Henry's arms. Then realizing that they must have already gone into the saloon for the kid's free drink, Henry headed for the back door. Passing the bedroom window something caught his eye, a soft reflection of moonlight that seemed for a moment to sway. He put his nose to the window and looked down and what he saw there turned his guts inside out, yet he could not turn his eyes away. Two moonlit hemispheres rising and sinking between two milk-white knees.

Henry shut his eyes and braced a hand against the wall for support. Something was knocking against the back of his skull. He opened his eyes. He stood at the window, eyes and mouth agape and watering. Harder still did his old heart pound when he saw her face, angelic in the

49

moonlight, eyes closed, mouth open yet making no sound for fear of Henry or someone else hearing across the wall of the saloon, and despite himself he was suddenly stiff as a wagon spoke. Henry watched with a pounding of his heart he thought might kill him, watched until at last the kid stopped moving and all was still.

Quietly he scampered back out into the brush and squatted behind a mesquite and did not stir from there until the soft sound of brogans stealing across the dirt had merged again with the silence of the desert. Then he stood up, paused for a moment, and made his way to the door.

ONE

Up and down and side to side in deft flicking motions, Rodriguez brushed with the tips of the feathers every inch of the painting and its gilded frame, in the fluted grooves of which Shakespeare's powdery alkali, as if irresistibly drawn to relics of the past, was forever settling. The woman in the painting was one of Stovall's ancestors, the Duchess of Gurovoc, a luminous being in a long green gown, two gaunt gray whippets to either side of her in a palace garden. The story of her death — a revolutionary's knife in the heart — never failed to touch Rodriguez while he dusted. He imagined the blade piercing her alabaster breast, her placid, regal expression changing to dismay, jewels of bright red blood spilling from her wound. The skin of the paint, as if in empathy with its tragic subject, was cracking over the entire surface of the canvas. This too seemed to Rodriguez a tragic thing.

After dusting the Duchess he ran the feathers along the wainscoting of all the lobby walls, dusting the other paintings and the parlor tables and all the things upon them as he went. He dusted the clock and the lamps. He dusted the reception counter and the keys on the hooks behind it. He dusted the bell. He dusted to the floor from the webs and dust of the windowsills that lined the front wall the dry bodies of dead flies. He dusted the banisters and balusters of the great mahogany staircase. If he could have reached it he would have dusted the length and breadth of the galvanized tin ceiling as well. He had dusted yesterday morning and the morning before and every morning of his employ as the Stratford's porter, and still everything was dusty and would be dusty again tomorrow morning and the day after. Sometimes in his dreams Rodriguez would forget to dust, and he would emerge from his room to dunes.

After dusting he swept the floor and the rugs and opened the double doors and swept out into dusty Avon his little pile of dust. With his rag and pine oil he polished all the wood, the tables and chairs and all the bare arms and legs of the upholstered furniture and the banisters and balusters of the great mahogany staircase. He straightened crooked things. He emptied ashtrays and wiped them clean and set fresh books of matches in them. He made sure the fibers of maroon velvet on the sofas and settees were running in the same direction, the darker one, erasing with a swipe of his hand all traces of previous guests.

When he was done with these tasks he stood at the foot of the staircase with his hands behind his back, his shirt crisp, his bow tie perfectly horizontal, eager to perform at a moment's notice any service that a guest might require of him. These things and others Rodriguez did with pleasure so that one day he might return home to his wife and child a wealthy man.

He had left the winter before last, heading north on his burro with the clothes on his back and the suit his grandfather had worn when he was head porter of the Mirador in Caja. He traveled the Territory from town to town, seeking the hotel that would hire him, to live out for himself the stories of his grandfather. Stories of serving great men. Men who had made history. From Pecan to Pit, Chloride to Sulfur, he sought but could not find the employment he so yearned for, working instead as a hired hand on farms and ranches, sometimes a day or two in a mine, but he could not stand mine work, the dark and the filth and the bastard gringos and their pranks. So when he heard about a man in a new camp called Shakespeare, forty-three miles southwest of Bird, in the heart of Indian country, a man who was building a fancy hotel said to rival in splendor the Grand Hotel of the capital, he turned his burro around and headed back south.

The final shingles were being set in the mansard roof on the evening he arrived. After such a long journey across the desert, the sight of the immense cut-glass chandeliers bathing the lobby in a luxurious amber glow was to Rodriguez like a glimpse of heaven, the beautiful woman in the painting nothing less than an angel, and he made his case to Stovall that very night. Stovall, having never employed a porter before, was pleased enough with Rodriguez's first week of unpaid work to keep him on at the generous rate of twenty dollars a month, plus free room and board and whatever gratuities he received from guests. Already Rodriguez had saved over ninety dollars.

Rodriguez rocked back and forth on his heels and cracked every knuckle of every finger, including the ones at the bases of his thumbs. Perhaps he should have taken more time dusting. If no guests arrived he would have very little to do for the rest of the day. Stovall didn't like paying Rodriguez for doing nothing. Nor did Rodriguez care for having nothing to do. More than anything

Rodriguez loved losing himself in his work. Then the days went fast, and Stovall was happier and made more jokes.

Rodriguez hummed to himself one of his grandfather's old portering songs. Across the street Mrs. Jonson was standing in the doorway of the Ore, as she did every morning about this time, staring toward the mountain. A passing miner waved at her. She did not wave back. Rodriguez admired Mrs. Jonson. She was what they called back home *una fuerte*, a strong woman. Guests from the East — it was rare that they came from other directions — having heard in saloons in transit about the woman who was the only woman in Shakespeare, and moreover that she was the one whose mattress, by now as legendary as she, had been abducted by Indians, were always anxious to cross the street for a drink at the Ore, but the stage from Bird arriving late in the afternoon they were always disappointed to learn from Rodriguez that unless she made a rare appearance that night they would have to wait until morning to see her. Some mornings she came to the well when Rodriguez was filling his buckets, but he never said anything to her, and she never said anything to him.

The night miners beginning to straggle into town, Mrs. Jonson turned from the doorway and went back into the saloon. Rodriguez, hands behind his back, hummed his song and waited.

Stovall came in from his quarters around nine, giving Rodriguez his usual morning greeting, a nod and a small wave from an unraised hand. He stood in the front doorway, back to Rodriguez, staring out onto empty Avon, the dark gray hairs at the base of his mostly bald head still wet from his bathing. He stood with his fists on his stout hips, his sleeves rolled up to his elbows, the waistline of his dark brown trousers, which the tension in his braces assured always stayed well above his navel, dividing into equal halves his sausage-shaped body. The stale odor of cigar smoke was so embedded in the fibers of Stovall's clothes that no matter how vigorously Rodriguez scrubbed them, the odor seemed only to gain strength with every washing.

All was quiet in Shakespeare save the steady clank of the blacksmith's irons. Taking a fresh cigar from his shirt pocket, Stovall sliced off the end with his pocketknife and lit it and puffed, shrouding his head in a cloud of blue-gray smoke. He smoked for a few minutes then turned and looked at Rodriguez and said: 'Where is this boom?'

Rodriguez made no answer, for he did not know.

Back in the lobby, an elbow cupped in a hand, two fingers stroking his lower lip, Stovall surveyed with consternation some aspect of the furnishings or the arrangement thereof. He asked Rodriguez to help him move the sofa to where the settee was and move the settee to where the two armchairs were and move one armchair closer to the front window and put the other by the painting of the Duchess. These motions completed Stovall eyed the result with displeasure and asked Rodriguez to help him move it all back. Then, with an air of resignation, Stovall stepped around behind the reception counter and, leaning his elbows against it, studied for some time the history of his hotel as set down in the register. Rodriguez continued to stand at the foot of the stairs, hands clasped behind his back.

Around noon Stovall took some folded banknotes from his trouser pocket and counted out twenty dollars and set them on the counter. He rang the bell. Rodriguez continued to stand at the foot of the stairs, hands clasped behind his back. Again Stovall rang the bell.

'Your pay is here,' Stovall said.

'Thank you, sir,' Rodriguez said.

'Come get it, please,' Stovall said after a while.

Rodriguez approached the counter and took the money and thanked Stovall again.

Stovall put his cigar in his mouth and took some more money from his pocket and counted out three dollars and handed them to Rodriguez.

'Go over to Blaine's and get some coffee,' he mouthed around the cigar. 'A pound. Watch him weigh it. And see if he has any bar chocolate.'

'Yes, sir.'

Rodriguez took the notes and was on his way out when Stovall stopped him.

'No,' he said. 'I should go myself. He'll cheat you.'

Rodriguez handed the money back to Stovall and returned to his post at the foot of the stairs.

He allowed a few minutes to pass before stepping around to the side of the staircase and opening the small door built into the wall there.

It was never intended to be a porter's quarters. The blueprint called it a broom closet. Hanging straight down from the low, slanted ceiling was a small picture of the Virgin in a tin frame. The other walls were bare. On the floor at the foot of a straw mat stood a three-legged wooden stool on which Rodriguez presently sat. He reached down and picked up a yellow cigar box from the floor, and setting it on his leg he opened the lid and took out a short stack of paper money. Adding the new bills to it, he counted the money. When he was finished counting he returned the money to the box and returned the box to the corner. *Never let them see you sit*, his grandfather used to say. Rodriguez sat on his stool for a few more minutes, resting his legs.

Back at his post at the foot of the stairs Rodriguez stood and waited, hands clasped behind his back, bow tie perfectly horizontal, waited for the guests to arrive.

He might not have noticed at all had there been any guests in the hotel, but a week had passed since the investor from the East had left, and Rodriguez, having nothing to do in the middle of the afternoon but stand at the foot of the stairs, hands clasped behind his back, could not help but notice the banker's nephew walking slowly down Avon, head down, as if milling something over in his mind. He walked past the Ore, where Shakespeare ended and the desert began, and there he stopped and stared at a mesquite bush. At one point he reached out and touched the leaves, which struck Rodriguez as an odd thing for a young bank teller to do in the torrid heat of a summer afternoon. After a while, as if to ensure no one was watching him, he looked around; then, with the resolution of one whom only after considerable thought has arrived at the only course of action, he walked briskly over to the north side of the Ore and disappeared from Rodriguez's view.

Rodriguez might have dismissed the teller's behavior, odd though it was, as an isolated occurrence had Mr. Jonson not stepped out of the saloon five minutes later and stood there rubbing the heel of his boot in the dirt, as if he too had something on his mind. Then, just as the teller had done, Mr. Jonson casually glanced up and down Avon and walked briskly around the corner of the building and disappeared from view. So it went, every other day or so. Ten or fifteen minutes later the teller would re-emerge from the south side of the saloon, still furtive but less so. Instead of returning to the bank, which by then was closed, he would walk south on Avon, all the way to the end of town, and from there carry on walking down the narrow road to his uncle's house a mile and a half away. Walking through the desert in the hottest part of the day, without even a hat to shade his face from the sun.

Over the course of a week Rodriguez saw these comings and goings of the teller and Mr. Jonson repeated three more times, each time with the same furtive glancings about, and while he could not say what any of it meant, he knew that whatever was going on between Mr. Jonson and the teller was a secret. A secret Rodriguez was happy not to know. He did not trust himself with secrets.

When he was a boy his sister had trusted him with a secret. The owner of the Mirador, Señor Juan Jose Gutierrez y Maria de la Cruz, as a gesture of appreciation for ten years of faithful service by Rodriguez's grandfather, and, it was rumored, as recompense to him for keeping secret Señor de la Cruz's well-known love affair with one of the hotel servants, had generously agreed to his son's impolitic desire to marry the girl he was in love with, the porter's beautiful granddaughter Lucinda. Rodriguez's mother and father, recognizing the honor that such a union would bestow on their humble family, counseled Lucinda to accept the de la Cruz proposal without delay. Lucinda's secret, which she entrusted to Rodriguez after he saw her kissing in a field a young man who was not the grandson of the owner of the Mirador, was that the young man she had kissed, Diego Echevería, a *vaquero*, was the only man she loved, not Raul de la

Cruz, and that she intended to elope with him before the family forced her to marry someone she did not love. Rodriguez promised his sister, whom among his eleven siblings he loved most, that her secret was safe with him.

After his lessons it was little Rodriguez's habit to spend his afternoons at the Mirador with his grandfather, helping him shine shoes or carry luggage up to the rooms. There were many secret passageways in the Mirador, left over from the days when it was a fort, and when Rodriguez's grandfather had time he would take his grandson into them and tell him stories of men who had breathed their last in those cool, dark passages, fending off the forces of rebellion. It was on such an occasion, in a narrow corridor between adobe walls, that Rodriguez's grandfather told Rodriguez that the Mirador and all its stories, all its history, would soon be a part of their own family. Rodriguez's grandfather took Rodriguez's hand and placed it against the cool adobe wall.

'This will be yours, too,' Rodriguez's grandfather told him.

'The Mirador? Mine?'

This struck Rodriguez as miraculous, that two different families could suddenly become one, their things shared, that the Mirador, the wonderful, magical Mirador, would become his.

'But grandfather,' he said without thinking, 'what if Lucinda did not marry Raul? Would the Mirador still be mine?'

It was not long before the whole family knew of Lucinda's plan to dishonor them and crush their hopes of a prosperous future for the coming generations of Rodriguez de la Cruzes.

Rodriguez could never forget the way Lucinda looked

at him when the family gathered to condemn her foolishness and forbid her from seeing the worthless *vaquero*. There was a painting in the church of Jesus being betrayed by Judas, Jesus' eyes brimming with sorrow and pity, the sorrow and pity of the coming crucifixion. These were Lucinda's eyes when she looked down at her little brother, the boy she had placed all of her faith in. Twenty years later Rodriguez had still not forgiven himself his mistake. Had he kept her secret she would have still been alive, married to the man she loved, not buried in unhallowed ground, a disgrace to the family.

'What ye buildin there, Henry?'

Henry took the nails out of his mouth.

'Store room,' he said.

He hammered another board across the uprights of the left-hand wall. The frame was about the size of the jakes, juniper posts fastened at the upper corners with strips of rawhide.

Henderson, his apron streaked and smeared with blood, nodded. 'Don't seem you'll be able to fit much in it.'

Henry bent down and sorted through the scrap until he found a decent board. He nailed it in place.

'It'll fit enough,' he said.

'You need some hinges?' Henderson asked. 'I got a couple I took off a old gate.'

'I thank you kindly,' Henry said. 'I got some. New ones. Wrought steel. I caint stand a squeaky hinge. Wouldn't want to wake the missus every time I come out to get another barrel, would I?'

Henderson nodded.

'Jest offerin.'

'Pardon me,' Henry said, moving over to the other wall.

'Then again,' Henderson said, 'squeaky hinges lets you know they's someone prowlin round your possessions.'

Henry nailed up another board. 'That's what locks are for,' he said.

Henderson nodded. He walked around and gave the bottom board of the right-hand wall a few kicks with the side of his boot. 'No tellin what a man'll do for whiskey.'

Henry had other visitors, come to admire and advise. All agreed it was a fine piece of craftsmanship and a necessary addition to a thriving saloon. Henry was glad someone was on hand to help him put up the door.

'That there's a quiet door,' he said, swinging it open and closed a few times. 'Man who built it was mighty clever, wouldn't you say?'

He nailed down the roof last, a single sheet of corrugated iron set at a slope. Free for the moment of advisors and admirers, Henry stepped inside and closed the door. It was warm and dark inside. Redolent of juniper sap. Thin lines of sky and ground striped the walls, contoured Henry's form. A knot hole here and there would have to be pitched.

Palms flat against the warm adobe bricks of the back wall of the saloon, Henry stood for a long time as a pilgrim come to some holy place might. He ran his fingers along the grooves between the bricks and cursed his foolish excitement. In time he went back out and swiveled the hasp over the hook and set the shackle of the padlock through it and clamped the lock shut.

Two

The Board of Directors of the Shakespeare Progress & Improvement Co. were men of wealth and standing who spent most of their time in the capital. No one in Shakespeare knew when one of the directors would be in town, or for how long. Sometimes they came for a day or two, sometimes longer, never paying their respects to the citizens of the town whose progress and improvement it was their wont to promote. What the directors actually did in Shakespeare was not well understood, for they seldom left their room at the Stratford, and yet no one could deny that when a director was in town there was a palpable feeling of progress, of improvement, in the air. Little else was spoken of. Every significant investment in the mines of the True Fissure District could be traced directly to a director's visit. The miners worked harder and drank less, spending money in places other than the saloon, which put the merchants in better moods and gave everyone in Shakespeare a feeling of pending prosperity. Frantic letters were written to wives and sisters back East, proclaiming now, *now* was the time to come to Shakespeare, and these letters were returned with promises of imminent arrival. As long as a director remained in town this feeling of euphoria persisted.

Then, as quietly as he had arrived, the director would leave, presumably back to the capital to fulfil his greater obligations, and once again Shakespeare would be left to fend for itself.

Over the course of these rare visits Rodriguez had developed a special relationship with the directors, for it was he who fulfilled the desires they were unwilling or unable to fulfil themselves. They sent him out to buy their cigars, their brandy, their tinned lobster. They asked him to bring to their rooms people they wished to speak to, more often than not the banker or the engineer. Rodriguez served them their meals, usually in bed, and he boiled and poured the water for their baths. Knowing that his cigar box was always filled with silver dollars by the time the director left, Rodriguez did these things and others with pleasure. Men who otherwise never went to the well at sunrise found excuses when a director was in town to come and fill their buckets and talk to Rodriguez, eager to know if he had overheard anything interesting in the Stratford, any talk of progress, of improvement. Seldom did Rodriguez have anything of value to impart. He heard snippets of conversations here and there as he passed the director's door with an empty tray, or when he carried the luggage of prospective investors, come to see the director, up to their rooms, but never did he hear anything that struck him as an obvious nugget of progress, of improvement. Rodriguez was certain that he would have known if he did, and it was always with sincere regret that he could not give to the men who asked it of him at the well the news of progress and improvement they so yearned to hear.

So it was with some excitement that Rodriguez, one midsummer afternoon, looked up from the floor to see a shiny black Concord with plate-glass windows and plush red velvet seats pull up in front of the hotel and a Director of the Shakespeare Progress & Improvement Co. step out squinting in the brightness and make his way into the lobby.

This Director was a man of advanced years with a full head of wavy white hair, though his skin, true to his Eastern origins, was smooth and pink, plumpened by the fat beneath. Without so much as glancing at Stovall, who was standing behind the reception counter with a welcoming mien, the Director walked past Rodriguez and labored up the stairs.

Rodriguez hurried out and fetched down from the roof of the Concord the Director's dusty, iron-bumpered oak trunk, and hoisting it up onto his shoulder he labored under its weight up the stairs and down the hall to the big room where the Directors always stayed.

The Director was standing at the window, gazing pensively down on Shakespeare.

'This woman,' the Director said. 'The saloonkeeper's wife. You are on friendly terms with her, I presume.'

Rodriguez set the trunk on the floor in a corner of the room and stood beside it should the Director desire it moved elsewhere.

'I see her sometimes at the well, sir.'

'Will you be so kind then,' the Director said, turning and taking a silver dollar from his waistcoat pocket, 'as to convey to her a message to the effect that I desire a word with her in my room, some time tomorrow, at a time convenient to us both. I trust you are familiar with my schedule.'

'Yes, sir.'

'That will be all,' the Director said, holding out the coin.

66

At dawn the next morning Rodriguez went to the well and waited for Mrs. Jonson to arrive. The well was at the north end of Avon, just beyond Henderson's Meat Market, the smell of entrails there thick and ripe. A low adobe wall encircled a hole that no matter how hot the day always emanated a cool breath of humid air. Rock wrens and black-throated sparrows were forever perching on the handle of the bucket, pecking moisture from the rope.

Hand over hand Rodriguez hauled up the leather pouch and poured the water into his bucket. He waited. He poured the water back into the well. Rodriguez had filled and emptied his bucket three times and was about to fill it again when Mrs. Jonson emerged from the Ore and headed for the well, her bucket bouncing gently against the side of her leg.

Rodriguez waited until she had filled her bucket and was turning to leave before he cleared his throat and said: 'Pardon me, Mrs. Jonson, please, for a moment of your time. I have a message for you.'

Abigail stopped and looked at Rodriguez with an expression of mild surprise. She set the bucket down and stood, arms crossed before her, waiting to receive her message.

Rodriguez cleared his throat again and, looking everywhere but at her face, said: 'The Director he would like to speak to you in his room in the hotel. He says this is very urgent, and it is very necessary you come today. This is what he says. He eats his lunch at noon, and he eats his supper at six, so these times would not be good times to see him. Also he sleeps for one hour at three. Between four and six you could come, but sometimes the Directors they are cranky at this time. You should not go very soon after supper. He may be working at his papers. Between seven and eight is best. This is when you should come. I will be waiting for you in the lobby of the hotel, near the big staircase, and I will show you to his room myself. Do you wish me to give to him any message from you before you come?'

Only now did Rodriguez glance at Abigail's face. She appeared to be giving his message some thought, but the sun burning bright behind her was making it difficult for him to see her.

'Your name is Rodriguez, isn't it?' she said.

'Yes, ma'am.'

'I was wondering when you would speak to me. I thought maybe you didn't know English.'

Rodriguez looked puzzled.

'Don't tell me,' Abigail said, 'your wife is on her way here as we speak.'

Rodriguez blushed at the mention of his wife. He cupped a hand over his eyes to block the sun. He had never seen Mrs. Jonson up this close. She didn't seem like the same woman. There was a little smirk on her lips, a look of amusement, as if she were laughing inside at some private joke.

'No,' he said. 'I tell her she cannot come. The Territory is a very dangerous place. And my son, he is a little baby. It is better for you to stay with your family, I tell her, until I come back a rich man.'

Abigail nodded and looked past Rodriguez as if peering at something in the distance.

'Don't you think it strange?' she said. 'Not a single woman here but me, and before me none. Doesn't that seem peculiar to you, Rodriguez?'

Rodriguez looked down at the ground. When he looked up, Mrs. Jonson was still waiting for him to answer.

'I have heard some things,' he said in a hushed voice, as if afraid someone might overhear. 'About the Madam of Bird. She does not want there to be any — how do you say it: *horez*? — in Shakespeare. Then the Shakespeare miners will not go to the Salon in Bird. The Madam knows many people all over the Territory. It is known that the governor himself has come many times to the Salon. Many people respect the Madam. If it is her wish to have no *horez* in Shakespeare, there will be no *horez* in Shakespeare.'

'I find that hard to believe,' Abigail said, somewhat perplexed that this little man, until now a perfect stranger, had taken it upon himself to educate her about the whores of the Territory.

'It is true,' Rodriguez insisted. 'I have heard it many times from the men who come to stay at the hotel. Any *horez* who wants to come to Shakespeare must come first to Bird. But no *horez* who comes first to Bird wants to work in Shakespeare. She wants to work in Bird. The Salon is famous. This *horez* travel very great distances to see the Salon. In their hearts they hope to work there. But only the best *horez* work at the Salon. The Madam picks them herself. Most of the *horez* who go to the Salon to meet the Madam are not good enough to work at the Salon. They must leave Bird and never come back. The Madam is a very smart lady. She knows that a *horez* who cannot work in Bird will try to go to Shakespeare. Shakespeare is her territory. If a *horez* does not listen to the Madam and tries to go to Shakespeare, the Madam will find out and—' Rodriguez sliced his throat with the back of his hand, making a squelchy noise in his cheek. 'These *horez* listen to the Madam because the Madam only says things once. They do not come to Shakespeare.

They go back to where they came from, or they go on to Molloy County, where the madams are not so powerful as the Madam of Bird.'

Abigail couldn't decide which was more outlandish: an invisible fence or an all-powerful madam who inhibited the free movement of whores.

She picked up her bucket and said she was pleased to have finally made his acquaintance, and, bucket sloshing, she walked back to the Ore.

Rodriguez remained at the well a little longer, wondering if it had been ungentlemanly of him to speak with her as he did, as if she were just another man.

'The Director?' Henry said, his spoon sinking back into his bowl of stew.

He rubbed his chin and looked at her. She dipped a corner of butterless bread into her stew and raised it to her mouth. She ate, looking into her bowl.

'What's he want to talk to you for?'

There was a distinct note of agitation in his voice. Abigail shrugged and took another bite. They sat quietly eating, their spoons tapping and scraping the crockery. Around them in erratic loops a horsefly buzzed.

His bowl empty, Henry leaned back in his chair with a quiet groan. Abigail took a few more bites then stood up and carried their bowls into the kitchen. She poured back into the pot what she couldn't finish and stayed standing at the stove, waiting to hear him leave.

'He's an important man,' came Henry's voice.

Abigail lifted the ladle from the pot and tapped it against the rim and set it on the stovetop.

'Never hurts to be on the good side of people like him,' Henry said.

70

Abigail lowered the bowls and the spoons and the ladle into the pail of water on the floor. Henry's chair scooted across the floor. Instead of leaving he came and stood in the doorway, watching her. Abigail dragged the sack of flour back to the corner.

'Man like that,' Henry said, 'if you manage to get on his good side, aint a bad friend to have.'

Abigail straightened up and, looking at Henry, said: 'I'll give him your regards.'

The sun was going down when she left the saloon, the bottle of whiskey in her hand catching the light and blazing like a lantern.

'Good evening, Mrs. Jonson,' Stovall said, straightening up and coming around the counter to kiss her hand, moved to manners by the formality of her dress.

She was wearing a sweeping blue serge skirt and a fancy shirtwaist with puff-top sleeves and floral designs in myrtle and pink. Her lips were painted red, and her hair, normally pinned back to keep it out of her face, was done up in convoluted swirls that wholly transformed her from the saloonkeeper's wife into something else entirely.

Abigail returned his greeting, then, one hand out as if testing the temperature of a bath, she seemed to float across the floor to the staircase, where, with a demure tilt of her head, she offered her arm to Rodriguez.

'Buenas tardes señora,' Rodriguez said, taking her arm and conducting her up the stairs and down the hall to the Director's room, where he knocked on the door and left her without another word.

The moment he heard the door close behind her Rodriguez came back from around the corner and tiptoed up to the door. There he knelt, eye to the keyhole, for quite some time.

The Director was sitting upright in bed, a heavy red-, black-and-white Indian blanket covering his legs. On the bedside table a brass lamp was burning low, giving his pale, fleshy face a sallow cast. He was wearing a white linen nightshirt, unbuttoned at the collar. A book was open, face down, in his lap.

The Director, smiling, gestured toward the high-backed, upholstered armchair a few feet from and facing the bed.

'I'm afraid I cannot accept your husband's gift, Mrs. Jonson,' the Director said as Abigail set the bottle on the bedside table and seated herself in the chair. 'Not out of a sense of propriety, mind you. The fact of the matter is that much of our success depends on maintaining an image of, shall we say, what I mean to say is that we have learned over the years that it is unwise for us to accept gifts of insignificant value.'

The Director looked at her as if he weren't certain she was following his line of reasoning.

'That is not to say that your husband's gesture is not most generous, in fact it surpasses the shall I say merce-nary... opportunistic... what is the... the self-seeking nature of the gifts we are unable to refuse for political as well as personal reasons having to do with the legacies both real and imaginary of our families. I'm speaking of myself and the other Directors of course. If we were to begin accepting small gifts from the citizenry, bottles of whiskey, wheels of cheese, fancy neckties, cufflinks, picture frames, door knockers, dog-powered butter churns and the like, it would be tantamount to embracing the commonly held notion that we are a sort of divine...

charitable... institution, let us say, for lack of a better word, able to give and receive political favors at will, which notion could not be any—'

The Director paused mid-sentence, a look of mild agitation perplexing his brow.

'Forgive me,' the Director said at length. 'I've lost my train of thought.'

'You were explaining why you are unable to accept my husband's gift,' Abigail said.

'Oh yes, thank you. Unfortunately, the more impressionable citizens of the illustrious hamlets of the Territory tend to attribute our somewhat reclusive natures to class snobbery. They believe us unwilling to mingle with the unwashed masses, and perhaps to some degree they are right, not that we have anything against miners and merchants, they are the backbone of the nation. It may have more to do with our breeding, our Eastern manners, each of our fathers in their day barons of one sort or another, great monopolists, whereas we, the other Directors and myself, have never lifted a finger for our wealth. Oh, we tried mixing with men of labor, salt of the earth, in our youth, to no avail. It's a matter of acceptance, I suppose. Knowing one's limitations. We have no desire to cause offense or engender reverence, but it is unavoidable that man in the absence of knowledge invents it. This is not precisely what I asked you here to talk about, though it will be easier if we dispense with it at the outset. The other Directors and I are in agreement on this point. Despite our prolonged absences due to commitments elsewhere, the people here are under the mistaken apprehension that Shakespeare is the only town in the Territory of any concern to us. Nothing could be further from the truth. The Shakespeare Progress & Improvement Co. is but one branch of many — in fact there is one in nearly every mining camp in the Territory — of the Territorial Progress & Improvement Commission, an independent body appointed by and under the aegis of the Territorial Legislature but by no means beholden to the strictures of that august body, in fact free to operate as we see fit, our aim being nothing less than the progress and improvement of the Territory as a whole, with the goal in mind of expediting its bid for statehood. Our role, apart from attracting Capital — the right sort of Capital, mind you, plenty of dirty Capital washing up on our... no... something more appropriate to our arid climate... winds, I suppose, blowing dirty Capital... herds of... no... you get my meaning, Mrs. Jonson, but Capital is only one aspect of progress and improvement — our role in any case is to assure the East that the Territory is well on its way to being self-supporting. So, please send my regards and my regrets to your husband, but I cannot accept his gift.'

With a stifled groan the Director leaned over and took from the drawer of the bedside table a bottle of brandy and two glasses. Setting the glasses on the table he poured into each a little spirit and handed one to Abigail. She took it, thanking him, and held it in her lap. The Director returned to his upright position and sat there for a moment with his eyes closed, recovering from his exertions. Then he opened his eyes, took a sip, and said: 'The matter, Mrs. Jonson — Do you go by that name? I suppose you do. It is best, I think, if I call you Mrs. Jonson to prevent any misunderstandings. I hope I haven't detained you from more important matters.'

'No,' Abigail said.

'Good. I will only take a few more minutes of your time, the matter being—'

Again the Director paused. He turned his head as if straining to hear something.

'Do you hear that, Mrs. Jonson?'

Abigail listened but heard nothing.

'Listen,' the Director said. 'Have you ever heard a more portentous sound? Nothing comforts the soul like the sound of a hinge squeaking in the wind. The corral gate, the shed door, the fence gate, the loose shutter. That is the sound of progress and improvement. The Indian cannot drive it away. If it were only a matter of money it would be different. Take as an example the savages whose land we share, formerly theirs, granted, but the tide of... winds of... civilization not so easily averted. Well, the Romans and Barbarians of course, but decadence they say on that score, overextension of Empire, another matter entirely. If we were to give the red man a million dollars — no, forget dollars, too small — an endless supply of Capital, to dispose of as he saw fit — forget for a moment their predilection for raiding and marauding and depredating and stealing and raping and plundering and pillaging and torturing and scalping and mutilating — and assume they had some notion of how to conduct themselves in the presence of an excess of Capital. Do you think they would make wise investments for the good of their people, building proper buildings, securing stores of nutriment against future drouths and famines, inventing and outfitting vehicles more suitable to this terrain than mangy unshod ponies? No, it is safe to wager that if they did not use it to fuel their fires, given it was in paper form and not bars of bullion or bricks of silver or other precious metal, they would expend every penny of it on armaments to widen the reach of their depredations. My point being that Capital alone does not by necessity lead to progress and improvement. Progress and improvement must go hand in hand with the march of... waltz perhaps more descriptive... waltz of civilization, the rule of law, Christian beliefs, monogamy, abstinence from illicit behaviors barring occasional gluttony and adultery but for the most part accepting that there is a right and a wrong way to go about things. In short: Civilization. At the heart of which must be Woman. Women. Many, many women. At least as many women as men, which is the standard in all of the great metropoli of the world. It goes without saying that where there are no women no civilization can exist.

'Shakespeare, as far as we know, is the only town or hamlet — I believe it has recently surpassed the status of mining camp — in the Territory whose dubious claim to fame is that it possesses not a single woman but yourself, and before you arrived, a period surpassing six months, no woman at all resided within a forty-three-mile radius of Shakespeare, nor did any dare or care or feel any urge to set foot anywhere near Shakespeare, which I think you will agree may be unprecedented in the history of, well, the history of anything. There must be a reason for it, though no one as yet has come up with an adequate explanation. It appears to be an instance of myth preceding and in turn shaping reality, for as far as we can see Shakespeare is no different from any other mining town on the frontier, no better, no worse, and yet even a mining camp as small as Pecan has its fair share of wives and mothers.

'My own wife refuses to accompany me to Shakespeare. When asked why she will not come she is unable to produce a reasonable explanation. Shakespeare is no place for a lady, she says, the heat is too extreme, the town is vulnerable to attack by Indians, it is nothing more than a watering hole for murderers and thieves, any number of outlandish reasons, none of which can be substantiated by facts. A most beguiling situation, I'm sure you agree. How can we be expected to convince men of wealth and enterprise of Shakespeare's prosperous future when we ourselves do not know if Shakespeare will even bear our own sons and daughters? Of course, the matter of procreation is only part of the problem. Which brings me to my second point.'

The Director raised his glass of spirit to his lips and took a sip.

'A curious kind of translation occurs,' the Director resumed, 'when facts leave the Territory in an eastward direction. You don't find this to be the case for westward traveling news, those west of the Territory generally being frontier types themselves or at the very least having passed through the Territory at one time or another and as a consequence understanding some of its more salient features, that is, like the waters flowing on the one hand to the west and on the other to the east as they traverse the Continental Divide, so too in people's minds, especially the minds of women, the facts seem to become muddied in their passage by all manner of fantastic flotsam and jetsam.

'In the end what reaches their ears are fables so irresistible to the Eastern imagination that no amount of reason can eradicate them from their minds, the effect being that one of the most promising new Territories this great nation has ever known, unsurpassed in its mineral wealth, its inexhaustible pasturelands, its mild and salubrious climate, its fertile valleys, its vast unpopulated and arable lands wholly unexploited by the savage or the sloth, its majestic snow-covered peaks, its veritable forests of virgin forest, its unmatched mile-per-man ratio, and much, much more, all of this overlooked, perhaps for good reason, nay not overlooked, never seen at all, in one ear and out the same, having not so much as tickled the brain in its aborted passage, in favor of an image of endless barren wastes of sand overrun by bloodthirsty savages, ruled by desperadoes and outlaws, and nary a woman to be seen, when in fact every town and burg save this one has a fair if not surpassingly fair number of members of the weaker sex in the shape of wives and sisters and daughters and mothers pursuing all of the professions native to their sex, not the least of which is the oldest if not the most honorable profession of them all, I can attest to that.'

Abigail took a sip of brandy and winced. It was vile. The Director coughed twice then went on.

'And so, Mrs. Jonson, Shakespeare has been and continues to be, if slightly less so now that you have come, a thorn in the side of the Territorial Progress & Improvement Commission, and I dare say the fly in the ointment... cog in the gears... metaphor of industry I'm looking for... you take my meaning, of the engine driving us to statehood. It is not my intention to make more of this tragedy than need be. After all, a mattress can be replaced. And I have no doubt that yours will be, in due time, most likely sooner than later, if not from Copes then some other vendor — I have a very good friend in the East who runs a large catalog of domestics, I'm sure he would be happy to oblige you.

'The point is, while I have no doubt that a strong woman such as yourself is not so easily distressed, the

78

matter of greater concern to Progress & Improvement is those who, even as we speak, are making more of this than it merits. Again I speak of the capitalists of the East. I'm afraid it is already too late to stop the news from leaving the Territory. The Eastern papers pretend that their principal interest is the massacre of the two boys, retelling every detail of that tragic day, from the moment they left Bird to the unfortunate choice by the younger one to fire his rifle for no apparent reason, thereby alerting the savages to their presence, but that is neither here nor there. Even to the Easterner these depredations have become all too common.

'The matter of greater interest in the East is the business of the savages absconding with your mattress. I can only imagine why people find this so enthralling, but judging by the tenor and volume of letters to the editor, it is unmistakably so. If this were any old mattress, I doubt there would be such interest. It is the fact that it was a matrimonial mattress that so enflames the Eastern imagination. Visions of savages in their mountain fastnesses cavorting on the very symbol of holy matrimony. None of this would be of any concern to myself or the other Directors if not for the fact that it is exactly this sort of thing that sets us back. Just when it looks as though we are making progress, something like this happens. The victory of your arrival is all but spoiled in an instant by this tawdry affair. What is to be done? I certainly have no desire to bother my brain about these sorts of things, but bother it I must if we are ever to see Shakespeare, and the Territory, achieve their true potential. Had the mattress arrived I am convinced that within a fortnight you would have been enjoying the company of new female friends in Shakespeare.'

The Director, with wistful, glazed eyes, studied Abigail. She gave him a small smile and resumed staring into her drink.

'Yes,' the Director said. 'This has surely set us back. What sane woman will bestir herself now to make a dangerous journey across the continent, believing that if she were to order a mattress she might very well never see it? What hope is there when married men cannot induce their own spouses to join them in an exciting voyage into the unknown, when not a single seamstress, not a cook or boardinghouse keeper or milliner or dressmaker, can be induced by the forces that have always brought men and women together to ensure the happy propagation of the species? What hope is there for civilization to take root in this already desiccated soil perpetually in need of irrigation, particularly in the uplands, untouched by rivers though blessed with artesian wells — what hope?'

His voice straining with emotion, the Director suddenly went quiet, as if guilty of revealing too much. Nearly a minute passed before he spoke again.

'Don't mistake me, Mrs. Jonson. It is not all gloom. I only feel compelled to give you a true and accurate picture of what it is you have come to. There are many men such as myself in the business of enticing Capital who employ a certain degree of, how shall I put it, exaggeration, her mineral resources by all appearances respectable but in no way unsurpassed, buried as they are deep in the earth. Lode mining requires men of patience. And yet it is precisely those who have none who flock to the Territory. Only those born in the Territory will be truly at peace with her. For them it will be heaven. The salvation their fathers sought will come only to them who knowing no other life know none better. Shakespearean tragedies. Is this what they came to the Territory for? To drink it away every night, guzzle down their lust for gold and wake up the next morning to slave for galena? It is hard to imagine a more loathsome profession, beating rocks in caves. Civilization. Progress. Improvement. I ask you, Mrs. Jonson, are any of us better off in the Territory?'

Abigail thought for a moment, then said, 'I'm not quite sure, sir.'

A volley of low booms rattled the windowpanes.

The Director stared at Abigail with tender, fatherly eyes.

'You needn't feel obligated to divulge the more personal circumstances of your life, Mrs. Jonson. I'm only curious to know why it is that you have succeeded where so many before you have failed.'

Again Abigail had no explanation.

The Director fell quiet, as if lost in thought, then he sighed and said: 'In any case. We have already decided that something more must be done to attract, lure if you will, too strong a word perhaps, against their better judgment if need be, more women to Shakespeare. Nothing can be done with the Territory until we have put this matter to rest.'

The Director put a digit in his ear and wiggled it violently for a few seconds.

'It is a matter of publicity in our opinion,' he said. 'Of advertising. A campaign aimed at attracting women to Shakespeare, along the lines of what we spoke of earlier. Civilization. Expressed as higher ideals, the Arts and the like. I intend to hold a town meeting to discuss the issue. If you would be so kind as to ask your husband to make his saloon available, I would be very much indebted to you. Your ideas will be taken very seriously, Mrs. Jonson, I assure you.'

The Director closed his eyes.

'Now I must get some rest.'

It was dark outside the window. The first whoops and hollers could be heard coming from the Ore. One half of the Director's face was bathed in a soft orange light, the other half in darkness.

Abigail stood up and said goodnight.

Rodriguez came to his feet and quickly limped away, his knees refusing to straighten as he hurried down the stairs.

Henry wanted to know everything the Director had told her. Abigail was tired. She couldn't remember everything the Director had said. It seemed to her that he spoke for a very long time but in the end said very little. More than anything she remembered his unusual way of speaking, his perpetual groping for the right phrase. That remained with her, and his plump infant skin in his linen nightshirt, his imploring eyes, as if she, Abigail, held the future of the Territory in her hands.

THREE

Passing the barbershop Andy ran his fingers through his hair and glanced through the window. The barber, Shakespeare's only Negro, whom Andy's uncle never tired of calling 'the Moor', was asleep in the chair, scissors half open in one hand, comb in the other, a fly crawling across his forehead. He looked dead. Like the rest of Shakespeare at that time of day. Andy carried on, walking past the blacksmith's and the bakery, then nearing the miners' tents at the edge of town he stopped abruptly. Heart suddenly pounding, he clutched at his back pocket. But the handkerchief was there. The wind picked up a little, blowing an empty tin slantwise down the street until it hit with a hollow *thunk* the pile of rocks in front of the assay office. Andy exhaled and walked on.

Three men he didn't recognize were standing in front of the hardware store, their dusty mules laden with gear, the lumpy bags and the shafts of picks and shovels jutting radially from them recalling to his mind bagpipes and their grating squeals, which he had heard once in a parade.

'Hey there,' one of the men said to the passing youth. 'It true they aint no whores here?'

By the looks of them they had been many weeks in the desert, their faces and hands dark as mud, the knees of their trousers, where not ripped, worn thin and caked with dirt. One of the men had a piece of cholla cactus stuck to the side of his boot. Their beards appeared to have been trimmed with blunt knives.

Andy stopped.

'I'm afraid so,' he said.

They looked at him as if he were somehow to blame for this state of affairs, then turning away from him and leaning against the mules they fell to discussing without enthusiasm their diminished range of options.

Andy carried on, picking up his pace when he thought he heard one of them say, 'I smelt what I smelt.' Twenty yards beyond the stables, where the pong of horse dung wasn't quite so strong, he took the yellow silk handkerchief out of his pocket and, still walking, brought it to his nose and sniffed. It was still moist, and, it was true, the smell of her was strong on it. He sniffed again. Strong enough for another man to smell? He walked on, sniffing, a feeling suffusing him as he inhaled that singular musk that made his heart not so much pound as squeeze with a peculiar insistence wholly new to him. He felt a stirring in his pants, the flesh therein still sticky and tender, and he put the handkerchief back into his pocket and left Avon for the narrow road through the desert, rutted by the daily comings and goings of his uncle's buggy.

The mesquite and creosote were sparser through this stretch of Shakespeare Draw than through the outwash slopes surrounding Watt Mountain a mile or so off to his left, and the full force of the sun radiating up from the blinding ground made him squint. He could see the house ahead, the tin roof glinting dully in the sun. The mulberry tree, bright splotch of fairytale green against endless shades of brown. The toy burro and toy mule in the toy corral. Off to his right the gypsum and scrub of South Soda Flat sprawled out to the rippling horizon, the far off mountains appearing to hover in thin air, severed from the earth. For the past several weeks the talk in town had been of rain, but the sky showed no sign of it. Only great bolls of cotton hovering high in the limitless blue. Whiptail lizards ventured from the cover of brush and froze in the road looking sideways at him through slit eyes, smug and indifferent, their long turquoise tails hair-thin at their length. Then, true to their name, tails whipping side to side, they scurried away.

Halfway to the house he came to the shredded gray disk of boot leather that before his uncle's buggy had flattened it nearly a week ago had been a horned toad, its juices long since devoured by ants and sun. The first time he had seen one was at the little stage stop south of the capital. 'Horny toad,' a man he was traveling with said, seeing Andy grinning at the strange little reptile scurrying across the dirt in the fitful shuffle peculiar to its species. And for a moment Andy felt as though he had slipped into a dream. It was an odd sensation. All the stories he had ever heard about the Territory, wild stories of cowboys and Indians, of mountains of gold and silver, of distances beyond human comprehension, of strange beasts and plants stranger yet, things he had yearned to believe in but could not, having never seen them with his own eyes, had suddenly, upon seeing this thorny little creature, become real, and in becoming real so suddenly and with such force the Territory had ceased at that moment to exist for him as merely an idea to muse on in idle moments and had become instead a land of waking dreams, a land whose only borders were the limits of one's imagination.

Andy stopped and stared at the dry little carcass. He imagined putting it in an envelope and mailing it to his mother as a souvenir of the Territory, but he feared she would not appreciate it, or, worse yet, read into it confirmation of her worst fears about the godforsaken place she had sent her boy.

The cry of a hawk drew his attention skyward. Wings black against the luminous blue, it glided in a wide gyre high on the boiling air. Andy watched it until his neck began to ache, then he looked down and walked the rest of the way home.

It wasn't every day. Sometimes as many as three days would pass before he would see among the bills of the deposit the note in her handwriting that told him to come after work. She made him promise never to come unless she asked him to. He understood her precautions — she also made him come by the north and leave by the south side of the building — but he could not understand why she insisted he come in broad daylight, when the saloon was quiet, rather than under cover of darkness. The first few times, in the bright stillness of mid-afternoon, he was so afraid Mr. Jonson would hear them across the wall that it had cost Abigail considerable effort to arouse him, and even then, after he was safely on the road back home, he told himself he would not go again. Never ever again. It wasn't worth dying for. But he did go again. And again.

It had been three days since Abigail had given Andy a note when one afternoon Mr. Jonson came into the bank himself to make the deposit. Seeing that wiry old man with his slow walk and hard face stride in where Abigail should have been gave Andy a terrible fright, and it was all he could do to swallow his fear and keep it down until Mr. Jonson had left.

'You're lookin good, young man,' Henry said jovially, setting the bag on the counter, and then to Crawford, 'I expect the climate's done him some good after all.'

'I'm not so sure of that,' Crawford said. 'Don't you think he looks a little gaunt?'

They studied him.

'Gaunt?'

'Like he's not getting enough to eat.'

Henry, head cocked, rubbing his chin, looked at Andy.

'Looks all right to me.'

Andy took the money from the bag and proceeded with quivery hands to count it, remembering as he did so his first time with Abigail, how he kept telling her he couldn't do it, she was a married woman, couldn't do it, it wasn't right, Mrs. Jonson, no couldn't do it, and how with each refusal she had found a new way to weaken his resolve, and afterwards, he couldn't believe what he had done, like she had cast some kind of spell over him, *the perfume and suppliance of a minute*, the feeling of all that skin, all that wetness, like nothing he had ever imagined and he had imagined it plenty, the smells too. He never should have gone the second time but he thought maybe she had wanted to talk to him, to tell him that they had made a mistake and that was the end of it, but then, just like the first time, she went down on the mattress and pulled up her dress, only this time she had nothing on beneath it, and the sight of what lay between her skinny white thighs had been too much for him. She made him wrap the handkerchief around himself, and when they were done it had stayed in her until she reached down and like a magician pulled it out and handed it back.

'Yes, sir,' Henry said. 'He's shapin up a real man. Kinda tragic they aint no more ladies than they is in town. Young Mr. Selgren here'd be a poplar man. Poplar indeed.'

Andy lost count and started again.

'You ever hear back from that gal with the...'

'I'm afraid not,' Crawford said. 'It's probably for the best.'

'Oh?'

'She certainly would not have lasted here as long as Mrs. Jonson, under the circumstances.'

Henry, still watching Andy count the money, shifted his weight to his other hip. After a while he turned around and stood facing the door, one elbow still on the counter.

'Be nice if them clouds'd make up their minds,' he said. 'Poor old Taggart's afraid his cattle caint take much more of it. Some a them gamblers are startin to wager whether or not we'll get any at all.'

Andy, finished counting, dipped the nib into the ink and brought it to the next empty line of the ledger, the numbers he set there marred by burrs and jags. He filled out a receipt likewise illegible and set it on the counter.

'There you are, Mr. Jonson,' he said officiously.

Henry turned and picked up the receipt and studied it with a perplexed look.

'Is everything in order, Mr. Jonson?' Andy said, a dry quiver in his voice.

Henry glanced at Andy.

'Good Lord, son, you look like you seen a ghost.'

Andy smiled feebly.

'Did I make a mistake?'

Henry looked at the receipt.

'Nope,' he said. 'Right as rain.'

Then he gave Crawford and Andy a little salute with the receipt and wished them a good day and left the bank.

FOUR

Rodriguez put the gristly chunk of pork shank into the boiling pot of beans and stirred it with the iron ladle. The fragrance of garlic and onion and green chile rose on the steam and filled the tiny kitchen and drifted out into the desert through the open door. Ladle to his lips he blew across the juice and sipped. He took a pinch of salt from the paper bag on the shelf behind the stove and sprinkled it into the pot and stirred again, then he sat down on the loose wooden chair against the wall and stayed there for some time, staring out the door.

The bellies of the clouds were dark as bruises, amassing in the morning over the mountains around the horizon, floating on the westerlies blowing across the Mendrugo Valley, marooning Shakespeare again and again on islands of shade only to plunge it once more into a sea of sunlight. By evening the clouds were gone, the sky empty. Day and night the distant thunder softly rumbled.

Rodriguez thought of his son seeing these very clouds, far away to the south, and he wondered what animals the boy would see in them. He wondered if his son ever thought of him at all.

He got up and served himself a plate of beans and

reheated one of yesterday's tortillas. He sat with the plate in his lap, dabbing pieces of tortilla into the beans, sweat dripping down his forehead. He ate quickly. The Director was napping but soon would be awake and wanting things. The feeling of Mrs. Jonson's arm in his as he escorted her up the stairs and to the Director's bedroom returned to Rodriguez with a little surge of warmth. At the time he had been afraid he might step on her skirt, but now it was the feeling of her arm against his that remained with him. Rodriguez wiped his forehead with the back of his hand.

When he looked up, the dog, a grayish tan bitch of indeterminable breed, was standing in the doorway panting. Rodriguez ate a little more then set the plate on the ground outside the door. The dog wolfed down the piece of tortilla and lapped up the beans and licked the plate clean then stood there looking at Rodriguez with upslanted brows.

Rodriguez pulled the bone from the beans and using the shaft of the ladle scraped away the loose pieces of meat and tossed the bone onto the plate. He knelt and petted and scratched the dog's head and spoke in gentle tones to it in Spanish. The dog trotted off, the joint sticking out of the side of her jaw.

'The Director wants a cigar,' Stovall said when Rodriguez returned to the lobby.

Stovall gave him some money, and Rodriguez walked across the street to the General Store.

Blaine was sitting on his stool behind the cash register, reading last week's *Bird Eagle*. A miner near the dry goods hoisted a twenty-five-pound sack of flour over his shoulder. Another man was pondering the merits of a gray wool blanket.

Rodriguez picked up a tin of green olives and a tin of tomatoes from a dusty shelf, comparing the heft of each with the other, then he blew the dust off of them and set them back on the shelf. After perusing other goods both durable and comestible, he made his way back to the front counter. Worst to best the tobacco and smoking articles were laid out on a shelf in the glass case.

'What can I get ye?' Blaine said, turning his ever-suspicious gaze up from the paper to Rodriguez.

Rodriguez pointed out the cigar he wanted, and Blaine, folding the newspaper and tossing it to the floor, took the cigar from the box and set it on the counter.

'Two bits,' he said, his hand resting on the cigar.

Rodriguez gave him the money.

'That Director gonna be at the meetin?' Blaine said, handing Rodriguez the cigar.

'I don't know,' Rodriguez said.

'Be a miracle if he was. Them sonsabitches don't give a damn about people. You can tell him I said that, too.'

'Now there's no need to be unneighborly,' the miner said. 'The man's workin day and night to get us a little progress and improvement. Aint that right, Rodriguez? Up till all hours of the night consultin with certain individuals.'

Rodriguez smiled but made no reply.

'I wouldn't mind doin a little consultin with a certain individual myself,' Blaine said.

'Hell,' said the other man, 'I'd consult with a bucket a lard round about now.'

'Now that there aint a bad idea,' the miner said.

'Over by the sugar,' Blaine said, pointing a lazy finger. 'Half a dollar a pound.'

The men were still laughing as Rodriguez quietly slipped out the door and returned to the hotel.

He waited until his uncle's buggy was leaving Avon before he stepped out from the lee between the bank and the assay office, tugged down on the front of his coat, and started across the street. A cooling, humid breeze, on which Andy caught a pleasant whiff of spicy beans was blowing through town. It had been thundering all day, soft rumbles like avalanches in the folds of distant mountains, all the uncannier to hear churning deep within the bruisy clouds overhead. A tarantula sat motionless in the middle of the street, as if unable to decide which side held the most promise. Andy nudged it with his shoe and it took a few fuzzy black steps and stopped.

There were six men, not including Mr. Jonson, scattered around the saloon at a number of tables, several asleep or drunk or both. Those awake watched with some curiosity as the young paying and receiving clerk, whom everyone knew was forbidden by his uncle from patronizing the saloon, stepped in and with some hesitation approached the bar.

Henry, his hands spread wide atop the bar, one leg crossed over the other, watched without expression as Andy stepped up to the bar.

'Afternoon, Mr. Jonson,' Andy said, addressing Henry's belt buckle. 'I'll take a whiskey, please.' His alacrity out of tune with the general torpor of the afternoon.

A little gust of breath, a fraction of a laugh, pushed through a nose at one of the tables. Henry squinted at Andy and grabbed a glass and set it on the bar and poured into it a shot of whiskey. Andy raised the glass to his lips and took a sip and winced, his eyes watering at once. He sniffled.

'Half a dollar,' Henry said.

Andy took a coin from his trouser pocket and set it on the bar. He raised his glass to Henry in a cordial way and went over to a table in the front left corner, by the window, and sat, his heart and stomach all aglow. He looked out of the window. The tarantula hadn't moved. The weeds along the street were bending in the breeze. He watched a dust devil swerve drunkenly down the street and sweep through the front door of the barbershop.

There in the corner, by the window, Andy sat and nursed his whiskey, his secret smoldering inside with every sip. See there, he told himself. Just an old saloonkeeper.

So it was that Andy, on the depositless afternoons, would sit alone in the front corner of the saloon, his back against the wall, and nurse a glass of whiskey. At times he pictured himself an outlaw, waiting for his moment, and he would glance toward the back wall, where he knew tomorrow or the next day, coupled in sin, he would lay his enemy's wife, and he would stifle a smile and take another sip.

Sometimes the miners, drunk or bored or both, would cajole him, try to get him to write love letters for them to sweethearts, no doubt wholly imaginary, in far away places. To which mocking proposals Andy would only smile and say no thank you.

One afternoon a drunk miner, getting nowhere with his offers to pay Andy a dollar a letter, said: 'Aint you a poet?'

'I wouldn't call myself that,' Andy said, flattered nonetheless.

'I didn't ask what ye called yourself.'

Andy demonstrated his equanimity with a nod and a smile. 'Right you are,' he said.

'Make me a poem,' the miner said.

'Well,' Andy said, 'I'm not much good at spontaneous composition.'

The miner turned to the other men. 'Sounds like a poet to me,' he said. He turned back to Andy. 'Make me a poem about a felloe.'

'A fellow, eh?' Andy said gamely. 'What sort of fellow?'

'Well, any sort a felloe. Aint much difference tween em far as I's ever seen.'

Andy gave this some thought. 'How big is this fellow?' he said.

'Big as most is.'

'What does this fellow do?'

'Same damn thing ever other'n does.'

Andy looked up at the ceiling. It was clear that the man was trying to make him the butt of some joke. It would be best, he thought, to play along.

'Is this fellow young or old?'

The miner thought for a moment.

'Old, I expect.'

'Thin or fat?'

'More thick than thin. Aint so much fat as curved.'

'Does the fellow in question have any hidden weaknesses?'

'I reckon all felloes have flaws of one kind or another, though if they's hidden ye caint rightly see em, can ye?'

'What about a name?' Andy said. 'Does this fellow have a name?'

'What kinda fool goes and names a felloe?'

'Well, the fellow's mother, I suppose,' Andy said. 'Or his father.'

At this the men burst into laughter, picturing the proud parents of the rim of a wagon wheel. Andy looked at

95

Henry, grinning himself, and laughed too, though he knew not at what he was laughing.

'Kid,' the miner said, 'you's pretty dumb for a poet.'

To Andy's mind this comment was uncalled for, and to the glow of whiskey was added the sting of incivility.

'Dumb but perty,' the miner said, grinning through a mouth of tobacco-blackened teeth. 'Perty dumb for bein so smart.'

Andy looked away, smarting from the insult.

'Look at his hands,' the miner said. 'All nice and clean. Them's some mighty slender fingers for a man. Skin all pink and rosy. He even smells sweet with that flower water on him.'

Andy considered getting up and walking out, but he didn't care to have his pride perceived, particularly by Mr. Jonson, to be so easily injured.

'How do you keep the dust off your clothes?' the miner said. 'Not a speck.'

The moment the miner stood up it was clear that he was drunk. He staggered over to Andy's table and standing there swaying back and forth said: 'Come over and look, Hobbs. I caint find a single speck a dust on his coat.'

The miner, eyes red and swimming in his sockets, conveyed in his every drunken atom such crudeness that Andy couldn't bare to look at him. He turned and faced the window. The man's smell was overwhelming, a mixture of overripe flesh and inebriation. Andy expected Henry any moment now to come over and remove the miner from the premises, but Henry did not, even when the miner began running his grubby fingers over Andy's clothes, in his hair, grinning maniacally.

'Soft as silk,' the miner crooned.

He went on running his hands through Andy's hair

until Andy, at wit's end, stood up and, not exactly facing the miner, shouted: 'Get your stinking hands off of me!'

It was probably no more than a few seconds, but to Andy the awkward moment that followed his outburst seemed to him an aeon. He looked at Henry, expecting to see in his expression something that indicated his thoughts on the situation, but if anything Henry seemed utterly indifferent.

By the time Andy looked back, the cold blade of the knife was already pressed against his throat.

'What's that you was sayin?' the miner asked with exaggerated politeness.

A warm stream ran down Andy's left leg into his shoe.

Henry set down his rag and walked around the side of the bar and stood where the drunken miner could see him. Andy had begun to breathe again, but his eyes were squeezed shut, his hands clutching the edge of the table.

'How bout I slit your perty little throat for ye with this here stinkin knife?' the miner asked.

'Get back to your table, Klemmet,' Henry said, 'and quit botherin my customers.'

Klemmet paid no heed. He tightened his grip on Andy's collar.

Without any notice of such Henry walked over to Klemmet and in one fluid motion grabbed his wrist and pulled it away from Andy's throat and knocked the knife to the floor. Henry stepped between Andy and Klemmet. Klemmet, waiting first for his mind to catch up with his eyes, bent down to pick up his knife. Henry set his boot over it.

'Pick it up on your way out.'

'I am on my way out,' Klemmet said, jerking his arm away and glaring at Henry and Andy both.

Henry kicked the knife out the door.

Klemmet spat on the floor in the direction of Andy and staggered out the door, Henry turning and watching him as he went. Outside, Klemmet picked up his knife and missed the sheath twice before he got it in, then cursing under his breath he staggered up the road.

'Don't pay him no attention,' Henry said to Andy. 'He's a decent fella, when he aint drunk.'

Andy looked around the saloon. All the miners were staring at him. A wave of humiliation washed over him.

'Thank you,' Andy mumbled to Henry, his mouth parched, and quietly left the saloon and started home, a cold, sharp line across his neck.

Andy was quiet at supper and quiet on the porch afterwards, Romeo purring in his lap, Crawford's words drifting over him without sense into the falling blue. Alone he watched the cottontails come one by one out of the surrounding dark to nibble the grass around the trunk of the mulberry tree, smudges of paler night, moon glowing in their eyes, until the tree was bibbed with them. Back in his room he took Theodore out of the trunk and set him on his knee and opened and closed his mouth a few times but said nothing.

The following evening, he left the house carrying a canvas bag in his left hand, its bulging, sharp-cornered contents clinking hollowly as he followed his gangly shadow through the brush, over the crusty sand. A hundred yards from the back of the house he stopped before a large mesquite. One by one from the canvas bag he took and hung on twigs and branches eight tin cans still smelling of brine, the red, white and green labels of Captain Aaron's Oysters, soiled and torn or missing altogether, lending a festive air to the bush.

Tins in place Andy walked back twenty yards and took the slingshot from his front pocket. He had ordered it from Peck & Snyder nearly a month ago, thrilled by the description in the catalog: *sturdy ash frame, heavy rubber tubes, soft kid pouch. Fell pigeons at 25m.*

Finding a suitable stone, he planted it in the pouch between his thumb and first finger. He held the pouch to his cheek and straightened his leading arm and held it trembling before him, *target between the top of the Y*, as the pamphlet recommended. The stone shot out with a flappy *thwop* and sailed wide of the mark.

Andy lowered the slingshot. He was not discouraged. All skills took time to master. He tried again. On his eighth try he hit a tin, and that bright *ping* in the otherwise *ping*less evening sent him racing back to the mesquite to confirm his progress. Each time he hit a tin he ran back to the mesquite and rubbed his finger with satisfaction over the small dent. From the green branch of a nearby mormon tea bush a wren watched with twitching head and blinking eye this man-child learning his weapon.

Five

The sound could be heard echoing off the high granite walls of Chirigota pass, a ceaseless jangling akin to a hundred out-of-tune wind chimes battered by a gale, growing louder by the minute, long before the burro pulling a cart antediluvian in crudeness nosed its way into the shady ravine. The wheels of the cart were thick slices of cottonwood trunk and as such were neither perfectly round nor of the same diameter, bits of stubborn bark all they possessed by way of tires. The axle was a branding iron. The body of this vessel was a confluence of woodscrap cobbled together with nails and rope, all the pieces of wood different colors, as if taken from the ruins of storefronts. From every side of this ramshackle conveyance, swinging and swaying in every direction like the tangled locks of a woolly mammoth, hung countless metal objects, some of them identifiable as goods of use to man, many defying classification altogether, all clinking and clanking with every list and lurch of the cart.

Atop this vehicle, easily missed from a distance, sat a man roughly half the size of a full-grown member of his race but otherwise perfectly proportional. The rifle across his lap was not much shorter than he. His name was Little John, and he was known throughout the southern half of the Territory for his gift of persuasion, a gift that more than once had delivered him into the bad graces of the law, from which he was presently absenting himself.

Pulling into the gorge he noticed up ahead, in the near distance, lying in the middle of the sandy ravine, a lumpy canvas bag besmeared with dried blood.

'Whoa!' he shouted, the pitch of his voice somewhere between a child's and a man's.

His trusty burro which bore no name came to an obedient halt.

Little John cocked his rifle, and that bright snap echoed through the canyon for many seconds to come. He sat perfectly still, waiting for his wares to settle, ears open and listening. It was late in the day, the wind calm. He looked high to the left, high to the right, but saw nothing save the history of the earth wrung through the strata. He turned and looked behind him. Reason suggested he turn around and find another way to cross the mountains.

Climbing down from the cart he told the burro to stay, and with tiny, cautious steps he stole across the sand over to the bag. It was a mail sack, the words TERRITORIAL POST stenciled across it in faded black lettering. Little John glanced around once more, then, dragging the bag off to the side, he untied the knot in the drawstrings and dumped a heap of bloodstained envelopes and parcels and other printed matter onto the ground. On one knee he idly perused the addresses for names familiar to him. Finding none, he sat down Indian-style and grabbed the nearest envelope and opened it and read the letter. Lonely for the words of his fellow man, Little John opened letter after letter and read them where he sat, it soon becoming apparent that these were letters from the loveless men of Shakespeare. Little John sat and read with an aching heart the desperate words of these men, for he too had been without a woman's love for many years.

Night was falling fast, the black clouds harrying the narrow run of sky above the gorge, promising a night of rain. Little John unyoked the burro and gathered dry branches blown down from the junipers bearding the lip of the bluffs and built a fire beneath an awning of stone. There he sat and by the warm glow of the fire proceeded to read the unread letters.

One of the envelopes he opened was addressed to the editor of the *Bird Eagle*. In it was a letter on Bank of Shakespeare stationery from one A.W. Crawford, to the effect that enclosed was his latest dispatch. Mr. Crawford expressed his hope that last spring's story of Miss Walker's arrival and subsequent marriage to Mr. Jonson had met with the approval of the newspaper's erudite readers. He also stated that he would continue to practice his unique, bracing style of narrative so long as the editor found no fault in it.

Little John tossed some more sticks onto the fire and settled back against the wall and read:

A Midsummer Night's Plea
by A.W. Crawford.

Shakespeare, the thriving little town at the heart of the famous True Fissure District, having not yet reached a plane of development adequate to the responsibilities and expenses that directly follow the severance of the bond through which we draw vitality and sustenance as if from the maternal bosom, was lately visited by one of the venerable, if not the most venerable, Directors of the Shakespeare Progress & Improvement Co., the express purpose of said visitation being to encourage the men of Shakespeare to redouble their efforts to attract to their hamlet members of the fair sex. To this end a historic town meeting was held in the Ore Saloon and Gaming House, every man and woman in Shakespeare attending.

At the behest of the Director the meeting was called to order and administered by your esteemed correspondent, owner and manager of the Bank of Shakespeare, majority stockholder of the Shakespeare Mining & Milling Company, and sometime author of regional enchiridia.

'Friends, Romans, Countrymen...' — alas the occasion did seem to merit such lofty diction — 'I trust you are aware of the grave situation our town continues to face despite our best efforts to produce a more balanced distribution of the sexes. Fellow Shakespeareans, something is rotten in Shakespeare, and its name is Celibacy.'

To this pronouncement came a solemn nodding of noggins.

'In our quest for answers we have scoured like scholars the brittle pages of our history. It is said that before the Territory came into being one old man and his dog kept a small flock of sheep on the land that today is Shakespeare and its environs. The old man had no wife, and legend has it that his faithful dog was also male, its name being Perro, which Mr. Rodriguez has kindly informed me is Spanish for Dog. That said, we the men for whom the study of history is a most sacred endeavor deem it highly unlikely that none of the sheep that the old man herded were ewes, and as such may rule out the possibility that some malicious whim of Nature has conspired to make this otherwise bountiful parcel of the Territory barren of females of all species, flora and fauna alike, a proposition which I think you will agree is patently absurd and easily refuted by empirical evidence. Even so, it must be said that there are some amongst us of exceptional imagination who do indeed cling like babes to the breast to ideas not dissimilar to the one I castigate.

'Now, seven months have come and gone since that first vein of native silver was discovered in what has hence become the Lear and the first miners and merchants came to found Shakespeare. To still be womanless, with all due respect to Mrs. Jonson, after all this time is, to say the least, disquieting. If we consult the biographies of men who have made themselves eminent, we see without fail that by their sides, to blunt their sharper passions, stood a woman. Lest any man claim to have prospered without a woman by his side, I submit that that man was no man at all but rather half a man, and that half not the better. What, I ask you, is an Antony without his Cleopatra? A Romeo without his Juliet? A Claudius without his Gertrude? Did God make Eve from the rib of Adam for the mere sport of it? I should think not.

'Hear me, fellow Shakespeareans, we are nothing without our women. Nothing in the eyes of the East, upon whom we depend for our daily bread. Nothing, it pains me to say, in the eyes of ourselves. Something must be done to purge this plague of womanlessness from our midst. Where will the future generations of Shakespeare come from, I ask you, if not from Shakespeare itself? We must find, and in many cases reunite with, our better halves lest we never become the men who won the West for our grandchildren's grandchildren. So I say to you, fellow Shakespeareans, in the name of God, think of something. Do something. Write to your mothers and your sisters and your wives and your fiancées and implore them, on your knees if you must, to join you on your adventure in Shakespeare. Tell them what they want to hear. Remind them of the salubrious qualities of our climate, of the wealth of opportunity in the feminine trades. Remind them how it feels to be young again, new again, full of vim and vigor. Tell them anything, but by God, get them to Shakespeare, or get them to a nunnery!'

And the miners and merchants, moved by this humble

entreaty, surged as one for the door, eager to be the first at their pens and paper, believing at last that if only they could make their better halves feel their desperation the women would come, and all would be forgiven, and babies would be born the following spring, and capital would likewise flow into Shakespeare's coffers, and in time the metropolis that Shakespeare is destined to become would be on its way to being. But, alas, patience was counseled, for there was business yet at hand.

Now the floor was opened to suggestions for a campaign aimed at changing the greater public's perception that Shakespeare is a town unfit for the habitation of women. Someone suggested building a church, which idea was hardly given a Christian hearing. Another man opined that women did not feel safe without a marshal on hand to enforce the law, a proposal no more kindly received than the previous.

'Something aint right if -------- won't even come here,' one man lamented. 'If Shakespeare caint attract -------- how can it attract respectable women?'

A murmur of assent circumnavigated the saloon.

Your correspondent reminded the illustrious citizens that there was a lady present, but the fair Mrs. Jonson, fair in all respects, protested that she would take no offense from a discussion of --------, and all the merry men of Shakespeare gave three boisterous cheers for Mrs. Jonson.

All eyes on Shakespeare's only woman, the crowd as one now asked Mrs. Jonson what she believed could be done to change the image of their town. Mrs. Jonson, not naturally inclined to public oratory, tried valiantly to deflect the attention of this concerned colloquium away from herself, but knowing that she was their best hope for success the long-suffering men of Shakespeare would not countenance any deferrals in the guise of good breeding. And so, giving due credit to the Director for her inspiration, Mrs. Jonson, in language more gentle than your

105

correspondent is capable of resurrecting, put forth the idea of inviting to Shakespeare a well-known theatrical troupe to perform one of the plays of the divine Bard himself, the idea being that the novelty of the enterprise would make for interesting reading back in the States and would perhaps shed a somewhat softer light on our town than it has hitherto enjoyed from the press.

If it is true that great ideas are seldom well received at their initial airing, then it is this correspondent's humble opinion that the absolute silence that followed Mrs. Jonson's suggestion is the truest measure of its merit.

'Someone needs to get hanged,' someone suggested. 'That's what this town needs. A good hanging. Look what it did for Hangtown. A good hanging, now that will attract young men and women who want to start families. A heritage to be proud of. And it's a hell of a lot cheaper than paying a bunch of actors to come all the way out from the States.'

Lamentably, space does not permit me the luxury of sharing with the readers of this esteemed periodical every idea that was proffered that night. Suffice it to say that no genuine display of civic enthusiasm was in evidence until one man suggested offering a reward to the man who brought to Shakespeare the most women in a single trip. As is so often the case in our wild and free towns, it was not long after this remark that things started getting lively.

Cries of, 'How much!' and 'Who pays!' flew up all around.

'Wanted: Women. Dead or Alive!'

'Wives Wanted. Apply within. Nobody barred!'

In his glee at so scabrous a notion, a miner (A) flung his arms back in laughter, inadvertently elbowing the man behind him (B) in the nose. B flew up in a blind rage and slugged A in the face. A stumbled back and careened into a table where four men (C,D,E and F) were seated, sending

106

glasses and bottles crashing to the floor. C,D,E and F, needing no more excuse than this to lash out at the nearest man, did just that, and soon every letter of the alphabet, and a goodly number of Roman numerals, were translated into a seething mass of flailing fists. Your correspondent hurried to safety behind the bar, where amongst the weak and wounded he watched unfold a contest of strength and stamina unparalleled in all the martial verse of Homer. Mr. Jonson, a veteran of battles deadlier than this, with the composure of the valiant knight of La Mancha, single-handedly steered the battle out of his place of business and into the freer arena of Avon Avenue, where it raged for some time to come. A lull in the battle gave your correspondent an opportunity to thank the gentle citizens of Shakespeare for attending the meeting.

'The Director' — who could be seen standing in the window of his hotel room — 'has taken note of your enthusiasm.'

Collars were freed from clutches, bloodied noses wiped with backs of hands, hats reseated atop heads. And with hard-earned shame the illustrious citizens of Shakespeare retired to their domiciles to while away the remaining hours of this otherwise idyllic midsummer night.

So engrossed in the narrative had Little John been that he failed to notice the first drops of rain thumping the sand. He quickly scooped the heap of letters back into the mail sack and pulled it under his shelter.

The image of that solitary woman of Shakespeare, a calm in the eye of a storm, stayed with Little John long into the night, even as the lightning strobed the deluge and the thunder blasted the canyon walls. He awoke deep in the night to see stars shining above. All the world black but for a thin belt of stars.

ONE

Stirred from her nap by a rumble that shook the floor, Abigail got up from the mattress, opened the back door and looked up at the sky. The leading edge of the front was passing overhead, dark as ink and ominously silent. A gust of humid wind blew against her, wrapping the fluttering hem of her skirt around her ankles. The chill in the air after so many days of relentless heat brought tears to her eyes, and she stood there in the wind, goosebumps spreading up her legs and down her arms, stood there breathing in the smell of rain, not so much remembering as feeling within her the memories of other storms. Gray skies like this one. The wind in her hair. Nerves alive and tingling. She went out to the clothesline, unclipped the clothes and carried them back inside and set to folding them.

His hair blown to the wrong side of the part, Rodriguez stepped back into the lobby and closed and bolted the doors. A piece of tumbleweed twirled in an eddy and flew up into the sky. It was gloomy in the hotel, the wind hissing and whistling through every breach in the edifice. He lowered the chandelier and lit all six wicks with the flame of a long wooden match and wound it back up to the smoke-darkened medallion on the ceiling. Upstairs he closed and clamped all the windows. In the Directors' room, now vacant, he stood at the window looking down on wind-swept Avon. Blaine and another man were quickly pulling twenty-five-pound sacks of flour from a buckboard and jogging them on their shoulders into the store. There at the window a memory of his wife's warm buttered tortillas returned to Rodriguez, and he closed his eyes and savored them again. Thunder rattled the chamber set.

Down in the kitchen he opened the back door and whistled, but the dog did not come. A bright flash momentarily blinded him. The sky ripped like rag linen and collided with the earth and rumbled. Somewhere a cock began to crow.

The leaves of the mulberry tree were shushing in the wind, the outer branches reeling drunkenly. The hot iron roof of the house thunked and plinked in the sudden chill. Above the storms in the far southwest the sky pooled molten gold over the leaden mesas of cloud and rain needling the earth with lightning. North of the Gable Range the sky was as blue as a medicine bottle, the desert dry and bright, all the bluer, all the brighter against the mounting gloom. Andy stood at the edge of the porch, watching the storm advance, reading into the diminishing gap between lightning and thunder tidings of divine retribution.

The first drops hit with a tentative patter, stippling to their darker shades all things naked to the sky. Drop by drop Avon shed its coat of dust, light percussion of *tap* and *ping* and *thump*, until a crack of thunder rent the heavens, pulling a curtain of rain across Shakespeare that hung rippling in the wind long into the night. Rain sluicing down in great curvy waves of gray. Rain pooling across the flat roofs and spilling in glassy sheets over the cheap crown moldings, slicing long rills into the mud. Rain pouring over the junk skirting the buildings, finding reservoirs never intended as such in all manner of abandoned things. Shovel scoops. Scale pans. An old black boot. All dark and heavy save an aureole of mist faintly luminous around the cracked glass fount of a derelict bronze hand lamp. Avon's dips and sags, hitherto unnoticed, soon were mirroring every flash of lightning.

The lightning closing in on the lodes, Kelly ordered the miners out of the Lear and back to town. Soon the saloon was packed, everyone wild with joy. Any man who wished to be heard by the man beside him had to yell over the roar of the rain and the ear-splitting thunder and every other man yelling over it all. Now and then the front door would fly open and in would stomp a breathless, sopping man, a crust of mud around the soles of his boots. Tilting his head to reach for his hat a veil of water would spill across his face, and some miner getting sprayed by the mist blowing in would yell at him to close the dadgum door. Henry could be seen throughout the night stealing suspicious glances toward the ceiling, but the old shepherd had proven himself a master mason of mud, which the effort Henry had expended digging a single adobe brick out of the back wall should well have convinced him of — not a drop came in by way of the roof. The floor was another matter. As the night wore on and the storm did not relent, water began trickling in under the door. Henry built a dam of rags across the sill, which, between people coming and going and fjords in the cloth, did little to keep the water at bay.

Then, sometime after midnight, a quiet stunning to behold suddenly descended over everything. No sound

113

from without save quiet thunder skulking away in the distance. From the front door of the Ore, Avon under the blackness of space appeared a river of tar, the flames of the Stratford's chandelier smoldering in the muck. A dim dog splattered by and was gone.

Abigail lay awake in the dark, listening. It seemed the breath had been knocked out of the world. No sounds even from the saloon. She closed her eyes. She had just begun to fall asleep when out of this stillness came a sound like the bleat of a lamb. Followed a moment later by another. Then another. Until suddenly the night was filled with a chorus of bleating. Each bleat as loud as a bugle blare. Wave upon wave of undulous bleating. Seemingly right outside the back door.

Abigail got up and lit the lamp. She went to the door and opened it and what she saw out there almost made her drop the lamp. The shore of a shallow lake began a few feet from the back door, the end of which could not be seen, and all across the ink-black water a thousand little eyeballs were glinting yellow in the lamplight. Blinking. Startled to silence by the intrusion of light. A sea of tiny greenish-yellow frogs, male spadefoots aroused by the thunder from their long, dry hibernation underground, crying out for mates to join them in a night's debauch before returning at dawn's first light, bloated with water, back into the ground.

She could have been made of stone, standing there like some Victory in her niche. The frogs as still as she.

She turned out the lamp, plunging herself and the frogs back into total darkness save the soft flickers of lightning.

The first cautious bleats seemed to inspire courage in the rest. Who knew when this night might come again? Abigail leaned a shoulder against the doorframe and stayed there for some time, serenaded from below by a throng of would-be princes.

'What the hell is wrong with that kid?'

Henry, shirtless, stopped pacing and was now standing at the window looking out, his arms crossed at his belly. On the wall beside him, a few feet to the right of the window, hung a framed chromo of Bardolph's 'Still Life with Oranges', two small holes the size of bullets in it slightly darker than the shadow of the bowl in which they lay.

Outside, the thunderheads were amassing again, the wind feathering brown pools of water in the scrub, everything brilliant yellow-green after four nights of rain.

Abigail tugged the needle twice, pulling it through the cuff, pushing it back through the opposite hole of the bone button.

'That kid don't know how lucky he is,' Henry said.

Three notes she had given Andy. Three times he had not come. At the bank he wouldn't look her in the eye, his manner perfunctory and professional, thanking her as Mrs. Jonson, sometimes saying nothing at all. Each time, after waiting in the shed for half an hour, putting the till at risk, Henry would come into the room irate and ask Abigail what the hell was wrong with that kid.

'Hell, there's a hundred men in this town who'd be happy to be in his shoes.'

Abigail knotted the thread and bit off the excess with her front teeth.

'Here,' she said, standing up from the sofa and holding the shirt out by the shoulders.

Henry walked over and took the shirt from her and buttoned it up.

'That dadgum kid oughta be payin you,' he said, tucking the tails into his trousers.

He straightened his collar and looked at Abigail, her silence all of a sudden heavy.

'That's what's called a joke,' he said.

In truth, Abigail was glad Andy had stopped coming. The things that had attracted her to him in the beginning, his innocence, his exuberance, his imagination, were now the very things that most annoyed her about him. He was like a puppy, incapable of sitting still. When he started dreaming aloud of their future together, of his Andy's Canteen, with her there beside him, she would feel a pressing urge to educate him about the hard truths of life, to make him understand that things were not what they seemed, that there was a man behind that picture watching them. He seemed to lack entirely any comprehension of the gravity of his sin, and this seeming absence of guilt, over time, had come to grate on her. Sometimes she was almost grateful when Henry stepped through the door and gave her that look of his, like an old, wild dog weary of the effort of living, wanting only to get at his meat, all the more startling after the exuberance of the puppy. This, at least, was how life really was. And when Henry was done he would lie there on top of her, as if crushed by the weight of his own wretched soul, sometimes for several minutes. Abigail would sometimes imagine he was dead, the strain of the effort at last too much for him, and she would wonder what she would feel, if anything.

She was glad Andy had stopped coming, and she didn't care why, though it only made her dwell all the more on the absence of women. It wasn't like the early days, when, like the men of Shakespeare before her, she had placed all

116

her hopes for happiness on the prospect of having another woman in town, if only one. She was glad those days were over. Sometimes she went days without thinking of women at all, drawing on hitherto unsuspected reserves of patience, feeling within her, now that she had suffered as long as they had before her, a growing bond with the miners and merchants. She was no longer the novelty she had been. She was one of them. But still, whenever the stagecoach pulled into town, even if she no longer made the effort to go out and watch the passengers alight, she could never refrain from stopping whatever she was doing and listening, her pulse quickening as she heard in her mind's ear those cries of joy that had greeted her own arrival.

TWO

They ate their beans and salt pork and licked their fingers and drank their coffee from tin cups, the sun warm against their legs and shoulders. It was not a particularly pleasant spot. There was no shade. They sat on rocks or on the ground. But they could see forever in all directions save the one behind them, and that was better than seeing nothing at all but dark walls of rock.

'I reckon they burnt it up,' one of them was saying.

'Burnt it? Why go and burn it? If they cared enough to make off with it in the first place.'

'Be a hell of a nuisance draggin across the desert with half a civilization huntin ye.'

There had been of late rumors of sightings of the mattress. In an old Spanish fort in the charred foothills of the Pitillo Mountains. Balanced on a pinnacle in the Chubasco Glyphs. High up a cliff in an inaccessible cave in the Aguja cliff dwellings. But considering who the bearers of these rumors were, notorious tellers of tall tales all, little stock was being invested in their veracity.

'What do you think, Kelly?'

Kelly, daydreaming of his fiancée, had been listening with only half an ear. After two years amongst miners he still hadn't become accustomed to their penchant for idle blather. At twenty-four he was younger than many of the men he supervised, a fact that his shaggy brown beard did little to conceal. If not for his hat Kelly might have had trouble commanding respect. A narrow-brimmed Galway, the hat had been given to him by an old Comstocker palsied by mercury poisoning who had taught Kelly amalgamating and retorting. After thirty years of exposure to the elements and innumerable applications of guar resin and other indignities both manmade and natural, the hat was neither brown nor black nor gray nor tan but was instead a muted tint of nothing. The moment the hat touched his head, all the sagacity and easy authority of his old mentor radiated out, as if his own, from young Joseph Kelly, M.E.

'What's that?' he said.

'You think that mattress is still out there, somewhere up in the mountains?'

'Playin at bein civilized,' someone interjected. 'That's all they's doin.'

'Ah hell, no Injun's gonna sleep on a mattress like at. They been sleepin on the hard ground all they lives. Mattress like at'd feel like bein buried alive to a Injun.'

'Decker's got a point there.'

'Even them squaws? You don't think they'd give it a try? I wager after a night or two on a real hair mattress they wouldn't care to go back to dirt.'

'Knowin Injuns they most likely ripped it all up and made ridiculous outfits of it.'

Kelly looked at his watch. He wasn't in the mood for the miners' foolishness today. He stood up and swiped the seat of his pants and went back into the mine.

Walking hunchbacked with his lamp before him, he followed the shaft fifty yards back, patting the mule's

119

forehead as he passed the pile of kibbles at the whim, then taking the left ventricle he started one-handed down a series of ladders, down through the white capping of dolomitic limestone, through the quartz ledges and trachyte fissures, the air cooling as he went. At the adit level he switched the lamp to his other hand and climbed down the winze through thick black walls of slate, down into the porphyry. A smell here of creosote tar and fired powder. Slouching again he worked his way back, navigating through a thicket of drills and sledges planted in haste by hungry miners. At the end of the workings he studied the drift of the vein, seeing in his mind probable bearings.

Of the mines being worked in the True Fissure District, including Crawford's other two paying properties, the Othello and the Hamlet, the Lear was the most promising. The present vein, a band of argentiferous galena six feet wide, two deep, extending well beyond the boundaries of the claim, was assaying as high as two thousand dollars a ton and was by Kelly's reckoning but a capillary in the sprawling mesh of ore-laden veins underlying the entire district. Why Crawford was having so much trouble securing the capital necessary to realize its potential Kelly could not fathom. His faith in reason did not permit him to believe, as so many of the credulous miners did, that Shakespeare's dearth of women was the culprit. It was a law as inviolable as the law of gravity that where there was profit to be made capital would flow. And yet the boom that Shakespeare had been sitting on for nearly a year, the boom that was guaranteed to launch Kelly as a mining engineer of the first rank, seemed to be wed to a fuse that would not ignite.

He chipped out a sample with his moil, wrapped it in a

small piece of oilcloth and put it in his pocket. He made some notes. He chalked the holes for the evening blast.

By the time Kelly left the mine at three o'clock, a soft, humid breeze was blowing in the thunderheads, stirring up from the desert the musty, resinous smell of wet creosote leaves. Riding his mule down the grade back to town he counted eleven storms tormenting the horizon, dark gray smudges scribbled over by lightning. All around him the desert fresh from its drenching was exploding with color. Bright yellow blooms bursting from the purple bulbs of olive-green prickly pear fins. Pink petals blazing the tips of yellow-fruited chollas. Long golden seedpods hanging like Christmas ornaments amidst the shivering pale green leaflets of honey mesquites. With the mule's every step silvery-white grasshoppers sprang into the air and flew a short way before landing and springing again. If not for Kelly's restraining hand the mule would gladly have eaten everything in sight.

Shakespeare below, dressed in amber sunlight, scrubbed clean by the rains, looked almost like a prosperous little town. All it lacked was a steeple. If only Nathalie could see how beautiful it was, he thought. She would surely come.

Mrs. Jonson was standing in the doorway of the Ore, in the same place she had been when he left for the mine in the morning, and he felt a surge of pity for her, down there all alone. No gentle friend to unbosom her soul to. He remembered the one dance he had had with her at the wedding celebration, how delicate she had seemed, like something blown there on the wind. The way she wouldn't look at him. And how she danced with miner after miner in this way, as if not really there, while all around her flailed the limbs of besotted fools. He

121

wondered if the real reason he hadn't gone around to the Ore for a proper introduction was that something about her intimidated him.

Kelly reached up and adjusted his hat. She was gone from the doorway when he reached Avon just ahead of the shadows of the clouds.

He had been sitting at his desk for nearly half an hour, listening to the rain, the sheet of paper before him blank but for the words, *Dearest Nathalie*, when the door opened and in walked Mrs. Jonson, her shoes caked in mud, beads of rain dripping down her face.

The office of the Shakespeare Assaying Co. was little bigger than a kitchen pantry, though given the volume of paraphernalia scattered across the desk and the work table — brass scales and weights, clay crucibles, cobbing hammers, lenses, jars of chemicals, all sandwiched between a bloated bookcase and a doorless cabinet choked with rocks and minerals — it seemed much smaller.

Kelly set down his pen and stood up.

'I hope I'm not disturbing you, Mr. Kelly,' she said, dabbing her wet face with the cotton handkerchief bunched in her right hand.

She glanced around the office.

'Not at all, not at all,' Kelly said with a bemused expression, coming hastily around the desk and clearing a pile of tools from the chair.

He apologized profusely for the disorder.

'How can I be of assistance?'

'Well,' Abigail said, seeming a little embarrassed. 'It's ridiculous really. Why I should bother a man of your expertise with such a thing. It's just that after the town meeting, and the way the Director left...'

She looked at Kelly.

'It really is silly.'

'I assure you, Mrs. Jonson,' Kelly said, returning to his side of the desk and taking a seat, 'no matter concerning the Director is too trifling for me to consider.'

'It's not so much about the Director,' Abigail said. 'There is a miner who works for you by the name of Hobbs.'

Kelly nodded all too knowingly. 'Say no more.'

'But don't you think it strange?' Abigail asked. 'All the same distance from Shakespeare?'

Kelly pressed his fingertips together.

'Mrs. Jonson,' he said. 'I have nothing against Hobbs. He's a good miner. After all, who wouldn't want to believe in an invisible fence whose sole purpose is to prevent women from reaching Shakespeare? It's wonderfully imaginative, don't you agree? The trouble with Hobbs is that he pretends to scientific rigor when in fact he lacks even the most rudimentary tools, intellectual or otherwise, to test his claims. He rides out to where one of the boys tells him a woman turned back — half the time they make it up just to get him going — and takes a look around and decides it's ten miles. When asked what method he uses to measure the miles, surveyor's compass or triangulation, he resorts to vague, offended mutterings which amount to little more than the expression of his desire that the distance of these incidents from Shakespeare be ten miles. Ergo, the existence of an invisible fence.'

Kelly, hardly aware he was doing so, had adopted the exact bearing and tone of his favorite university professor, Professor Warden — one arm across his waist bracing the other at the elbow, fingers thoughtfully clawing the hairs of his beard — and postured thus he proceeded to refute Hobbs' theory, on the premise that if he did not do so he was allowing to exist without argument an ontological conundrum of the profoundest sort.

'But let us assume for the sake of argument,' he said, 'that Hobbs' measurements are right, that every time a woman attempts to come to Shakespeare she is turned back at a ten-mile radius. Unusual, but facts are facts, are they not? Does it then follow that the only possible explanation for this series of events is the existence of an invisible fence which somehow apprehends the difference between a man and a woman? Are there no other properties of this fence that can be verified by the senses? No other tests but the one? Would, for example, this fence be visible in the rain, or in a dust storm? Could we dress a woman in a man's clothing and sneak her across? How high is this fence? Would it be possible to catapult a woman over it? You laugh, but how else are we to verify the existence of such a fence if not by some tangible proof?'

Outside, the clouds had parted and the sun was glistening over all the bright wetness of Avon's buildings.

'And I might add,' Kelly continued, hitting his stride. 'A point which hardly merits mentioning. If indeed Shakespeare were corralled by this invisible fence, or I should say if women were corralled out by it, one of two things would follow in regards to you, Mrs. Jonson. Either you alone know how to cross the fence and are jealously guarding the secret, or you are not a woman. As both conclusions are patently absurd, we must conclude again that there is no invisible fence. And if this fence has no material existence, can it truly be said to exist? Perhaps what Hobbs is trying to express in his unsophisticated way is some kind of inner fence, a fence existing only in the minds of women who attempt to come to Shakespeare. In which case the fence is nothing more than a convenient symbol for some ultimately incomprehensible process of thought resulting in the termination of a woman's progress toward Shakespeare at an arbitrary if perhaps roughly uniform distance from it. Such a thing, while difficult to imagine, is not altogether inconceivable. Yet it remains to point out how such a belief might be established rationally, let alone empirically.'

Kelly opened a drawer of the desk and took from it a photograph of Nathalie, one he had taken himself two years ago. She was wearing her thick wool coat, the ground covered with snow. She had been cold standing there, waiting for Kelly to set up the equipment and take the photograph. They had quarreled earlier, and some of that upset remained in her pouting lips and impatient eyes.

'Hobbs also fails to mention that most of the women who don't make it to Shakespeare never bother to try,' Kelly said, handing the picture to Abigail. 'My own fiancée, for example.'

Abigail took the picture.

'She is pretty,' she said.

'Thank you,' Kelly said with a small, proud smile. 'I've been trying to get her to join me for over two years. That's a long time for a man to be away from the woman he loves. No matter where I am, Shakespeare, Bird, Chloride, towns with as much to offer as the one she's stuck on, she refuses to come. She has never once set out to see me, even when I was only a day from the railroad terminus. Her excuse is that her father is too old and she can't bear to leave him should he die in her absence. And yet she professes her undying love for me in her letters and says how much she misses me and, When are we going to be together? and, When are you going to come back to me? I write to her again and again, explaining to her the sacrifices my profession demands of me, but she doesn't seem to appreciate my position. I fear in the end she will win and I will be forced to give up mining altogether and settle into some dismal clerkship back home just to be with her.'

Kelly had worked himself to the verge of tears and was now quite embarrassed.

Abigail handed the photograph back to him.

'Anyway,' he said dismissively, 'my case isn't so unusual. Half the men in Shakespeare have wives and fiancées who have never bothered to leave their home-towns, let alone be turned back by an invisible fence.'

Slowly the clouds drifted back over Avon, blotting out the sun.

'Thank you, Mr. Kelly,' Abigail said. 'I feel better.'

After she had gone, Kelly wondered what had come over him to make him speak as if he hadn't spoken to another human being in years, a torrent of ridiculous babble about an invisible fence, from he, a man of few words.

He sat listening as the rain started up again, then he dipped the pen into the ink and tilted a little to the left the patiently waiting sheet of paper.

Kelly had written to Nathalie four times since the letter announcing Abigail's arrival and as yet had not received a reply. But mail was long in coming to Shakespeare from the East, and there were many opportunities for a letter to get lost along the way. Still, Kelly was confident that his letter had arrived, and that Nathalie was preparing at last to join him. She might even surprise him by sending herself instead of a letter. He was sure she would have come sooner had he not been such a fool and written, in a moment of naked pride, that she could very well be the first woman in Shakespeare. That had been in the early days, when everyone was still certain that Shakespeare would follow the example of other mining camps in the Territory and attract its fair share of women. Kelly, like many another man in town, was convinced that his own would be Shakespeare's first marriage. Odds indeed had been in his favor, for at the time he had been the only man officially engaged. So it had come as quite a blow — Kelly had not realized how much of himself he had invested in this game of chance — when he had received her letter stating that she had no intention of being the only woman in a mining camp, and only when the situation had changed would she come.

Now Kelly wished he had been as wise as Henry. Not only had Henry deliberately left out any mention of women or the lack thereof from his letters to Abigail, but he had also enlisted the aid of Crawford's nephew, purportedly a talented writer, to help him compose the letters. At the time, Kelly had privately condemned this behavior as dishonest. But he could not argue with the results. Henry had earned his rightful place in the history of Shakespeare and was now enjoying all the fruits of matrimony while Kelly and everyone else were still setting aside money for their monthly trips to the Salon in Bird.

Kelly lowered the pen to the page. He wrote, as he always did, that he missed her and that life was incomplete without her and that as soon as they were reunited all of her unfounded fears about living in the Territory would evaporate. He described the beautiful thunderstorms that had been dousing Shakespeare every afternoon for the past week, and how wildflowers of every color bloomed overnight. He asked after her family and told her to give his love to his.

When his letter was finished he folded it up and placed it in an envelope on which he wrote the address he knew by heart.

THREE

'What in God's name is he selling?' Crawford was saying.

Andy came around from behind the counter and stood at the door beside his uncle. The pedlar, a midget in a brown suit and top hat, had stopped in the middle of Avon, down toward Henderson's, and was standing on the seat of his cart, gesticulating wildly, crying his wares in a voice like a goat's. Miners and merchants were emerging from doorways and venturing through the stagnant muck the better to hear the pitch of this charismatic stranger.

'I'll go down and have a look,' Andy said.

Sticking to the narrow archipelago of dry ground abutting the storefronts along the west side of the street, Andy worked his way down to within twenty feet of the pedlar's cart, a rickety contraption burdened by the most amazing gallimaufry of metal objects he had ever seen. A half-starved burro yoked to the cart stood hoof-deep in mud, enduring the swarms of freshly hatched flies.

'And in this vision,' the pedlar was bleating, 'in this vision in the wilderness, God instructed me to bring unto the men of Shakespeare for the relief of their suffering my copious assortment of Feminized Utensils!'

Miners and merchants exchanged dubious glances.

'The one among you named Decker, whose sister yearns for your return, your suffering can be alleviated. Charlie Barrett, whose wife recently brought into the world a strapping baby boy, your suffering can be alleviated. Edward Stull, whose mother daily pines for the return of her favorite son, I say to you, your suffering can be alleviated. Hear me, Shakespeareans, for I speak the truth when I say that every last one of these utensils has been touched by the hands of a woman. And in so doing, the magnetism of the finer half of our species has passed into the atoms of the metal, causing them, as so eloquently elucidated by Dr. Emmett Longfellow in his treatise, *The Healing Properties of Magnetized Tractors*, to vibrate at a frequency uniquely beneficial to the hearts of lonely men. These apple corers, a little touched by corrosion having lately come from the tarnishing airs of the East. These radish graters. This sap pail. How can these things possibly take the place of a woman? you may be asking yourselves. While it is true that I cannot affect a permanent relief to your woes — only the Good Lord has that power — until that promised day should come to pass, why labor under the burden of heavy hearts? Come forth, I say. Come forth for a free demonstration, any man among you with the courage to embrace happiness. Feel the healing radiance of the Feminized Utensils! Come forth! There is no harm in trying.'

Hobbs stepped forward and selected from the cart a long-handled gravy strainer. The pedlar asked the miner to bare the skin of his chest, and when the miner had done so the pedlar began rubbing the gravy strainer in methodical circles over the area around the miner's heart. The effect was immediate. The miner's eyes brightened. His chest expanded. He inhaled deeply and smiled and bellowed: 'I'm healed! I'm healed! Sweet Jesus, I'm healed! Go to hell, Louise! I don't need you anymore.'

A commotion, equal parts guffaw and groan, agitated the rabble.

'How much'd he pay ye, Hobbs?'

'Me next!'

'We could use that there muffin tin.'

The pedlar held up his hand to quiet the crowd.

'Again I say to you, this is not a cure but only a salve, as opium is to a man in mortal agony. A gift from God. Naaman the Syrian could not say why the waters of Jordan should be better than Abana and Pharpar, Rivers of Damascus, but since experience proved them so, no reasoning could change his opinion. So too with Feminized Utensils.'

The pedlar, addressing Hobbs again, said he was welcome to the gravy strainer for the trifling sum of two bits. Hobbs eagerly parted with his money and returned to the crowd, the men nearest him trying to get a hold of his Feminized Utensil.

'As soon as you feel your loneliness for female companionship beginning to return,' the pedlar explained, 'simply repeat the procedure. You too, Mrs. Jonson.' She was standing in the doorway of the Ore. 'Should you feel the ache of longing for the bosom of a boon companion, you too will benefit from a Feminized Utensil.'

Blaine stepped forward and said: 'I don't know who the hell you got our names from, but you put on a entertainin show. Here's a dollar. Give me that corn popper.'

Other men likewise came forth, willing to part with a bit or two for the amusement the midget afforded them.

Andy bought a pancake turner, but when later that

night he rubbed it in slow circles over the skin of his chest, it did little but make him cold.

Wrinkles of frustration lining his brow, the old man staring back at him from the looking glass scowled. Tilting and swiveling uncertainly around the tuft, the scissors retreated, approached, wavered awkwardly in the air. The old man switched hands, to little effect.

'Sonofabitch,' Henry muttered, turning with a grunt from his reflection.

She had offered to do it for him. He didn't want her cutting his hair. Didn't want any woman cutting his hair, feminized scissors or not.

He was sore at her. He had told her yesterday evening, after hearing it from some damn miner, that it wasn't his business who she visited with when she wasn't at work, but there were some things she ought to know about. The thing was the perception of people. It wasn't that Henry cared that she had decided to take a walk in the rain and then stop in and pay a visit to Kelly, but she had to understand that people were bound to misinterpret things. Henry wasn't about to say it, but what he meant was he feared he was losing control. She said she understood and wouldn't do it again. But that was the way with her. He never knew what she was actually thinking.

Henry spat, then stood up and walked out into the saloon and kept walking, through the morning crowd of miners, past Abigail reading the *Eagle* behind the bar, out the door, leaving unanswered a volley of good mornings.

Avon was still a stew of mud and clabber, churned and cratered by man and beast, and it was beginning to smell like the banks of a slow-moving river. Running all through the darker, thicker shoals were labyrinthine reefs of lighter, harder mud, favored routes of navigation. In particularly bad spots boards had been laid down, now all but indistinguishable from the mud.

Weaving an erratic path down the street, Henry labored heavy-booted through the muck, down to the barbershop, muttering to himself along the way.

'Mornin, Mr. Jonson,' Duncan said as Henry stomped his boots at the sill and sat down on the bare plank bench against the sidewall.

'Good morning, Henry,' Crawford said, sitting bibbed on the stool, a motley carpet of hair clotted in dried mud on the floor around him.

'If you say so,' Henry said.

Duncan, elbows and a pinky held aloft, scissors snipping the air with the chirrupy persistence of a baby bird, gently nudged Crawford's head forward with a thumb.

'I guess that midget didn't get too far, did he,' Duncan said.

Henry, shooing a fly from his face, mumbled something vaguely affirmative.

'Feminized Utensils,' Crawford said with disgust. 'It serves him right. Hornswoggling men of honestly earned pay with that quackery. And to not even have the basic human decency to return the letters. That's what galls me most. Here I was casting aspersions on the editor of the *Eagle* for not printing my dispatch when all the time it was in the possession of this low-down confidence man. He's lucky they didn't given him more than a hiding.'

'Uh-hm,' Duncan agreed.

'It's people like him that give the Territory a bad name,' Crawford said.

Duncan guided Crawford's head back and nudged it to the left.

'My own nephew bought a pancake turner,' Crawford said, 'if you can believe it.'

'You don't say,' Duncan said.

'He was doing so well, too. I'm afraid the shock of his father's death is finally beginning to sink in.'

Henry squinted a little at these words.

Duncan, nodding empathetically, picked up a comb from the small shelf cluttered with the tools of his trade and ran it through Crawford's hair, the pale palm of his other hand smoothing close behind.

'You boys hear what happened to old Jenkins comin over from Chloride?'

'No,' Crawford said. 'What?'

'Had him three hoes tied up on his buckboard headed here to start us a little cathouse when right round the bend in the road one them hoes says she gots to make water, caint hold it no mo, so Jenkins pulls up and unties the one and lets her down to do her diddlin off behind a rock. Course then them other two decides they gots to do it too, so Jenkins figures he gone let em down one at a time, not wantin to stir up no trouble with a swarm a hoes. That's when the first hoe lets out a scream to raise Cain and his brother both from the grave and comes runnin round from behind the rock yellin she been bit by a snake. Right on the rump.'

'Good Lord,' Crawford said. 'Where will it end?'

'That aint the end of it,' Duncan said. 'Old Jenkins knows what he gots to do, only thing is he aint the one to do it, so he unties one them other hoes and tells her if she wants her friend to see the light of another day she best get down on her godfearin knees and start suckin out that venom.'

Duncan sighed laughing, tears brimming in his eyes yet again.

'Well, this suckin and aspittin goes on upwards a half a hour but the rump jes keeps on growin and a growin till it's damn near the size of a prize-winnin punkin. And all three them hoes cryin and carryin on. No choice but to turn round and head back to Chloride, get her to a doctor.'

'That's the fifth time I've heard that story,' Henry said. 'Each time a different man, a different animal, a different number of whores.'

'Reckon one of em gots to be true,' Duncan said.

Crawford's haircut finished, Duncan tugged aside the bib and shook the hair to the floor. Crawford nodded approvingly into the polished tin held before him, then paying and thanking Duncan for his services, he said, 'Gentlemen', and left.

Henry took a seat on the stool.

'Not so damn short this time,' he said.

The bib floated down over him, and Duncan set his scissors in motion.

Standing outside the barbershop after his haircut, Henry managed half a smile. For the first time in four months he could face the sun without feeling like a Sunday roast. Count your blessings, old man, he counseled himself.

Crossing to the other side of the street he worked his way down to the bank and went in. It was only the kid there, Crawford having other business to attend to after his grooming. He didn't look well. A crop of acne had sprouted across his waxen forehead and astride his nose. His eyes were puffy, his lips chapped. Whatever spirit he possessed seemed to ooze out of him as Henry approached the counter.

'I need a draft for fourteen dollars and eighty-five cents,'

Henry said. 'Payable to J.D. Copes & Sons Domestics. Take it from the account, if you would, please.'

Henry looked up at the painting of the governor as Andy busied himself with the draft.

'That sonofabitch Klemmet aint botherin you, is he?' Henry said.

'No, sir,' Andy, head bent to his task, said.

'You aint come in for a drink since, I was just wonderin.'

'My uncle frowns on me drinking.'

Henry nodded.

'Long as it aint on account of some fool miner. A man oughta be able to have a drink when he wants one. No other form of amusement in a town like this.'

Andy went on writing.

'Kid your age, a little whiskey'll put some hair on your chest.'

Andy smiled obligingly.

'Come round any time you want,' Henry said. 'It don't have to be your birthday to stop in on Mrs. Jonson neither. She gets mighty lonesome sometimes.'

The draft made, Andy set it and the pen on the counter and asked Henry to sign it.

'I guess you can figure what this is for,' Henry said, signing.

'No, sir,' Andy said. 'I wouldn't speculate on the private affairs of the bank's customers.'

'Well,' Henry said. 'I'd appreciate it if you kept it to yourself anyway.'

Andy said he would.

'And don't let some jackass like Klemmet keep you from comin round. Just go on round back and say hello. People are gonna talk no matter what. Let em talk, I say. I'll set em straight.'

Henry stood there for a moment, looking at the top of Andy's head, then he left.

'If I were married to the only woman in town,' Crawford said with an air of scandal upon his return, 'I'm not so sure I would be as trusting as Henry Jonson is. Letting her go off with Kelly like that.'

'Kelly?' Andy said, shedding in an instant his mid-morning grogginess.

'He wouldn't tell me what it was all about. Some kind of tour of the country or something. All he said was he would be gone for the better part of the day.'

'Just Kelly and her?'

'I'm sure he'll behave himself,' Crawford said. 'He's a man of the utmost honesty and integrity. I wouldn't have hired him if he wasn't.'

Andy stared abjectly out the window.

'Still,' Crawford said, 'Henry certainly doesn't know Kelly as well as I do. He has a weakness for the ladies. I can vouch for that.'

A cold lump of jealousy sank into Andy's stomach and stayed churning there the rest of the morning, coming up again during lunch back at the house.

'You don't think Kelly...'

'Oh heavens no,' Crawford said between bites, the leaves of his mulberry tree showing their first touch of brown through the window. 'Though it's probably for the best that Henry doesn't know what a rake our young engineer once was.'

Andy's spoon stopped halfway to his mouth, dropping slowly back into his beans as his uncle began his story.

'He and I spent a weekend in the capital last winter, peddling our prospectus.'

Crawford wiped the ends of his moustache with his napkin and placed his elbows on the table.

'I guess we'd been in Shakespeare about a month. His fiancée, whom at that time he'd already been engaged to for over a year, was due to arrive any day, and he'd been going around boasting to the miners that he'd won the bet, offering them his sincere condolences and generally behaving like a fool, which is uncharacteristic of him. Then during our trip north he went strangely quiet, and I couldn't help but notice as we walked the busy streets of the capital how his eyes lingered on every woman who crossed our path, even the wretched squaws hawking their trinkets on the plaza. These were no ordinary glances, but deep, penetrating stares filled with emotion.'

Crawford, reliving the moment, affected the same haunted stare and went on.

'After supper that night he told me he had a personal matter to attend to, he would meet me in a few hours back in the room. I waited up for him until midnight, somewhat concerned that he hadn't returned, then unable to stay awake any longer I went to bed. When I awoke the next morning to see his bedclothes untouched, I feared something had happened to him. I was all set to go make an inquiry at the Sheriff's office when in he walked, looking somewhat the worse for wear, mind you not injured or anything, but clearly unhappy and exhausted.

'"What the devil happened to you?" I said, but he didn't want to talk about it.

'It wasn't until several weeks later, back in Shakespeare, that I found out what happened that night. He came by one evening under some pretense or other but ostensibly to unburden his conscience before his fiancée's — this time certain — arrival. Sitting at this very table, he confessed that he had spent that night in the capital in a brothel. I laughed and assured him that how he spent his nocturnal hours was no concern of mine. But he felt the need to justify his behavior to me so I wouldn't think him a Lothario. As I suspected, he had received news before we left Shakespeare that his fiancée would not be coming, which put him in a foul frame of mind after all of his boasting. He confessed that he had consorted with no less than five soiled doves that night. Five! You'll laugh when you hear his rationale. It is so like Kelly to reason out an equation for every action, even in so squalid an atmosphere as a brothel. The consummate engineer, that's our Kelly.'

'"Why five?" I asked him.

'So he told me. Five was the number of times his fiancée had promised she was about to join him in the Territory, and five the times she had not come. Five drams of bitter disappointment roiling around his insides, making rancid the sweet milk of their vows. So, he reasoned, he would purge the poison from his heart all in one go, while he had the chance.

'I couldn't help but laugh. "Oh dear," I said. "And did this remedy restore a healthy blush to love's bloom?"

'He replied smiling that it had, but at the expense of a canker of guilt gnawing at his spirit. Hence his need to confess to me. I dare say, once we tapped that canker there seemed no end to the ooze that issued from it. That young man has known women, let me tell you.'

The lump in Andy's stomach slowly turned to stone as his uncle went on making light of Kelly's long battle with the demon of lust, from the age of twelve onward. Kelly was no stranger to brothels, nor to other men's wives and daughters and servants. If it was female, Kelly had coupled with it at one time or another.

'What is Mr. Jonson thinking?' Andy nearly shouted.

'Oh, it's not as bad as all that,' Crawford assured him. 'I'm sure he's behaving himself. He vowed he was done sowing his wild oats and wants nothing more than to settle into the role of domesticated husband.'

'Why didn't Mr. Jonson take her himself?' Andy said, scarcely able to conceal his outrage. 'The man really doesn't pay her enough attention. I can't fathom why she married him.'

Crawford leaned back and set his napkin on the table.

'It's called a marriage of convenience, my dear boy,' he said. 'They're quite common.'

They finished their lunch in silence.

They rode east across the blinding alkali of South Soda Flat, passing a small flock of snowy egrets standing in an ephemeral lake a few miles out, unblinking eyes watching in profile atop long sinuous necks. Skirting the outcrop hillocks of the Little Bullocks they rode through the remnants of Rainbow, an old mining camp long abandoned, nothing left but piles of rusted tins and a small wooden cross canted east, the being thereunder rendered nameless, robbed even of duration by the wind. They turned northeast, following the trend of the mountains up a gradually sloping sediment plane, pale green mariola and buffalo gourds softening the glare of the ground.

She rode as a man would, legs astride the saddle. The pants she had bought at Blaine's, hemming the waist to better fit her shape, were as stiff and coarse as sandpaper, chafing the tender skin of her inner thighs with Whiskey's every step. One of Henry's blue moleskin shirts, sleeves buttoned at her wrists, and a gray felt cowboy hat that for two months had been waiting under the bar for its rightful owner's return, completed her protection from the sun. The thought that from a distance she would likely be mistaken for a man amused her a little.

'I only mean,' Kelly was saying, 'that none of us realized how accustomed to living without female companionship we had become.'

They had hit the old Copper Trail, once a busy thoroughfare for Iberian miners, now running indistinguishable from the surrounding brush through an arm of vanished Lake Mendrugo. Off to the left rose the imposing blue-gray peaks of the Mendrugo Range, to the right the more modest Little Bullocks.

'Since you've come, our eyes have been opened to our condition. We're even more miserable now,' Kelly chuckled.

'Why thank you, Mr. Kelly,' Abigail said.

'Oh, it's not your fault. It's just that to see how happy you and Henry are makes us feel... how shall I put it?'

'Jealous?'

Kelly grinned.

'Well, yes, I suppose. That and sorry for ourselves. As I'm sure you've gathered by now these men out here, these miners and prospectors, lack a basic degree of refinement, to put it mildly. They don't think it fair that Henry should be the only man in Shakespeare enjoying the fruits of marriage. They hold it against him. I hear their grumblings in the mine.'

'And you, Mr. Kelly? Do you hold it against him?'

Kelly went quiet for a moment. He reached up and lifted and reseated his hat.

'At one time, yes,' he said, 'I did. I'm embarrassed

to say. I was convinced, as many of us were, that my Nathalie would be Shakespeare's first woman. This must seem like so much hubris to you, men betting on love as if it were a game of cards, but I assure you, it wasn't like that. Sure there were times when we made jokes about it, but we all wished each other well. In the end we knew it was in everyone's interest to attain a more balanced ratio between the sexes as quickly as possible. I had no idea how invested I had actually become in the idea that mine would be Shakespeare's first wedding until I saw you step down from the stagecoach. Then, yes, I did hold it against Henry. I'm over it now. I laugh to think of myself as I was in those days. So earnest and arrogant. In the end I think it best I wasn't the first.'

'Why is that?' Abigail asked.

'I'm not sure I would handle as well as Henry does being married to the only woman in a town full of miners.'

Abigail smiled but otherwise refrained from comment. It was pleasant being out in the desert, far from Shakespeare. They rode for a long time without speaking, no sound but the gentle clink of bridle on bit and the steady clomp of hooves in the sand.

'But don't you think if she really loved you,' Abigail said as they began working their way down a mild grade dense with flowering yuccas, 'she would have come long ago?'

'I don't think that's a fair statement,' Kelly said, unable to conceal the defensiveness in his voice.

'I was only asking.'

'It's asking a lot of a woman to leave behind her home and family, to cross a continent to live in the middle of nowhere, in a desert peopled by hostile Indians. Even for love.'

'Yes,' Abigail said, 'it is.'

'The circumstances are more complicated than you know, Mrs. Jonson.'

'You're right,' Abigail said. 'I spoke out of turn. I apologize.'

Kelly looked ahead, clearly disconcerted by his outburst. Then he looked at Abigail.

'No need to apologize,' he said unconvincingly. 'Come on, we have some ground to cover yet.'

They reached Yucca Springs around noon, startling into southern flight a flock of Canada geese. The spring was small, running only a short distance before sinking out of sight in a circular basin of black soil. A low platform of volcanic rock extended around the north and west sides of the basin. In the damper soil stood a clump of reeds and tule rushes a few feet high, in and out of which half a dozen black-tailed gnatcatchers were swooping, catching midges where they hovered above the shallow water. Otherwise no sign of life animated that dry, desolate plain exactly ten miles northeast of Shakespeare.

Kelly dismounted and led his mule to the water. He stood at the edge of the basin looking east, grimacing against the brightness.

'Just over there,' he pointed, turning to look back at Abigail, who was still sitting in the saddle.

Kelly walked over to help her down.

'Aren't you getting down?' he asked when she made no move to dismount.

'I shouldn't have made you do this,' Abigail said.

'Come now,' Kelly said.

He held up his hand, but Abigail did not take it.

'I want to go back,' she said.

Kelly blinked a few times.

143

'We've come this far,' he said. 'What's another hundred feet?'

'I said I want to go back,' Abigail said.

Kelly, running his fingers through his beard, looked east then again at Abigail.

'I insist that you get down and walk to the other side of the spring. I didn't abandon my duties at the mine to ride all the way out here only to turn around and go back.'

'I thank you for your efforts on my behalf, Mr. Kelly. And I'm telling you that I'm satisfied. There is no invisible fence. I don't need to go any farther to see that.'

Kelly walked around in a small circle. He stopped. He fidgeted with his hat then looked up at Abigail.

'You know what this is about, don't you?' he said. 'You are proving by your intransigence that you do in fact believe in the fence. You're afraid you might actually find it.'

'What nonsense!' Abigail laughed. 'Why walk even a foot to prove the obvious? You go, if you must.'

'Me go? You're the woman, not me. And why are you suddenly so sure it isn't there? You can't actually see an invisible fence, can you?'

'It sounds to me, Mr. Kelly, as if you are the one who needs to disprove the existence of the invisible fence, not me.'

Kelly shook his head and walked back to the spring to get his mule.

'It was stupid of me to do you this favor,' he said over his shoulder. 'You are a stubborn woman.'

Just then Abigail dug her boot heels into Whiskey's ribs and whipped the reins, bolting off at a charge. She raced past Kelly, catching only a glimpse of his startled face as she splashed through the spring, scattering birds and midges, and rode up the bank into open country, Kelly's voice, small and high beneath the pounding hooves, calling after her in alarm.

Kelly, baffled by her behavior, stood watching her speed across the desert, a small cloud of dust rising behind her. He was beginning to think he had better get on his mule and go after her when at last she halted the horse about a hundred yards out and turned to face north, as if she were contemplating racing off in that direction next. Then she turned and started back at a canter.

'Crazy damn woman,' Kelly muttered to himself, swinging up into the saddle and walking the mule through the spring and up the bank, where he waited for her to return. When she was abreast he turned the mule and fell in beside her.

'Satisfied?' she said, and did not wait for him to answer but rode on, through the spring, back the way they had come.

FOUR

All he seemed to want to do was talk. Henry couldn't make out what he was saying, but there was a pleading quality in his voice. He was holding Abigail's hands in his, peering into her eyes, talking and talking in this pleading voice. Henry could see it was making Abigail uncomfortable. She looked aside. The kid stood there lost in thought then recommenced his pleading.

'For Christ's sake,' Henry muttered under his breath. 'Get on with it, you dumbshit.'

Then the kid was kissing her passionately, and Abigail after some initial resistance was kissing him back, both of them wrapped in each other's arms, kissing. Henry wasn't sure he liked that. Then came a frantic shedding of clothes, Abigail pulling all her layers off over her head, Andy hopping on alternate feet to get out of his shoes. They stood naked before each other for a moment, as if sweetening by delay the pleasures to come, then fell to kissing again.

Henry shifted his weight to his other leg and grumbled.

They were a long time at this kissing, their hands moving over each other's bodies in tender, loving strokes, before finally sinking down onto the mattress.

Henry cupped his hands around his face and pressed his forehead into the coarse adobe.

Only this time it was different. Gone was the kid's nervous rutting, his perpetual readiness to bolt at the slightest hint of danger. In its stead had crept a quality of leisurely possession, of savoring a thing rightfully his own, and Abigail did not seem at all opposed to it.

Watching through the brickhole this unwelcome development, after so long wondering if he would ever get to do it again, Henry felt nothing. No arousal. No rage. All he wanted was to get back to the saloon before someone made off with the till. At that moment it seemed to him that being married, at his age, to a woman hers, was more trouble than it was worth. He didn't have it in him to keep dredging up such passion from the barren drifts of his soul.

Henry stifled a little cough, the memory of his first love stuck in his craw. She was the daughter of the farmer one field over. The spring before he left home they often met down at the creek separating their fathers' properties, a mile from each other's houses, alfalfa on his side, cabbage on hers. He could still see her face, after all these years. Plain but open and alert. A little scar on her right cheek where a goat had gored her once. The way she gave him sidelong glances walking along beside him. The same day they had seen two male ducks pinning a female by the neck and waddling and flapping to mount her in turn, he and she kissed for the first time under the chestnut tree on her side of the creek, his young heart pattering away like a tiny locomotive. They met under the chestnut tree as often as they could, every time like the first and last, such were the words of longing and devotion they poured into each other's hearts. She wanted to give herself to him, those were the words she used. He said it wasn't right until they were married. It became a game. No matter what she said or did, he knew she was only testing his resolve, and his love for her was the only thing that gave him the strength to resist her.

Then one day in early summer, in a moment of weakness that he thought was something else, he gave in. Afterwards they sat on the ground under the tree, telling each other how nice it had been, all the while their dour faces filling with shame. They continued to meet at the tree but it was never the same. They lied to each other, painting bright pictures of their future together, of all the wonderful years that lay before them, but she would not give herself to him again, no matter how much he pleaded. They met less and less often. The last time they saw each other he tried to have his way with her again. She slapped him hard across the face. The word shot out of his mouth without thought. *Whore!* Then she was gone, running back across the field of cabbages gone to seed, her stinging handprint slow to fade from his cheek.

He had felt at other times in his life the stirrings of love, had dreamed of settling down with a woman, but it was never the same as with Rebecca. Always something would come between them, some twist of fate, and eventually Henry would get over her and move on. This was the pattern of his life, and it seemed to him now as he stood there watching the kid make love to his wife, stood there seeing again with his own eyes what young love looked like, that it was finally over for him.

He bent down and picked up the adobe brick and slid it slowly back into the wall.

She waited for a while then got up from the mattress and dressed and went outside. The lock on the shed was fastened. She stood at the door, feeling abandoned, then went back in and started her chores.

She kneaded the dough and set it in the pans and covered them with towels and set them on the shelf to rise. She swept the floors and sorted the beans and cleaned the tub, but she could not rid herself of the feeling she had been abandoned.

She admitted to herself while she was chopping potatoes that over the course of these months with Andy, believing all the while that she had found a way to make Henry pay for luring her out there on false pretenses, she had been growing closer to Henry. He was like the desert he had brought her to. It took time to see it, but it was full of life. She had grown accustomed to his looser, thinner skin, his wiry muscles, his smell. She had learned to appreciate his terse sense of humor, his foul mouth. It was Henry, watching them from the other side of the still life, whom she thought about when she was with Andy. Everything she did with Andy she did for Henry, always trying to drive him to greater jealousy, greater desire, knowing what pleasure it brought him to overcome his debility. Without seeking it she had found in the sequence of young then old the full spectrum of the man, all the years in which she had never known him. His youth and his age.

He came in from the saloon toward nightfall and told her he didn't want the kid coming around anymore.

She closed her Bible and asked him to sit. They could talk about it. Henry didn't want to sit. There was nothing to talk about.

'Why?' she said. 'Why this sudden change?'

'Because I said so. That's the only reason you need.'

There was a quality in his voice that said, *Don't argue.* And she didn't.

Andy's face went an ochre color and he gaped at her as if she had just given him the news of his own death.

'But, but,' he stuttered. 'What about yesterday?'

'We can't keep going on like this, Andy. It's too much, going around all day terrified Henry is going to find out.'

'We'll run away together,' Andy said. 'Leave Henry. Leave Shakespeare. Leave the Territory if we have to.'

'Don't be ridiculous.'

Andy took hold of Abigail's hand and squeezed it hard while he sat there trying to find a more hopeful interpretation of her words.

'Please,' he implored her. 'Just think it over a little longer. I know I'm young and all, but I have potential. You said so yourself. In a few years our ages won't be so far apart.'

Abigail pulled her hand away from Andy and looked straight ahead.

'Don't make me say it again, Andy. You go on back home and forget this ever happened. There'll be other ladies for you here soon enough.'

Andy sat silent for a while, staring at the floor, then he said: 'If you believed that, you wouldn't have gone out to try to find that invisible fence with Kelly.'

These were not words Abigail wanted to hear.

'Now look here, Andy,' she said, turning to face him with growing impatience. 'I'm not one of your little puppets that you can just take out of the trunk and play with whenever you feel like it. When a woman tells you she doesn't want you coming around anymore, that's exactly what she means. I'd hate to have to tell Henry I've got an unwanted admirer.'

Two big tears spilled over Andy's eyelids and ran down his cheeks. Abigail looked away. Andy stood up and nodded to himself, wiping his cheeks with the heel of his hand. He straightened his coat. He nodded again and started for the door. Abigail followed him, the sight of the clean-shaven nape of his neck making her feel cruel.

At the door Andy held out his hand for Abigail to shake, but the gesture struck her as so pitiful that she couldn't bring herself to take it. She kissed him on the cheek instead, causing fresh tears to glisten in his eyes. She tussled his hair, as she might a child's she was sending off to play. Then he was gone.

FIVE

The rains gone, the desert retreated back into itself. The petals of the flowers curled out, dried up and blew away, taking with them their brief bursts of color. The sky sucked up the last of the standing water, the ephemeral lakes and rock pools, killing all the delicate plants sprouting as if by magic around them. Avon dried and hardened, leaving casts of boot and hoof prints baked into the street. Once again cumulus clouds floated brilliant white and silent across a cerulean sky.

Now the nights grew cooler, the days shorter. The sun day by day set farther south of Watt Mountain. Crawford began construction on a two-story boarding house down beyond the tents, intending it to be finished for the miners before the coming winter, all the lumber shipped at great expense from the mill at Pinos Grandes, high in the Aguja Wilderness. Miners willing took a cut in pay for the chance to work outdoors in the warm sunshine, trading their sledges for hammers which in comparison seemed made of nothing.

Three days before Abigail's twenty-first birthday Henry announced he was taking her to Bird. They set out at sunrise two days later in the stagecoach with two other passengers: Henderson's brother, who was returning to the States to settle his affairs before coming back for good in the spring; and a lawyer named McCollock who lived in Bird and had been in Shakespeare on some legal errand for Crawford. Henderson's brother, not nearly as tall as Henderson, was still in a state of euphoria over his discovery of the Territory and spent much of the trip gazing rapturously out the window and proclaiming that no words could describe it to a man who'd never been there. McCollock, a middle-aged man with an air of ennui about him, kept up a cough the entire trip, his only means of protest against the dust, which his lowered shade did little to prevent from turning his polished black shoes a dull, gritty tan. This was the very stagecoach Abigail had traveled in from Bird to Shakespeare a million years ago. She recognized the faded green seat cushions missing all their buttons, and the way the right-hand door rattled without end, swinging open with the right combination of jolts and lurches only to slam shut again and rattle on. She sat in the same place, on the left side of the forward-facing seat, across from McCollock, who nearly succeeded in not looking at her once during the trip. Just before leaving, Henry told her it might be chilly in Bird, to bring something warm to wear, so she had taken from her trunk her old black woolen jacket, still smelling of the button factory, and put it on. By ten it was off and folded across her lap. Against his own advice Henry brought no coat or jacket, his custom being never to wear one until the first day of winter.

For the first few hours of the journey the passengers kept their thoughts to themselves, rocking sleepily with the swaying coach. McCollock broke the silence around nine o'clock, telling the others in the strictest confidence that surveyors were at that very moment scouring the lower third of the Territory for a suitable route for the transcontinental railroad, which topic kept the three men talking for the rest of the morning. Running the railroad through Bird was out of the question. It was too high in the mountains, though no one doubted that an auxiliary line from Bird to the main line in the lowlands was essential. Of the towns in the lowlands, Shakespeare was closest to Bird. It also had the advantage of broad, open basins to the east and west, with only the occasional isolated mountain like Watt to work around. Other possible candidates were Chloride and Pecan, though it was widely accepted that their mineral wealth was not as promising nor as extensive as Shakespeare's, their futures as mining centers less secure. The benefits of a railroad to whatever town it passed through could not be overstated, though the three men in their exuberance for the subject came close to succeeding. Abigail, not especially sleepy, could not keep from yawning.

Shortly before noon they pulled into Roadrunner Wells, the stage station at the foot of the Big Bullocks. Charlie, the station master, whose only companion was a green-and-red parrot named Borracho who, to their invariable delight, insulted passengers in Spanish, changed the mules while Buddy and the passengers went in and ate a lunch of jerked beef, raw onions and rock-hard biscuits at the narrow table inside the little adobe building. Then they were back in the stagecoach and climbing, McCollock and Henderson's brother clutching the leather straps dangling from the ceiling. For a long time Abigail watched McCollock battling to keep his sleepy head from dropping to his chest, until at last, conceding victory to gravity, his swiveling, bobbing head echoed freely every tilt and jolt of the coach.

It was a long, monotonous afternoon. No sooner would they crest one hill than they would start up another. There were times when they could have walked faster than they were rolling. Outside, cactus and creosote gradually gave way to buckbrush and manzanilla. Black-tailed deer stood breast-high in swales of burrograss. The din of Jerusalem crickets rose and fell as the stagecoach rolled through their swarms, one of the ugly brown bugs every now and then flying into the coach and bouncing spasmodically against the walls before finding its way back out. Sometimes when the coach made a sharp turn, a vista of the plain below and all its far-flung mountains would open just long enough for the dozy passengers to sit up and lean toward their windows, only to see it slide out of view as the coach turned away. Henry patted Abigail's leg a few times, asking her how she was holding up. She assured him she was fine. She was touched he had decided without any suggestion from her to close the saloon for three days and nights, to suffer the discomforts of stage travel, to spend money they needed for the plot, on her behalf. She knew it was partly his way of putting the past behind them, reasserting his authority, but she didn't care.

Around three o'clock the stagecoach leveled and slowed as it entered the deep sand of Pheasant Canyon.

'This is where...' McCollock began to say then cut himself short with a sheepish glance at Abigail. At the foot of one of the walnut trees set back from the road stood a small white cross, the ground around it strewn with dark gray husks.

'Where what?' Henderson's brother asked.

'My mistake,' McCollock said.

Henry didn't bother to look out the window.

155

Nothing else was said.

Leaving Pheasant Canyon they resumed their climb, rolling in and out of the elongating shadows of peaks, the air growing cooler with every passing mile. Soon the bright smell of pine was wafting through the coach, carrying on it the whistles and trills of green-tailed twohees. The brisk mountain air reinvigorated the men's tongues, and they fell to discussing eastern winters with a kind of reverence that belied their gladness to be quit of them. Henry made several efforts to snare Abigail into the conversation, but she didn't take the bait, preferring over their frozen pictures of the past the world passing by outside her window.

The last three hours passed quickly, the stagecoach looping around the mountains, coursing between wind-carved megaliths that looked to Abigail like creatures from another planet, pitching into and out of ravines, passing with increasing frequency other men traveling the road in quest of their fortunes.

As golden afternoon faded into blue evening it grew dim inside the coach, the air through the window sharp against Abigail's face. The smell of woodsmoke, the burning resins of piñon and juniper and cypress, seldom encountered in Shakespeare, preceded by a quarter of an hour the first of the placer camps outlying Bird.

In that falling light, cold, clear and blue, Abigail saw for the first time in six months another woman, stooped over a fire, stirring a steaming pot of soup or stew with a ladle. Watching this woman stir and stir in slow circles, Abigail felt something twist inside her, as if the woman's ladle by some quirk of magnetism had leapt its bounds and was stirring instead Abigail's own innards. She sat back and closed her eyes, her heart thudding hard under the thickness of her jacket. She concentrated on her breath, afraid she might be sick, and in time the queasiness passed. Then she was back at the window.

She stayed at the window for the rest of the trip, eyes devouring the silhouettes of women around fires at every camp. The fingers of her left hand and the right side of her face were aching from the cold by the time the stagecoach finally jerked to a halt at the top of steep, cobbled Silver Street in downtown Bird.

They stayed at the Hotel Regis, across from the Bird News Depot on Second Street. A creaky wooden building partially rebuilt after the back half was gutted by fire, it wasn't as splendid as McCollock (whose brother-in-law coincidentally owned and ran it) had led Henry to believe, but the room did possess a large iron bed and, as Henry didn't tire of pointing out to Abigail, a real wool-filled mattress. The window looked out over the south side of town, stretching down the hill and scattering across a small, grassy valley a hundred feet below, walled in by juniper-stippled hills. At night all the fires and lamps flickering across the landscape mirrored in yellow-orange the cold white galaxies above.

That first night, at supper in the hotel dining room, Abigail hardly touched her veal. She couldn't keep from staring at the women at the other tables, feeling in the pit of her stomach the same welter of emotions she had felt on the way into town. She was amazed that human beings could be so beautiful. She looked at their faces mostly. Smooth, rounded expanses of bare skin disconcertingly naked to the eyes of men. Full, delicate lips the color of overwarm fingertips. Acquiescent eyes. More than once she was forced by uncomfortable glances to look away.

Henry thought the agitation of the long trip was to blame for her poor appetite. She didn't suggest otherwise.

Neither of them had a restful night. Henry spent the night fidgeting, getting in and out of the squeaky bed to gaze out the window, pacing around in the dark. Only after Abigail rose at sunrise and began to dress did Henry finally settle back onto the mattress with a sigh, wishing her a happy birthday as he succumbed to a deep sleep.

Shivering in the brisk morning air out on bustling Silver Street, Abigail gorged her eyes on women. Women at their shopping. Women gossiping on the sidewalks. Women dragging along fussy children. Women, women, women. They seemed to her, these flocks of women, like actors costumed for the stage, so striking was their dress, so mannered their carriage — so unlike her, she couldn't help feeling with an almost nostalgic ache in her throat — in their wide-swept silk and serge skirts lined with colored taffetas that rustled with every step, their velvet capes and sateen shawls fringed with lace, their chocolate-colored button shoes, their straw hats trimmed with silk violets, satin rosettes, ostrich feathers. So accustomed to the filthy rags and lumbering gait of drunken miners had she become that it seemed to her as if these beautiful creatures arrayed in delicate folds of fabric were not so much walking as floating down the sidewalks.

Outside the confectioner's shop she watched in a trance as two little ringleted girls in tartan dresses sucked on pieces of sugar candy. She smiled at the sight of an elderly lady in an old-fashioned shawl and bonnet, resting on a stack of silver bullion bricks in front of a bank, her face shriveled as a rotten potato. Through the milliner's window she watched a shy young woman try on hat after hat, frown after frown. Outside the greengrocer's

158

a woman brandishing a frilled silk parasol interrupted Abigail's fixed gaze on a woman choosing oranges to say hello and ask her where she was from. The expression that stole over the woman's face when Abigail told her spoke volumes beyond her 'I see.' The woman made a few more pleasantries then went on her way.

Feeling hungry and sorry for herself Abigail bought a lemon pastry from the confectioner and stood at the window watching pass in all their finery, like the taste and texture of that sweet, flaky delicacy on her tongue, the flowery women of Bird, and it struck her that she must have looked, gaping as she was, just like the miners in the Ore.

It wasn't until she found herself standing across the street from a stately home fronting First Street, a few blocks north of Silver, that the self-pity swelling within her all morning began to recede. The two-story, red-brick house with green wrought-iron balconies encircling the upper casements might have been transported intact from the East, so old and grand did it seem in the dappled shade of two tall poplars. On a plaque over the red front door, written in fancy gilt letters on a black ground, were two words: *The Salon.*

Abigail had been standing there for some time, remembering with mild amusement what Rodriguez had told her about the Madam of Bird, when a fashionable middle-aged woman with a fox stole draped across her shoulders left the house by the front door and ambled with an air of profound contentment up the street. This seemed peculiar to Abigail, given the nature of the premises. She glanced up at the balconies, half expecting to see garishly clad harlots parting the tapestry curtains. When a little while later another respectably dressed woman came along and opened the front door without knocking, Abigail decided she had to see for herself why society women were coming and going from a whorehouse.

She crossed the street, hesitated briefly at the door, then opened it and went in.

A wave of warmth smelling of pomade and heated hair bore her into an atmosphere as dusky as it was luxurious, the shallow flames of a chandelier's jeweled globes dimly glimmering in sterling silver hairbrushes, in glass-stoppered phials filled with tonics and oils and elixirs, in waving and crimping irons, in every facet of scores of cut-glass atomizers bunged with colored rubber bulbs. Here and there on shelves and pedestals, wigs, waves and bangs lent panache to porcelain heads otherwise devoid of expression. On the right side of the long, narrow room two ladies in Louis XIV armchairs, their shoulders covered with grenadine bibs, sat before cheval glasses reflecting back to themselves their own placid visages. Behind each of them, wearing black foulard wrappers trimmed with gold braid, an attractive young coiffeuse stood fretting their hair.

Abigail had already turned to leave, laughing inwardly at her mistake, when one of the hairdressers turned from her ministrations and in a heavy French accent bade her good morning.

'I'm sorry,' Abigail said. 'I have the wrong address.'

'Please,' the hairdresser said, gesturing with her comb toward a dark green velvet sofa set against the left-hand wall, 'do make yourself comfortable. Madame will see you shortly.'

Abigail, seduced as much by the sonorous lilt of the hairdresser's voice as by her casual authority, acquiesced, deciding her legs could use a rest. She unbuttoned her jacket and hung it on the lacquered coatrack behind the door.

The moment she sank into the deep plush of the sofa she began to drowse. The source of the almost oppressive heat in the room was a stove deep in the shadows of a back corner, its embers glowing brightly through the dampers. Every now and then a little girl emerging from some unseen room would feed the stove a new log, stoking the already blazing fire to a fiercer burn. Abigail closed her eyes, and in that toasty darkness the gentle murmurs and languorous combing lulled her into a deep slumber.

He awoke to the noise of the stamp mill in the valley below, a sound like a slow train banging over rail joints. Seeing she wasn't there he put on his boots and shirt and, slicking back his hair with a spit-moistened palm, went down to the lobby to find her not there either. He wound his watch, comparing its time to the ugly porcelain clock on the shelf behind the counter. It was almost or just after ten.

Out on the corner of Silver and Second he stood for a while watching for her. He was no lover of crowds, and all the people thumping by over the boardwalks and brushing up against him with polite apologies made him edgy. Especially all the women in their fancy clothes. They made him feel, by doing nothing more than rustling by, that he was in need of reform. The men too, not only the well-to-do in their worsted suits and alpaca frock coats and stiff black top hats but also the miners and men of the soil and other trades, seemed to Henry both compelled and constrained by some higher purpose, something deliberate in their stride and gaze, conspicuous by its absence in the men of Shakespeare.

Bird had boomed since Henry was last there in the spring. Two new steeples, one to the east, the other to the north, ensured with the older ones to the west and south that salvation was within spitting distance of every corner of town. Those seeking more earthly pleasures had sixteen saloons to choose from, which number comported with the views held by some that a ratio of four saloons to every church was the truest measure of a town's progress and improvement. Two new banks, First Territorial and Bird Savings & Loan, were advertising their surety by stacking eighty-pound bricks of silver bullion three feet high against their cast-iron lower facades. There was so much traffic in the streets that wagons and buggies were getting tangled up in the intersections, provoking their drivers into shouting matches, which, when added to the unbroken clatter of iron-shod hooves striking the cobbles and the drumroll of heels and toes beating the board-walks and all the resounding voices of happy men and women, made for a nerve-wracking cacophony. Over all this noise Henry could hear the telling blasts of dynamite coming from camps and claims in every direction, giving Bird a genuine right to call itself a boomtown.

Heading north up Silver, glancing through the windows of the shops he passed, Henry became aware of a mild twinge of concern, all right of jealousy, warming his joints, and he wondered if he shouldn't welcome it. His original plan had been to deal with the mattress later in the day, giving him a chance to investigate his freighting options, but as morning wore on and he still had not spotted Abigail amidst the throngs, he decided to go ahead and get it taken care of.

Turning onto First he headed west on Platinum. The newly rich, as if to assure Eastern investors that their town was there to stay, had lavished their wealth on architecture as seemingly indestructible as it was ornate: on brick and granite and slate, on gabled and mansard roofs, on windows crowned with carved pediments, on elaborate wooden cornices, shutters and moldings and long limestone friezes peopled with men and beasts of Attic cast.

At the corner of Fourth and Platinum Henry stopped and stood for a moment, staring up at the sign on an older wooden building with oak sideboards and buffets lined up out front. The ghostly '& Sons' on the sign had a chilling effect on the storefront and, to a lesser degree, on the ones adjacent. Henry cleared his throat then crossed the street and made his way into the store.

It was a large showroom with broad windows running the length of the front and left sides, nearly every inch of its floor space occupied by all manner of furniture and domestic goods, from couches and armchairs to stacks of linen and drapery, displays of china and silverware, sewing machines, feather dusters, cuckoo clocks. The man Henry took to be Copes, a balding, middle-aged fellow with curly, reddish hair, his hands held obligingly behind his back as he escorted a young man and his wife through a passage of upholstered sofas and settees, didn't match the picture of the man Henry had formed in his mind's eye.

Henry strolled around, idly surveying carpets and bath screens. After a while, unable to find the mattresses, he went and stood near the front windows should Abigail happen to pass. Tacked to a notice board beside the window, amongst ads and bills less exclamatory, was a playbill for *Helen of the Nile* — *Clad in Scenic Garniture of Uncommon Beauty* — being staged at the Bird Opera

House by the renowned tragedienne Samantha Darling and her Traveling Thespians. For the paltry sum of fifty cents (dress circle and parquet one dollar) this drama promised to deliver into unrivaled raptures of enchantment even the most critical lover of the arts. Henry wondered if this was the sort of thing Abigail liked. He stared out the window. A steel-wheeled surrey clattered by ferrying three fat men in batwing collars and bowler hats.

When at last the young couple had gone, Henry walked over to the counter at the back of the store, where the man he took to be Copes was busying himself with some papers.

'Are you Copes?' Henry asked.

'Yes,' Copes said.

He seemed eager to please, but as soon as Henry introduced himself a searching look stole into Copes' eyes, and they went a little moist. Henry feared the man was about to succumb to grief.

'We came up here,' Henry said, 'my wife and I, on account of it's her birthday. I figured since I was in town I'd go ahead and pick up the mattress myself.'

Copes returned his pen to its holder.

'I've been meaning to write to you, Mr. Jonson,' he said, 'but things being what they've been...'

'Ah, hell,' Henry said, and looked around, discomfited by the emotion in the man's voice.

'The fact of the matter,' Copes said, 'is I don't carry mattresses anymore.'

Henry rubbed the side of his jaw.

'Oh?' he said.

Copes explained that at the outset it hadn't been intentional. After the tragedy he had let all the mattresses he had in stock go without ordering any more. It was only later, after people started asking him for mattresses again, that he realized he would never be able to sell another, and over time that had become his policy.

'Yours was the last,' he said, as if this were something Henry might be pleased to know.

'Course I never got it,' Henry said, trying hard to sound pleasant.

Copes nodded sympathetically.

'I trust you received the moneys owed you?' he said.

'Yes. Yes, I did,' Henry said.

'I do apologize, Mr. Jonson,' Copes said.

'That's all right,' Henry said. 'I woulda done the same thing myself.'

Copes was kind enough to cash Henry's draft and suggest he try at Mahoney's, on the south side of town.

'He charges a little more, given he's the only one carrying them, but he'll give you a good mattress. Use my name and he may give you a discount.'

Henry pocketed the money and thanked Copes for his time, and they told each other how nice it was to have finally met.

She could not have been asleep long — the same two ladies were still having their hair set — when she was awoken by the touch of a hand on her shoulder. She opened her eyes to see standing beside her in a black velvet dress with a high starched collar an older woman with a Flemishly oval face, her eyes in that wan light as dark and solid as polished jet, all the darker under the stripe of scalp as pale as bone parting the center of her graying black hair. Festooning her stiff bodice was a silver chatelaine, at the end of which hung a monocle. Abigail couldn't fathom why this imposing woman with raven eyes should be staring down at her so intently.

'Happy birthday, Mrs. Jonson,' the woman said as if she and Abigail were old acquaintances, adding a moment later when Abigail made no response, 'You can't keep secrets for long in towns like ours.'

Still somewhat disoriented, Abigail took the chilly hand offered her and exchanged squeezes.

'I'm Dorothy Dumaine,' the woman said. 'Everyone calls me Madame. That's Isabella's doing, I'm afraid.'

'Hello,' Abigail said, unable to think of anything else.

With a gentle tug and an almost imperceptible tilt of her head Madame Dumaine coaxed Abigail up from the sofa.

'If you'll follow me, please, Mrs. Jonson,' she said, 'we can get started.'

Abigail, trying without success to think of a polite way to say she didn't belong there, followed Madame Dumaine to the back of the salon and into a small chamber separated from the salon proper by a curtain of black Spanish lace. A Turkish couch of burgundy silk damask spanned the middle of the room, wisps of steam rising from a porcelain basin on a table at its head.

'Let's shampoo, shall we?' said Madame Dumaine, guiding Abigail down onto the couch and setting the back of her head on a velvet-lined head rest at the lip of the basin.

'I don't mean to be impolite,' Abigail said, 'but I don't have much money. I hadn't actually planned on coming here. I was out for a walk and...'

'My dear,' Madame Dumaine chastised her, 'money should never enter a lady's mind on her birthday. It's your

166

day to be spoiled. You just lie there and think pleasant thoughts.'

As Madame Dumaine unpinned Abigail's hair and dipped it into the steaming water, Abigail was struck by the uncanny sensation that she was dreaming. From that angle all she could see besides the shadowy ceiling was a banquet lamp whose column was a plump, naked Cupid, the oak handles of a curling iron protruding like a rabbit's ears from its softly glowing chimney. More than once during the shampoo this lamp dimmed as if it had reached its last drop of oil only to surge back to full glow.

Taking a thick sponge from the basin Madame Dumaine wetted the top and sides of Abigail's head, the excess water trickling down with a mellow resonance into the basin. She poured a dollop of lavender-scented shampoo into her palm from a blue rectangular bottle and began rubbing it briskly into Abigail's hair, kneading her scalp with strong fingers, her monocle tapping her bodice as she rocked forward and back.

'Your poor hair,' she lamented. 'All that dust isn't good for it. We don't get much dust here in Bird. The dust storms through Shakespeare are something to behold. So I'm told. I've never been there myself of course.'

Abigail, in a stupor of contentment, murmured something unintelligible. Madame Dumaine went on scrubbing, working from the scalp clear down to the ends of the hair, her breath rising and falling with the level of her exertions.

'It's a mysterious thing, why one town prospers and another doesn't. I've lived here long enough to know it has little to do with potential. It's all about luck. Like those poor boys. That was just bad luck. Then all that business about the mattress.'

Scrubbing and scrubbing she spoke in a soft, soothing voice.

'People come up with all sorts of amusing reasons why no other woman but yourself has decided to live in Shakespeare when, as I see it, there is no reason but chance. They need these reasons, if only to settle their minds. Am I right?'

Abigail nodded.

'If you weren't in Shakespeare no one would think twice about its lack of women. It's all too common. It's the fact of there being only one that so enthralls them.'

Taking up the sponge again Madame Dumaine rinsed Abigail's hair and poured more shampoo into her palm, resuming her scrubbing with extra vigor.

'In fact, Mrs. Jonson,' she said. 'You and I have something in common.'

'Do we?' Abigail said.

'Yes, we do. I was the first woman in Bird.'

Abigail opened her eyes.

'You were?'

'Yes, I was. Granted, I wasn't alone nearly as long as you've been, you poor thing. When I came here Bird wasn't more than a couple of tents and a man selling whiskey by the cup from a jug. Things take time out here. Everyone expects things to happen overnight. Very few people in the Territory have the patience required to succeed in their enterprises. It doesn't help when people from the East read about the bricks of bullion stacked up in front of our banks, as if they were just swept there from around the corner, blown there on the wind. That mentality infects everything else, a disease. Everyone's got a scheme. The men and women who make it don't have any schemes. They identify a need and fill it. People don't want to believe it's that simple. It takes away the thrill, eliminates the need to hope. They are so smitten with their own cleverness, so in love with their own hopes, that they would rather suffer for a chance to express them than admit the truth.'

Madame Dumaine scrubbed.

'I wouldn't worry too much,' she said. 'You're young. You have your whole life ahead of you. I think people just need something to talk about. People want to know who you are, where you are from, what it must be like for you being the only woman there.'

'What do people say about me?' Abigail asked.

'Oh dear, all sorts of absurd things that don't merit repeating. I'm afraid it has become a sort of self-fulfilling prophecy. It's almost as if all the attention it has been given serves as a warning for women not to go there. I listen to the ladies that come here. Some fanciful notions, a lot of speculation about you, Mrs. Jonson, it may surprise you to learn. You are spoken about here with considerable interest. Whenever a man from Shakespeare is in town he can't walk two feet without someone asking about you. Needless to say, I'm sure none of it bears the slightest resemblance to the truth.'

Squeezing the excess suds from Abigail's hair, Madame Dumaine exchanged the basin of soapy water for an identical one of clean and began rinsing Abigail's hair.

'What do people say about me?' Abigail asked again.

Madame Dumaine clucked her tongue a few times.

'Really. I wouldn't pay them any heed.'

'Still,' Abigail said, 'I'd like to know.'

'What difference would it make?'

'Perhaps there's some truth in it.'

Madame Dumaine chuckled dryly.

'I doubt that very much.'

'They talk about my husband and I, don't they?'

'My dear, they talk about everything. It stands to reason your husband would be mentioned now and again.'

'What do they say?'

'You are persistent, aren't you,' Madame Dumaine said, clearly more than happy to have lost this particular battle. 'If you must know, they say what is always said when an older man marries a younger woman: remarks to the effect that time is not on his side. Now, please don't ask me to repeat any more of the idle chatter of ladies who have nothing better to do than speculate on the intimacies of people whom they have never laid eyes on.'

Abigail knew that this was probably the least of what was spoken about her.

'Well, I've heard some things about you as well,' she said.

Madame Dumaine smiled.

'I'm sure you have, my dear. It never ceases to amuse me to hear how I am perceived far and wide to be a kind of baroness whose very words strike such fear into the hearts of whores that they would sooner starve to death in the desert than risk my wrath plying their trade in Shakespeare.'

Madame Dumaine laughed.

'No, I have far better things to think about than trying to keep track of every two-bit trollop traipsing across the Territory seeking her fortune. Of course, I'm flattered to be invested with so much power, and no doubt some of this mystique has contributed to the success of the Salon, but I profess my own bewilderment at the situation in Shakespeare.'

Madame Dumaine, finished with the shampoo, helped Abigail up, and with the softest, warmest towel Abigail had ever felt she rubbed and fluffed Abigail's hair until it was nearly dry.

'I've asked Isabella to give you a Cleopatra Swirl. It's all the rage in the cities. You have the perfect face for it. And not a word about money, you hear.'

Madame Dumaine's rebuke melted into a smile as she offered Abigail her hand.

'Now, Mrs. Jonson,' she said, 'I have other matters to attend to. It has been most illuminating. And if ever you need anything, please don't hesitate to write. Women should always give each other help. Wouldn't you agree?'

Abigail shook the small hand, and thanking Madame Dumaine for the shampoo she parted the lace curtain and stepped through it.

Henry wasn't in the room when she returned to it shortly after noon.

Standing at the window, watching the smelter's tail of black smoke fraying across the sky, Abigail wondered where he was, if he was thinking about her, maybe buying her a gift. Her hair felt strange all coiled around her head like snakes. She wanted it out, didn't feel like herself, but Isabella had put so much work into it, curling and waving and crimping it, that she didn't have the heart to undo it.

It was another hour before Henry returned.

'He don't sell mattresses anymore,' he said, stomping in, hardly glancing at her he was so irate. 'Come all the way up here and he aint got a one. I felt like wringin his dadgum neck, the way he was lookin at me like I was to blame for what happened.'

Abigail was sitting on the bed, arms crossed. Henry

171

looked at her, his eyes lingering momentarily on her hair, then he looked away without comment and walked over to the window and sighed wearily.

A warm lump of indignation began to throb in Abigail's chest. Neither spoke for a while. It was quiet in the hotel, everything still but for the distant bangs of ore being crushed at the mill.

'I thought maybe you'd run off earlier,' Henry said. 'I wouldn't of blamed you.'

'Run off on my honeymoon?' Abigail said, trying to dispel the gloom, but the note of bitterness in her voice only added to it.

If Henry had any opinion on this remark he didn't make it known. Again there was a long silence. Abigail fiddled with a corner of the quilt. She was about to suggest they go and have a look around the shops when Henry spoke again.

'Listen, Abigail,' he said quietly, turning away from the window.

Abigail, hearing a strange tremor in his voice, turned to face him and was taken aback by how upset he looked, as if he were struggling hard to hold back his feelings. That wasn't the Henry she knew, and it made her uneasy.

'Things don't seem to be workin out the way I thought they would,' he said. 'I don't mean just us, but the saloon, Shakespeare, everything.'

He paused, rubbing his chin, and looked down at the floor.

'It aint fair to you,' he said. 'Livin like we are.'

She wasn't sure what he was driving at, but she wished he would hurry up and say it.

'You aint happy,' he went on. 'I aint happy. I caint go on like this, and you caint either.'

He was looking directly at her now, the burden of some unspoken truth taking its toll on him, making him look truly old.

'What are you saying, Henry?' Abigail said nervously.

'You're goin on back home and forgettin this ever happened.'

And saying this, he turned around and faced the window again.

Abigail felt a sudden urge to throw something, anything, at him. It was the word *home* that hit her hardest, spoken as if all her time in Shakespeare had been little more than a holiday, all her time in the saloon, all those leering miners, all her loneliness, something she was just supposed to forget.

She stood up and, addressing his back, said: 'You've got some nerve.'

Henry turned around, stone-faced.

'A little trouble and you give up,' she went on. 'Ship me back. Postage paid.'

Henry made no reply. He swiveled his head slowly to the side as if he were about to spit then swiveled it back.

'My name aint Henry Jonson,' he said matter-of-factly. 'It's Lester Dawson. The man you married don't exist.'

The look Henry gave her as he spoke these words implied more or less that there was nothing more to be said, that the only appropriate response on her part was shock and dismay. Abigail did not comply. She had heard enough murmurings and whispers in the saloon to gather by now that Henry had not led an exemplary life in his youth. And while she did experience a weird, disorienting sensation upon hearing this other name, she wasn't about to give Henry, not the way he had slung it out at her like some ace up his sleeve, the satisfaction of seeing her flinch.

She turned aside, took a few contemplative steps, then turned again to face him.

'You can't get rid of me that easy, Henry Jonson,' she said.

'You have no idea what you've gotten yourself into, woman,' he said, lowering his voice almost to a growl.

'Oh, I think I do,' she said. 'Henry Jonson may not exist on a piece of paper, but he's standing right here in front of me.'

Henry, shaking his head in consternation, turned back to the window and placed his hands on the sill. Abigail kept thinking he was about to say something, but he just went on staring out the window. She stood there looking at him, wondering what it was about this man that called up in her, against all her better sense, such resistance to be quit of him.

'This is about your debility, isn't it?' she said, trying to think of something to break the silence.

Henry turned around, his face red.

'No, it aint.'

'You wouldn't be doing this if it wasn't.'

'Is that all you can think about?'

This comment, or more so the mean way he said it, hurt Abigail more than anything else he had said.

'You make it sound like I'm some kind of whore,' she said. 'Is that what you think I am? Your whore? Done her job, now send her back where she came from.'

'Whoa now,' Henry said, raising his hand to petition innocence. 'Hold on one minute.'

'Is that why you sent me out to Yucca Springs with Kelly?'

'What are you talkin about?'

'You know what I'm talking about. You can't just

dangle me out in front of the next man when the first one quits his job.'

Again Henry swiveled his head slowly to the side as if he were about to spit.

'Kelly was the only one I could trust not to go blab the whole dadgum thing to everybody in town. Invisible fence. You expect me to close the saloon for a whole day on a fool's errand? Accusin me of treatin you like a whore. Hell. I think you pretty well earned that one on your own.'

'You sonofabitch,' Abigail fumed. 'Begging me to get the kid back, telling me to send him away. Sending me out with Kelly. And the nerve to call me a whore. You don't give a damn how I feel about any of it.'

'How you feel! Any other man woulda killed you both the first time. I think I've been pretty darn fair considerin.'

'Fair! Fair? Get your damn clothes off! Get on the mattress! You call that fair? He could have been raping me for all you knew. It was all about your debility. You weren't even jealous!'

'Like hell I wasn't jealous. Jealous is all I been since I met you. Look at me when I talk to you, woman.'

Abigail glared at him.

'You think I like watchin some jackass kid plowin my wife? You have any idea how humiliatin that is for a man? Jealousy's the only thing gets my blood up enough to do it myself. Maybe if you were more of a woman I wouldn't need to get jealous.'

This remark flew past Abigail unchallenged, and though she knew he was only trying to shift the blame for his debility onto her, she couldn't help feeling, despite her knowledge to the contrary, that perhaps he was right.

'How am I supposed to know that's what you're thinking if you don't tell me?'

'What do I got to tell you everything I'm thinkin for? Hell, half the time I don't know what I'm thinkin my own self.'

They continued to argue over various unacknowledged injustices, their voices growing louder as they closed the distance between them, but the heart of the matter having been aired, the rest was little more than standing ground. There was an awkward moment when they ran out of space, ran out of words, and they looked at each other like strangers, then Henry was clutching at her shirt and she was helping him out of his pants, and seeing his erection there without the aid of betrayal she felt her knees go slack with desire, and afraid that it might deflate she grabbed hold of it with both hands while Henry went on pulling off her clothes, causing little tearing noises where he couldn't find some catch, and he was kissing every swatch of bare skin he could get his lips on while she stroked him and they fumbled about in a clumsy jig, Henry practically weeping with desire for her, and she for him. When they were sufficiently unclothed she told him to lie down on his back on the bed, and she climbed on and straddled him, and the light that gleamed in Henry's eyes, the light of his cure, burned into Abigail as she rode him remembering the feeling the day she bolted out into the desert beyond the invisible fence, a feeling of freedom unlike any she had ever known, out there in the desert, the air rushing past her, the endless world before her, the power of the horse beneath her, free, and she remembered thinking that she was the only one who could come and go through the invisible fence. The only one.

It was a long and tedious play. The audience, clad in more scenic garniture than the play itself, proved in the end a more entertaining spectacle than the drama on the stage. One man in the proscenium box remained standing the entire evening, overcoat on arm, stovepipe hat poised on the thumb of his left hand, dourly awaiting the arrival of his date. All throughout the performance people kept tramping into the theatre, each new arrival heralded by a flourish of banging seats. When not openly damning Theoklymenos or sympathizing with Helen, the play-goers were heaping scorn on the monuments to millinery obstructing their views, trying to arouse snorers from their slumbers, getting up in the middle of the acts to take in some fresh air. The high point of the night came when Menelaus, intending to flood the hearts of the audience with pathos, stumbled onto the stage wrapped in a torn sail, provoking gales of laughter. Helen and her Chorus hardly garnered more respect in their clinging chitons.

Mr. and Mrs. Jonson, seated in numbers three and four, row B, parquet circle, were decidedly more subdued than the local patrons of the arts. Mr. Jonson, his eyes glazed, seemed lost in an inner world infinitely richer than the one at hand. Mrs. Jonson, for her part, knowing it could very well be a long time before she laid eyes on a woman again, made no efforts to follow the confusing story. Instead she painted portraits of Helen and the Chorus in her mind's eye, to take out and gaze on in the long, cold months to come. Helen, in limelight, pining for Menelaus before the tomb of King Proteus. The six women of the Chorus dancing in a circle with their flutes and lyres, sea-green chitons swirling. Helen cutting off her hair in feigned mourning.

When at last the play was over, Mr. and Mrs. Jonson filed out with the crowd into the cold night air, the sounds of carousal spilling over them from all the surrounding saloons. Arm in arm they strolled under the twinkling stars, back to the hotel, an easy silence between them. That night they slept for the first time side by side, in the same bed, for most of the night.

At dawn the next morning they boarded the stagecoach with a miner and a gambler, who, not knowing who she was, told Mrs. Jonson that the town she was bound for left something to be desired in the way of female society.

All the way back to Shakespeare, down the mountains and through the canyons, past the old black walnut tree where the Copes boys met their end, Abigail was unaware of the world changing outside her window, so lost was she in her own thoughts.

ONE

One after the other, as if by common consent, they dropped to the ground like stones. By dawn every branch was bare, a shallow pile of brittle brown leaves quilting the ground where once their shade had lain, the cold light of the east penciling in a spray of wiry twigs.

By the time Crawford emerged, dapper in his black wool overcoat and bowler, the leaves were gone, scattered across the desert by an icy north wind. He stopped short of the steps, faltered by the sight of his beloved mulberry raped of its foliage, his eyes misting over as if on the verge of some profound apprehension. Had he any artistic talent, he mused wistfully, he might have chosen this solemn tableau — barren tree, windswept crags, marble sky — as a fit subject for a watercolor in the manner of the great English Realists. A cruel yet moving parable of the life of Man. But his was a literary imagination, prone to spontaneous overflows of feeling; as such he dimly perceived through the skeletal limbs of his poor naked tree the armature of a sonnet on the theme of Solitude. He stood transfixed for several minutes, snagged on the word *deciduous*, then, feeling time's gentle nudge, he stepped down from the porch and fell to the business of the day, promising himself he would take up his humble little poem again that evening, perhaps enlisting the aid of his nephew.

All through the morning feathery cirrus clouds gusted high across the stratosphere, each hair fringed with a faint suffusion like the iridescent nacre of a shell. Around three o'clock the wind ceased entirely. Shreds of smoke scarcely distinguishable from the sky around them wavered over chimneys in the sudden calm then rose unperturbed like ghostly umbilicals between Shakespeare and the clouds. In the woolly quiet that ensued, dogs shuffled up and down Avon casting wary glances skyward. A cold light sifted through the vast extent of the clouds, suffusing the world with a strange yellowish tint.

By this light Abigail read in a whisper of an old king gone mad in a lonely and meaningless world. From time to time the fire popped and she would raise her head and listen, as if straining to place some faraway sound. She closed her book and sat gazing vacantly at the sulfurous gray light seeping through the window. In time she got up and went to the parlor and opened her keepsake box and took from it the small sheaf of envelopes bound by a strip of white lace.

Back in her chair in the kitchen she untied the lace and found the oldest letter and began to read. She read again from first to last all six letters, penned by Andy but seemingly from some nameless voice of desperation reaching out to her across the miles, to whom she once was, not so long ago in days but forever in lifetimes, the picture he painted of the pleasant little town, *lots for a woman to do*, the beauty of the country, and he spoke glowingly of Crawford and Kelly and Muldoon, which reminded her less of those people than her own feelings when she had first read about them, how they had seemed like characters in a dime novel, as if the town she was bound for was no more real than its name suggested, but rich beyond compare in love and life, and reading the letters again she felt around her heart a warm ache of sorrow for what might have been.

When she was finished she folded the letters back into their envelopes and sat holding them in her lap. Then she opened the stove and set the envelopes on the glowing embers. They blackened at their edges and smoked then caught fire and curled, and watching them burn she felt some part of herself scatter and vanish.

She had just returned to *King Lear* when three soft knocks landed guiltily on the back door.

Although he never came into the saloon during her shift, she knew of Andy's nightly bender and increasing eccentricity. 'There's somethin wrong with that kid,' Henry kept saying, telling her how Andy had taken to sitting off in a corner, staring fixedly at him as if intending to paint his portrait, or else coming up and shaking his hand and not letting go until he had made some offensive remark about women or old men. She had long since stopped making the deposits herself, put off by Andy's exaggerated friendliness, the way he held before his own true feelings a sort of dummy of his uncle, replete with overbroad smiles and kisses to her hand.

Cursing under her breath, Abigail got up from her chair and carried the lamp through the rooms to the back door only to see when she opened it, standing there holding his hat in his hands, not Andy but Kelly, the low angle of the lamp casting shadows upward across his face.

'Evening, Mrs. Jonson,' he said.

'Well, don't just stand there,' Abigail said when he said nothing more. 'You're letting all my heat out.'

By the length of his hesitation it was clear he had not called with the intention of coming inside but had planned only to say his piece in the briefest possible manner then quickly depart. Stepping in he glanced down at the mattress, furtively took in a few other details of this, the domicile of Shakespeare's only married couple, then came to his point.

'I'd be surprised if you didn't have some inkling of what has happened.'

'I confess I don't,' Abigail said, her tongue still soaked in Shakespeare.

If not for the seriousness of his expression she might have added, *my lord*.

'Well,' he said, his voice and bearing steeped in guilt, 'you were right. I resented you when you questioned the sincerity of Nathalie's love, but you were right.'

He went on to explain that he had received in Tuesday's mail a letter from Nathalie to the effect that one of his dearest childhood friends, a man whom he had trusted implicitly, had asked for her hand in marriage, which she had duly accepted.

'I'm sorry,' Abigail said.

'No,' he said, 'it's you who deserve an apology. I behaved abhorrently that day. Clearly I wasn't equal to the task. I thought of nothing but myself, failing entirely to see what a difficult moment it was for you.'

'I'd forgotten all about it,' Abigail said.

'Nonetheless,' Kelly said, 'I feel that none of us, me especially, have made any effort to understand what it must be like for you being here. We think of nothing but ourselves.'

'I assure you, Mr. Kelly, I am quite content.'

'I'm relieved if that is the case.'

'It is.'

Kelly glanced down and turned his hat a quarter-turn clockwise.

'In any case,' he said, 'I didn't come here to burden you with my private grief, only to say that if there is anything I can do for you, anything at all, please don't hesitate to ask.'

With that he apologized once more for the intrusion, put on his hat, said goodnight and left.

Abigail stood for a while with her back to the door, somewhat perplexed by this visit, then, a chill running up her legs, she returned to her tragedy.

They stepped out of the saloon and inhaling deeply the sharp night air, lit their freshly rolled cigarettes and smoked standing there in the cold.

'You hear that?' the older one said when the ruckus of the saloon subsided for a moment.

'Hear what?'

'Be still,' he said, hand raised, head cocked to the side. 'That. Hear that?'

They looked toward the window above the assay office, the light within curtained green. From that direction they could hear distinctly now the high reedy whine of a violin, strains of a meandering lament evocative of some grand old world in decay.

Carefully, over frozen pits and ruts, grasping each other for balance, they crossed Avon by the light of the Ore. Backs against the front wall of the assay office, they smoked, heads down the better to hear the music above. Gazing into the soft puddle of light on the ground before them they stood entranced, as if remembering misfortunes or pondering those still to come, the dampering effect of

185

wood and glass serving only to increase in their hearts a strange, ineffable longing.

Oblivious to the cold they listened for some time to the sad, enchanting melody, not even lifting their cigarettes to their lips, not moving at all until a harsh note raised their heads a little. They exchanged glances. Over and over the music foundered on the same passage, snagging each time on the same harsh note, until at last a terrific yell, in all regards like the roar of a bear, erupted from above, followed by a sharp, ringing crack.

They looked up. Another sharp crack. The bright timbre of splintering wood, jangle of screeching strings. Then silence again.

The older one dropped his cigarette and ground it out with his boot heel.

'You ever been in love?' he said after a while.

'Once, I reckon. I aint sure,' the younger one said.

'Then you aint loved. If you aint ever been broke up like at you aint loved.'

A little time passed before the younger one spoke again.

'I kissed the dugs of a cow this little old gal used to milk.'

'What was her name?'

'Emily.'

'Never did like that name.'

'They weren't aimin to please you when they named her.'

Silence again.

'Why didn't you marry her?'

The younger one took a drag on his cigarette.

'A woman made me, and I preciate it. She brung me up, and I thank her for that too. As for the rest of em, I figure they's better off without me. Like my old man used to say, *You caint mistrust a woman if you don't trust a one to begin with.*'

The older one nodded appreciatively at this polished nugget of wisdom.

A shadow passed across the puddle of light, then the ground went dark, leaving but a shard of moon to silver their frozen breaths.

They sat at the tables stiff in their coats, hands in their pockets, their frosty breath fogging their faces. It was after two in the morning. A few of them hot with liquor had shed their coats, and what little warmth the walls retained was rightfully theirs.

'She upset about it?' Hines was asking.

'She don't seem to be,' Henry said.

Hines took a drink.

'You'd think the Director askin they might a come,' he said.

It is with our deepest regret, Crawford had read aloud that afternoon, *that we, the players of the Overland Theatrical Troupe, and its most esteemed director, Oliver Gidding, inform you that in consideration of the greatness of distance and the recent Indian depredations, the management of the Troupe deems it unwise at this time...*

'Another?' Henry asked.

Hines scooted his glass forward.

Around three o'clock the silence came. For almost half an hour no one moved. No one drank. No one lifted a hand to scratch an itch. To a man they all sat or stood, still as statues, as if captive to waking dreams.

It happened every third or fourth night, always at this the coldest, darkest hour, this strange pall of silence that fell over everything, not just the men but the world itself

187

and all things in it. Had any man sought to break it he would have failed, for it was a silence born of the dead of night and thus impervious to will. Standing behind the bar in that terrible silence, Henry surveyed man to man the miners' hard, cold faces, cropped by the shrubbery of ragged beards, sharp clean lines slashed across powder-blackened foreheads, their own selves the rubble they wrested from the earth. Short stalks of steam puffing from their red noses the only testament to their animate beings. His eyes came to rest on the hands of a recent arrival. Smooth clean hands not yet mangled by the mine, spread flat on the table around his glass. Running over her skin they wouldn't chafe her, these young, healthy hands not long enough in Shakespeare to have forgotten the feel of a woman. He saw these hands undressing her, taking off piece by piece all of her clothes until she stood naked before him. He saw these fingers touch her breasts, circle them, squeeze them. Saw them slide down her belly, curve under, press up into her soft white flesh...

A moth thumped the window. The sound of Henry's breath stretched out into the silence. Someone sniffed. Then the men were talking again and calling for whiskey.

'Railroad'll change everything,' Hines said.

'Hmm,' Henry said, and poured the man his drink.

Two

Ice crystals in his beard, Buddy jumped from the stage and fairly burst into the Ore, proclaiming between gasps that there was a hell of a storm blowing in, he'd nearly got snowed under in the mountains, snow already two feet deep through Pheasant Canyon, couldn't see the heads of the mules even.

Henry poured a whiskey.

'You don't say,' he said.

Half an hour later it began.

Thin and sparse at first, the snow came scudding straight down Avon in horizontal flurries, growing denser by the minute, scrimming with ice anything with a northern face. Every now and then some dark shape clutching a hat would flicker past like a figure in a zoetrope. There one moment, gone the next. The storm soon bled from the sky what frail light still struggled through the clouds. Not yet six o'clock and black as midnight. Only a soft luminescence emanating from the thickening carpet of snow as if from some subterranean moon.

At his usual table in the corner of the saloon, Andy sat nursing a whiskey, a book open before him.

Men caught by the storm at various removes from town kept gusting through the front door, the wind of their arrivals threatening to make off with anything not nailed to the tables. Stomping their boots and brushing the snow from their extremities they would remark on their way to the bar on the mighty fine weather they were having.

His glass empty Andy stood up, a digit marking his place in his book, and made his way to the bar.

Henry poured the whiskey and eyed him warily.

'You won't get far walkin in that tonight,' he said.

'Ah, snow,' Andy said philosophically. 'Pure, virginal white, unblemished as the soul of an honest woman. I love snow. Don't you?'

He took a swig and exhaled loudly. Henry returned the bottle to the shelf.

Coming back from serving other customers, Henry asked Andy what he was reading.

Andy looked up from his book.

'Just a little essay on Man,' he said in a pompous tone, not unlike his uncle's. 'A satire, though it isn't particularly humorous. He's especially savage on old men. He finds their wrinkled skin and weak hams as comic as their stubborn adherence to outmoded traditions and their steadfast conviction that in the presence of a woman they are half their true age. All of which are obvious to anyone with eyes, which makes me wonder why the author felt compelled to write it in the first place, much less publish it. Shall I read you some?'

Henry thanked him no. He folded his arms across his chest. Andy resumed reading. It wouldn't take much, Henry thought. A minute at most. Crush the windpipe with his thumbs, or...

'You say somethin?' Henry said, noticing out of the corner of his eye a miner at the bar trying to get his attention.

'Four, I said,' the man said.

Henry set the glasses on the bar and poured the whiskey into each.

At length Andy stood up and buttoned his coat. He tucked his book under his arm and surveyed with fraternal pride the company he had come to keep. Then he saluted Henry and left the saloon, the force of the wind nearly toppling him as he pulled open the door and leaned out into the storm.

Ducking under the stemple Kelly carried on stoop-backed and awkward down the drifts to the workings, the box of cartridges and the fuse reel under one arm, the lantern hanging from the other. When he had reached the tail of the group he gently set his cargo on the ground and approached the nearest team.

'It's coming down hard,' he said.

Cooper, naked to the waist and sweating, planted the sledge on the ground. Ralston pulled the drill from the hole, pivoted toward Kelly and said: 'Where's Hobbs?'

'I'll set them tonight,' Kelly said.

He turned and whistled to the other teams, and a wave of expanding quiet rolled domino-fashion down the line. The miners began snuffing out their candles and carrying their gear out of the blast zone on the long slog back to the main shaft, some moving by touch and sound alone, so intimate were they with every stope and bulge of these the bowels of the Lear.

After he had carried the fuse and cartridges and the tool tray to the end of the workings, Kelly knelt down beside the lantern and pulled the mochila from his shoulder and took from it the bundle of envelopes addressed to him in a feminine hand. Working methodically from hole

191

to hole along the face, he wrapped a letter, sometimes two, around each cartridge before ramming it with the baton to the butt of the hole, piercing the compound with the nail and inserting into it a length of fuse. Then he stemmed each hole with clay and tamped it flush to the collar. From time to time in the quiet between his motions he stood listening to the sound of the wind resonating through the chambers of the mine, a sort of soft sustained tolling, as of mourning bells carried on the wind from the next village over.

At the last hole Kelly took out of the mochila the photograph of Nathalie in the snow. He peered at it for several minutes, a lump swelling in his throat.

A heavy snow had fallen the night before but that day it was sunny and almost warm, reams of snow melting from headstones and dripping onto dead and shriveled bunches of flowers, the bark of the sycamores black with damp. She was in her gray woolen coat and black boots, her cheeks and nose rosy in the cold. They visited the graves of their forebears and resurrected family lore long since dead to themselves. A great-grandfather who had lived for three months with cannibals on a South Seas island. A grandmother who had survived a lightning bolt only to die of rabies. A great-uncle who married his brother's wife after the brother's suicide. Kelly could find no words to say at her mother's grave, visions in his mind of a squalling life killing in delivery the woman who bore it.

They walked some more. He liked how the shadows of the trees lay in the snow across the pointed black rods of the fence. He set up the tripod and took the camera from its case. All lacquered metal and bellows and glass, the camera seemed incongruous in the snow and stone of the cemetery, a toy of the living amidst trappings of the dead. It was new to him, a gift from his father, and he was long in setting the plates, in balancing the light between iris and shutter. She grew bored and cold waiting for him, and perhaps it was in frustration that she asked him bluntly if it was true he consorted with prostitutes in the city.

He straightened up and stammered, then said with some ire: 'Who said that?'

'Is it?'

His temper seemed to amuse her.

'I want to know who told you this.'

'No one told me,' she said.

'Then why did you put that question to me?'

She scooped up some snow and packed it into a snowball.

'I thought that's what university students did.'

'I most certainly have not,' he said, 'and I don't think it a proper topic of conversation to be having in a cemetery, a stone's throw from your mother's grave at that.'

He returned to the viewfinder, his fingers quivering, and asked her to stand by the tree and occupy her mind with thoughts of a more pleasant nature. Her snowball missed a nearby cross. He brought her into focus and squeezed the bulb.

'I'm sorry I upset you,' she said back in the buggy.

He looked at her and saw in her eyes that she knew the truth, and the knot in his chest began to loosen.

He wanted to tell her everything, how sometimes he would go to the same brothel two or three nights a week, how the girls called him by his first name, that some of the happiest moments of his life had been spent in the clutches of whores, how he loved watching them undress before his eyes, whatever shape, fat or thin, short or tall, that only between the legs of a whore had he ever felt he was seeing life as it really was, teeming with unspeakable urges, and afterwards, walking back in the dark, the city quiet, the sound of his footfalls echoing in an alleyway, he would sometimes wish the sun would never rise again.

But he could never tell her these things. Not his sweet, beautiful, innocent Nathalie. He closed his eyes and kissed her warm lips, and when the kiss was over he asked her to marry him.

Kelly pulled the picture from his lips and slid it into the hole with the cartridge.

When he had finished tying the fuse to all the rattails hanging from the collars he cleared the tools from the area and unreeled the spool down to the winze. He lit the fuse with the snuff of his lantern and started up the ladder, the flame hissing below like a nest of angry snakes.

He barely heard it when it blew. A roll of soft *whumps* under the howling gusts. He hunkered over the mule, clutching his hat against the driving wind and snow, putting all his faith in the nose of that good, loyal beast to guide them back down to Shakespeare.

Reading of Probus, who in his six-year reign restored peace and order to every province of the Roman world, and who in an ill-fated effort to stem forever the tide of barbarians erected a high stone wall over hills and valleys and rivers some two hundred miles between the Danube and the Rhine, Crawford sat in his armchair by the stove, stroking the back of Romeo's head. Warm, soft bundle of purring fur, a little wheeze from some accident when he was a kitten, nose wet, eyes half lidded in pleasure, Romeo gently clawed Crawford's dressing gown.

Crawford licked his thumb and turned the page and read some more.

Midway through the account of the vices of Carinus, Crawford's mind strayed from the course of words and came to rest somewhere in the uncharted white of the page. He slowly stroked the left tip of his mustache, coiling it to a point. The wind was shaking the roof tin, screeling in wild crescendos through every groove not yet bunged with snow, as if determined to hit some impossible note.

They surely wouldn't have let Andy leave the saloon, he thought. He looked toward the window, dark and slick with frost, snowflakes swirling in the lamplight like frantic moths. He stroked Romeo and listened to the wind. Then with a long, exasperated exhale he surrendered once more to Gibbon's sober prose.

But he could not concentrate. Crawford closed the book and set it on the arm of the chair. Dislodging Romeo, who made an offended little pule as he thumped the floor, he got up and went over to the dining table on which his dirty supper plate, a bottle of wine and two glasses still sat. He poured himself some wine and stood with the rim of the glass to his lips, peering toward the window, the clock tick-tocking with ominous insistence above the sound of the wind. Romeo gazed up from Crawford's slippers with a plaintive meow and questioning eyes.

Fetching the lamp from the reading table he went to his bedroom and took from the armoire the knee-length buffalo robe he'd won from an Indian agent in a faro game, the dark brown fur all bunched and burred, the musty smell of the beast still strong on it. With some reluctance, not knowing what deadly disease it might be harboring, he put it on. He could barely get it buttoned, the sleeves were so stiff.

Armored thus he opened the front door and stepped outside, hard squalls of snow flurrying the side of his face and shredding the lamp flame. Clutching the post he stood at the edge of the porch and squinted townward. He could see nothing at all save the snow gusting around him.

'AN-DROOOOOOO!' he bellowed, fully aware of the futility of it.

The storm all but swallowed his voice. He stood there squinting in the darkness. Hearing nothing save the wind, he turned, telling himself he had done all he could, and started back for the door, which he was annoyed to see he had left wide open, only to hear what sounded like a faint cry buried deep in the wind and snow. He rushed back to the edge of the porch and yelled again.

'AN-DROOOOOOOOOOO!'

'Un-kuuuuuuul!' came the feeble, faraway reply, somewhere off to his left.

The next moment he was lunging through snow halfway to his knees, lurching side to side, arms wide and swinging in his heavy pelt like some crazed ape come to find itself on the wrong side of the world. He headed for the road, stopped, yelled again. Andy, still no closer, yelled back.

He lunged on, comparing in his mind the lay of the road in better weather with that which lay before him now. He knew that the road as it approached the house passed through wide stretches of desert as barren of vegetation as the road itself, so that buried as it was in a foot of snow it was nearly impossible to tell what was road and what wasn't. Nor did it help matters that he couldn't see more than ten feet in front of him. Still he lunged on. Only after several more shouting exchanges, realizing that Andy had

196

clearly lost it himself, did Crawford abandon altogether any effort to stick to the road and set out in the direction of Andy's voice.

'THIS WAY, ANDREW!' he shouted, sure that Andy could by now see the light of the lamp. 'THIS WAY!'

The brush here was denser, mesquites and creosotes looming ghostlike out of the frenzied dark, long spiny ocotillo limbs whipping violently in the wind, every dim yucca mimicking a frozen man. Only when he saw the awful sight of a prickly pear colony half buried in a drift did Crawford realize that he was still in his slippers.

He stopped, yelled again, lunged on.

At some point not long after abandoning the road, encouraged by the rising volume of Andy's replies, Crawford bolted forward and in so doing kicked a buried rock and stumbled to the ground. Sailing out in a wide, graceful arc the lamp plunged into the snow and extinguished without a sound.

Crawford raised his head and blinked. He thought for a moment he was underground, fallen through the snow into a pit, the world was so black. He came to his knees, ice running down his neck. The wind blew hard against his face. He groped around blindly for the lamp but could not find it.

'Un-kuuuuuuul! Where are yooooo?'

'I'M HERE, ANDREW! THE LAMP WENT OUT! I WILL STAY RIGHT HERE!'

It didn't last long, two or three minutes at most, but this brief period, standing there shouting at ten second intervals *I'M HERE!... I'M HERE!*, his left foot throbbing, snow gathering on him, the black diffusing ever so slightly to a deep, soft gray, these few minutes were oddly satisfying to Crawford. With each *I'M HERE!* he

197

was struck anew by the irony of those two words, belted into the heart of a blizzard, as if they were the sum of his existence. Never would he be a great poet, never rule an empire. *I'M HERE!* was all he was, and it seemed to him in those fleeting moments, waiting for his nephew to appear, that he was happy just to be alive and wanted to go on living until he could live no more, if that meant shouting *I'M HERE!* to the end of his days.

Then Andy was there, as if congealing out of the storm itself, inches from Crawford's face, his face calm, almost angelic. Snowflakes in his eyelashes. He too, in his mute placidity, seemed somehow exalted by the absurdity of the situation.

Not a word passed between them.

Crawford removed the buffalo robe and wrapped it around his nephew's shivering shoulders. Only then, as they took their first steps together, did it dawn on Crawford that he had no idea how to get back.

Rodriguez lay in his little room under the stairs, listening to the howling wind. He could feel the cold draught blowing in under the door. It was very late. He wished he had never shown Mrs. Jonson his room. It was harder to sleep in it now. He was more aware of the pressure where the walls touched the bottom of his feet and the top of his head. He could not understand why Mrs. Jonson had wanted to see his room. She gave him the impression that she did not approve of it. She didn't say anything to that effect, but that was the impression he got after she had looked at it.

He had just begun to doze when he thought he heard someone whisper his name, as if directly into his ear, and he felt the pores of his scalp pucker. He sat up, heart thumping, and clutched the Virgin.

After a while it came again. The voice. Whispering his name above the wind, as if right outside his door. He saw his sister, hanging from the viga. Eyes bulging. Face blue. Her fingers straight and swollen as cow's udders. Come at last to curse him.

'Rodriguez,' came the whisper again.

'Lo siento! Lo siento!' Rodriguez pleaded.

The door opened.

'Come out of there, Rodriguez, it's too cold. You'll freeze to death.'

'Mr. Stovall?' Rodriguez said, though still he could not see him.

'Come to my room,' Stovall said. 'I've got the stove burning. Bring your things.'

Gathering up his mat and pillow he more than happily followed Stovall back through the kitchen and into his room.

The heat in Stovall's room was stifling, the dim orange glow from the embers making all the lavish furnishings appear twice their normal size. The enormous bed, a four-poster draped entirely by a grizzly bear pelt, seemed to recede deep into its own shadows.

Rodriguez unrolled his mat on the floor at the side of the bed and thanked Stovall very much for his kindness. Stovall climbed with a noisy shiver back under the pelt and said goodnight.

On his back, eyes open, Rodriguez gazed up at the soft smudges of orange light playing over the ceiling and listened to the moaning wind. He couldn't sleep. He wasn't used to so much space around him, and the room smelled strange. Sweet and dark, like molasses.

Again he was seeing Mrs. Jonson peering into his room. 'Is that where you sleep?' she had asked him. 'In the closet, under the stairs?' That morning she had come to borrow his bucket — hers had cracked — and she had caught him just as he was leaving his room. This embarrassed Rodriguez. He didn't want people knowing he slept under the stairs. Mrs. Jonson wanted to see his room, if she might. Rodriguez had no intention of showing Mrs. Jonson his living quarters. They weren't fit for the eyes of a woman. Mrs. Jonson said she would be the judge of that and walked over to the door. Rodriguez rushed to the door and standing before it told Mrs. Jonson that Mr. Stovall would be upset to learn that people were observing his room. Rodriguez did not relent until Mrs. Jonson seemed disappointed that he could be so childish. He opened the door and asked her to be quick. She looked in, nodded, then thanked him and left with his bucket.

It was the first time anyone but Mr. Stovall had ever seen his room. Now that Mrs. Jonson had seen it, the room's shortcomings were more apparent to him. The room seemed smaller than before. It could have used an airing out now and then. Again Rodriguez saw in his mind's eye Mrs. Jonson's disapproving glance. She made him think of his wife and son, and it seemed to him that he was not in Shakespeare for the reasons he thought he was.

'Rodriguez,' Stovall whispered.

Rodriguez opened his eyes.

'Are you still awake?' Stovall asked.

Rodriguez wasn't sure if he should answer. Wasn't Mr. Stovall's hospitality best repaid with a deep slumber? But growing uncomfortable with the deception, he said: 'Yes. I am awake.'

'Come up to the bed,' Stovall said. 'It's more comfortable.'

Rodriguez, sensitive to the fact that even in the middle of the night, in a raging blizzard, Mr. Stovall was still his employer and not to be denied, got up and slipped under the heavy covers and sank into the thick, soft mattress, a substance like none Rodriguez had ever experienced, so completely did it yield to the weight of his body. He thanked Stovall again and turned onto his side and closed his eyes.

Still he could not sleep. He could hardly move under the covers, they were so heavy.

He was starting to wish he was back in his room under the stairs when he felt Stovall's hand come to rest against his back. It was very warm, the palm flat against his skin near his left, his higher, shoulder.

Rodriguez wondered why Mr. Stovall's hand was touching his back. Maybe it had strayed there in his sleep, he thought after a while. He soon grew used to its presence and decided he didn't really mind having the hand on his back, and at last he fell asleep.

The embers were almost out, the wind still howling, when Rodriguez was awoken by the heat of Stovall's belly pressed up against his back and a heavy arm draped around him. Though he reasoned that it was, after all, a very cold night, and it was only natural that they should lie closer together for warmth, in truth Rodriguez had no hope at all of sleeping under such conditions. Stovall felt like a furnace against him. Rodriguez considered slipping out from the covers, back to his mat on the floor, but he didn't want to wake Mr. Stovall, who might take offense at such ingratitude, so he just lay there listening to the moaning wind, wishing now that he was back in his cold little room under the stairs.

Not long thereafter Stovall's hand slid down

Rodriguez's belly, down to his crotch, and took hold in his firm grasp of everything there and squeezed such that Rodriguez, now wide awake, surmised that Mr. Stovall was not asleep at all and likely never had been. Still Rodriguez did not move. As far as he knew Mr. Stovall thought he was asleep, and the sensation for the most part being a pleasurable one Rodriguez thought it best to remain still rather than give Mr. Stovall the impression he was willingly submitting himself to so sinful a practice.

So it was that Stovall stroked and fondled Rodriguez for quite some time, Rodriguez vaguely aware of what felt like a corn cob pressing into his lower back, until Stovall seized the cob with his free hand and, giving it similar attention, one hand on Rodriguez, one on himself, brought the situation to its natural conclusion before returning with a sigh to his own side of the bed.

Dawn. A blush of rose over the soft white face of the world. The sky vacant, hard as polished turquoise. No wind. Watt Mountain rising like an iceberg from a frozen sea, the white broken here and there by clumps of dull green and brown, streaks of ochre, patches of bald gray. Peaks on every horizon capped with snow, looking much as they must have when woolly mammoths roamed this land, the dark brown rectangles of Shakespeare the only thing shattering the illusion of the Pleistocene.

The door opened with a sharp crack and caught on a ramp of frozen snow. She shoved it back and forth until the space was wide enough to stick her head through. Sapphire blue in the long, leaning shadows of the buildings, Avon lay fluted by the winds into smooth, undular furrows of snow. Down in front of the boarding house a rope as stiff as a branch was pointing due south from the crossbeam of the hitching post. Everything still, white, silent. A blank page awaiting the pen.

She stood in the doorway, the cold stinging her cheeks and ears, and watched the sunlight fire orange the thick slabs of snow bunting the roofs of the buildings on the other side of the street, a feeling of childish excitement sweeping through her.

She closed the door and lit a lamp and stood behind the bar holding her hands to the glass, the play unfolding in her mind.

THREE

'The cat?'

'That's what Crawford said, swear on my mother's grave.'

'I never. In that squall?'

'He reckons they weren't but fifty yards from the house.'

'Fifty yards or fifty inches, it aint a cat's inclination to brave blizzards for a man. He could be the King of England and it wouldn't make no difference to a cat.'

'Well, this one did, by God. Went out, found em, brung em back.'

They all sat there pondering these assertions with looks of mild offense. Henry had opened the door to let some fresh air in and one of the stray dogs was sniffing about the doorway in the hopes of inheriting the remnants of a plug of tobacco.

'Hold on. Aint that cat white?' one of them said.

By noon the snow had begun to melt. Jewels of dripping water glistened in the brilliant sunshine, making a steady patter of *plop* and *plunk* all up and down Avon. Men and beasts trundling by in their comings and goings churned up the dirt and slush with every step, turning the road into a slurry of cold sludge that refroze at night into rock-hard chunks and ridges that sprained more than a few drunken ankles. Gathering snow from the shadows a group of miners built in front of the Ore a three-tiered snowman with lava rock eyes, a medicine-bottle nose, and five charred corks set in a rakish scowl. They lent him a black scarf and a black hat and leaned a branding iron into one of his mesquite-root arms and called him the Outlaw and greeted him with accordant respect until nothing was left of him but an assemblage of his relics encased in mud. Only in the shade between the buildings did the snow lie whole and clean for weeks to come.

The nail gave with a dry screech. Wedging the claw of the hammer between the planks Henry pried up the board and set it on the floor. From the hollow thus revealed he brought out a small wooden box with dovetailed corners and the words *Assorted Fine Creams* printed in fancy lettering across it. He brushed away the delicate bud of a dead spider and, knees crackling, stood up and carried the box over to the stove and removed the lid, moving with haste lest she wasn't long out.

It lay corner to corner across the box, a scattering of .38 caliber cartridges crowded around it like a hungry brood. Nearly yellow now, the stock was one he had fashioned himself from the tusk of a javelina, the blued barrel all nicked and scarred, the hammer and trigger grimed almost black. A strong smell of chocolate wafted up as he lifted the pistol and gauged with easy jerks its cold heft in his hand.

So what'll it be now? Farmin? Ranchin?

Don't rightly know. I always had a dream of runnin a saloon. Settlin down. Wife and a kid or two. Easy retarment.

His partner snickered and shook his head. *Retarment,*

*hell. Runnin a saloon's more work than rustlin anyday.
And a sight more dangerous.*

Slipping the gun into his front pocket he grabbed a handful
of cartridges, closed the lid and returned the assorted fine
creams to their resting place beneath the floor.

'I don't want you to take this the wrong way,' he said to
her one night. 'I know sometimes things don't come out
the way I intend em to, but you said you'd like to know
what all I'm thinkin, and I'm thinkin maybe we oughta
consider the kid again.'

Abigail was sitting in front of the stove, reading *As You
Like It*. She had been expecting this request for some time
and had already formulated her thoughts on the matter.
They had both tried to make light of it, telling themselves
it was probably only a temporary relapse, but when a few
days after their return from Bird they tried again without
success, the truth by then was clear. The most upsetting
thing for Abigail was knowing that it didn't have to be
this way. Those few moments with Henry in Bird had
changed entirely the way she thought about him, changed
everything, his ridiculousness, his bitterness, the cloud of
doom forever hanging about him, shed in an instant. He
was still the same man but suddenly altogether different.
Having experienced that, if only once, without the kid,
she had no desire to go back. She made a few attempts to
talk to Henry about it, but it only made him angrier. He
would come in when there was a lull in the saloon and,
standing over the pot in the kitchen, wolf down whatever she had made for supper, exchange a few words,
then head back out. Abigail, knowing that brooding on
it would only make things worse, tried many things to
cheer him up. She polished his boots. She feigned interest

in his homeopathic medicines. She made a cushion for his stool. And though Henry thanked her for her little kindnesses, he could not hide his despair.

She closed the volume and sat there thinking for a while.

'I don't know,' she said. 'It doesn't seem fair to him.'

Henry nodded.

'I spose that's true, one way you look at it. But you haven't seen him the way I have, drinkin himself drunk and mopin about, insultin me, insultin miners. You'd have to be blind as a mole not to see it's you he's broke up about. Maybe it aint fair gettin his hopes up again only to let em down later on, but maybe it aint fair lettin him suffer the way he is either. I don't know.'

Henry rubbed his chin and shifted about uncomfortably.

'That aint so much my concern,' he said, 'as, I mean the kid and all, as much as, well, your own thoughts about it.'

'My thoughts?'

'Whether or not it's somethin you're interested in or if you've had enough of all that foolishness and me to boot.'

Abigail looked at Henry, standing there almost bashfully in petition, his hands down at his sides looking as though they needed something to hold. She looked at him, and he looked away.

'I'll have to think about it, Henry,' she said.

Henry nodded.

'Take as long as you like,' he said. 'We aint got anywhere to get to in a hurry.'

'Again,' Muldoon said, pressing the ice-cold bell of the stethoscope against the other side of Andy's sweating chest.

Andy, wincing, took a deep breath. Muldoon gently thumped Andy's chest, his eyes moving to and fro as he listened, tapped elsewhere, listened again.

'Well, my boy,' he said at length, pulling the earpieces from his ears and wrapping the tubes around the rods, 'you've earned yourself a first-class case of pneumonia.'

Andy's eyes widened at this news but he said nothing. Muldoon pulled the sheet and blanket back over his patient, then taking a pencil and a small pad from his shirt pocket he made some notes to himself, saying as he wrote: 'You should be grateful I've denounced allopathy or you would now be bled and blistered.'

Andy made no show of gratitude. He closed his eyes and only after nearly a minute had elapsed did he open them again to see Muldoon still there, looking down at him with unsettling tenderness.

Muldoon smiled at Andy then reached into the well-worn black leather bag resting beside him on the bed and brought out an egg and a measuring glass, saying: 'Allow me to demonstrate a fact of nature.'

Into the measuring glass he cracked the egg.

'The white of an egg,' he said, 'consists of pure albumen.'

He reached into the bag again, this time retrieving a small, blue rectangular bottle. Uncorking the bottle with his teeth he poured an ounce of clear fluid into the measuring glass, which after a deft little swirl he held above Andy's face.

'Notice how the white of the egg has already begun to coagulate,' he said, 'to harden and turn white in the presence of the alcohol. Just as if it were being cooked. It so happens, it may surprise you to learn, that albumen is a substance common in the nerve tissue of the human body. In other words, every time you get soused you are cooking your own insides.'

A series of weak, phlegmatic coughs scraped in quick succession through Andy's throat, bringing tears to his eyes.

'There, there,' Muldoon said, 'I won't be much longer. Then you can get back to sleep.'

He set the measuring glass on the bedside table and interlaced his fingers around one knee.

'When I was a student,' he revealed fondly, 'I had the good fortune of conducting a postmortem examination on the cadaver of an alcoholic. A man of about forty, I'd say. Upon slicing into the subject's blackened, spongy liver, an organ which in a healthy man is bluish-red in color and smooth as silk, I was assailed by the unmistakable stench of whiskey. This being several weeks after his demise, mind you. Every organ I opened was the same, so saturated with whiskey that the vulgar among us joked we could wring them out and bottle the stuff. Ha ha... Oh my! Heart, kidneys, digestive organs, the brain itself, all pickled in alcohol.'

Muldoon sighed in fond remembrance.

'Nectar of the gods, eh? I've never been able to understand it myself, the amount of whiskey these poor sots drink out here, gallons of the stuff, barrels of it. When I was a young man, and this is back East I should add, we were more diverse in our choice of beverage. A glass of beer perhaps, some wine with a meal, a little spirit on special occasions. The sheer volume of imbibing that takes place in these Territorial towns staggers the imagination. I knew a Cornish fellow once whose habit was to drink from an old Spanish helmet he'd found in a cave. Needless to say he is no longer with us. I would be without a profession if these temperance folks ever convinced the miners to give up drink. Every last dollar guzzled. For what? These men could be building something for themselves, saving their money for some enterprise of their own. Instead they drink it all away then complain about their lot in life. Fools, every last one of them.

'Now a boy your age...'

He paused.

'A boy your age. That is another matter entirely. That is a tragedy. For seldom does a man who discovers the bottle in his youth ever escape its tyranny.'

Unclasping his fingers Muldoon now leaned over Andy, bracing his hands on either side of the mattress, and said: 'Perhaps my point is better made by analogy. Imagine if you will a man reared in entire ignorance of women. In such a case, though he knew not what he desired, our unfortunate man would yet crave their flesh, and his passive desires would instantly be stimulated into activity by their presence. So it is with man and alcohol. It provokes the desire, but it takes away the performance. The craving for intoxication is instinctual, much like a man's desire for woman. When, however, an instinct is not opposed by counteracting traits, when man is as a ship in a maelstrom, every circling eddy of which draws him nearer to destruction, then the diseased condition of the physical man becomes engrafted on his spiritual nature and there follows a general impairment of all his moral faculties. A sort of moral prostration if you will, characterized by paralysis of the will power. Convictions of duty, right action, grow feebler. Reason, what is left of it, dashes to extremes, either filled with alarm and restless agitation, or stupid indifference and depression, until all elements of his higher nature fall progressively and he ceases to be a man at all.'

Muldoon sat up, shoving the mattress for emphasis. Sighing deeply, he picked up the stethoscope and put it back in his bag.

'No, my boy, pneumonia is nothing compared to this, the father of all diseases. As your friend and your physician I ask you to abstain from any further drinking. If that means taking up other forms of personal recreation I strongly suggest you do it. As my own father used to say to me, "Hear these words of instruction, my son, while you are sober, for it is not possible to be taught when you're tight."'

With that Muldoon patted Andy on the leg and, his bag in one hand, the measuring glass in the other, wished Andy a restful sleep and departed.

From his bed Andy watched the sky brighten in the window, and he watched it fade to darkness. Day bled into night, night into day. At times the ache in his lungs and the endless stream of sputum it spawned seemed less an ailment than a sort of sensate being temporarily in residence inside him, devouring him, without malice. Only deep in the night could he admit the truth. He was being punished for his cowardice. Not by God or Fate or any other Dispenser of Poetic Justice but by this thing that had been within him since her first visit to the bank. This, not drunkenness, was Muldoon's fabled malady. Love. The father of all diseases. No stethoscope existed that could detect its sound. No thermometer to measure its heat. No homeopathic remedy to root it out of the blood.

Night bled into day, day into night. He held the

handkerchief to his cheek, her scent long since faded, and closed his eyes and remembered with an exquisite suffusion of pain the feeling of her skin against his. He slept much of the day and woke in the night and lay listening to coyotes and wind. One night a wildcat paced the roof, its claws clattering like hailstones across the tin. Back and forth it paced, harrying the night with yowls to raise the dead.

Crawford stayed home the first two days to nurse his nephew, bringing his meals to him on a painted tray, wiping his feverish forehead with a damp washcloth, making sure he drank at the appointed times the vile solution of aconite and bryonia alba, but even that brief closure of the bank disgruntled the merchants and confirmed some of the miners' suspicions that the Shakespeare Mining & Milling Company did not rest on solid financial ground, that Kelly was cracking up and Crawford losing faith, the end result being yet another exodus of miners. Andy, wanting only to be left alone, assured his uncle he would be fine by himself.

The stove burned hot all day in the front room. Now and then he got up and went and stood looking through the front window at Watt Mountain and the empty sky and the dead tree, as if looking long enough might soften their brittle edges. The light bright and cold. When by the third day she still had not come to see him he accepted she would not. He poured himself a glass of wine and drank it and poured himself another. *Cowards die many times before their deaths; the valiant never taste of death but once.*

Looking at the photograph of his mother on the mantle he wondered if in the future pictures could be made to move, the people in them to come and go as they did in life, to speak even. He stood at the stove in the kitchen eating hard crumbly cornbread from the cast-iron skillet thick with the grease of bygone meat. His teeth and scalp aching. He listened to the ticking of the clock. Fatigued from his exertions, he returned to his bed and lay there breathing shallow breaths, Romeo by his side.

'It's your fault. You know that, don't you?'

Romeo purred.

He wrote a long overdue letter to his mother, not mentioning his illness or anything else of personal relevance, telling her instead that the raiding party had returned to the reservation; that he was happy working at the bank with Uncle Albert, there was still so much to learn; that winter in the desert was colder than one might think; that as soon as it warmed up a team of surveyors would be arriving to chart a route for the railroad; that the saloonkeeper's wife was still the only woman in town. He felt sad writing to his mother. He missed her. Missed his old home. The trees. The river. His innocence. He wept.

Muldoon rode out every afternoon, striding in with his black bag and jovial mien to listen with his instrument to Andy's heart and lungs, to take Andy's temperature, to pronounce yet again an improving prognosis for his patient and a victory for homeopathy, always leaving a little wedge of chocolate on the bedside table on his way out. As soon as he heard Crawford pull up, Andy would pretend to be asleep. His uncle's ministrations exasperated him to no end; he seemed all too happy to have Andy bedridden, bringing home from Blaine's each afternoon a different tinned delicacy: succotash, marrowfat peas, plum pudding, corned beef, sardines stuffed with truffles. Always humming while he cooked. The more Crawford fussed over him the more Andy felt like strangling him. Never were Andy's cravings for Abigail so strong as they were the first few minutes after Crawford's return.

Day by day his breathing came easier. He felt his strength begin to return, and with it the will to live.

FOUR

'It's out of the question. It would undermine my authority with the miners.'

'Why do you say that?'

Kelly set the cobbing hammer back on the desk and brushed the stray chips of ore into a neat little pile with the edge of his hand.

'A mining engineer has a certain image to uphold. And gadding about on a stage isn't part of it.'

'Are you that selfish,' Abigail said, 'that you would put your vanity before the needs of your miners? Wouldn't a real leader do whatever it took to cheer them up?'

'Entertaining miners isn't in my contract,' Kelly said flatly.

Abigail said nothing, her petulant expression speaking well enough for itself. A prospector approaching the door, seeing Kelly engaged, veered from his course and tacked nonchalantly Oreward, whistling.

'Why me anyway?' Kelly said, picking up the little steel hammer. 'Can't you get one of the merchants? Muldoon has a commanding presence, a strong voice. Henderson. Blaine even. Any of them. Why are you so intent on me?'

'Because it's you the miners need to see making an

effort on their behalf. Not Muldoon. Not Blaine. You've been moping around like a lost lamb ever since you got that letter.'

Rolling the handle between thumb and forefinger Kelly twirled the head of the hammer.

'They'd be better off somewhere else anyway,' he half mumbled.

'Somewhere with more women?'

'I didn't say that.'

'You may as well have.'

He tapped the butt of the handle a few times against the desk and, measuring her with an inquisitive eye, said: 'Am I mistaken or does this have nothing to do with the miners?'

A slight rearrangement of herself in the chair as much as confirmed Kelly's conjecture.

'Did you not come to me and say,' she said, '*If there is anything, anything at all, I can do for you, please don't hesitate to ask?*'

Kelly set the hammer down, interlaced his fingers and smiled. The smile of one ensnared in the trap of a worthier opponent.

'Ten dollars?'

'Maybe more,' she said. 'If everyone likes it we'll do it again the following weekend, and that would be another ten dollars.'

The rising sun shone coldly through their frozen breaths, sparkling the frosted ground around the well. Grabbing the brittle rope Rodriguez hoisted the sloshing pouch up and onto the wall.

'Still,' she said, 'I don't know about some of these miners for actors. They don't seem to think about

216

anything but themselves. An actor needs to know how to put others before himself, don't you think?'

Rodriguez, nodding, poured the water into her bucket.

'Someone who understands the importance of appearances,' she said.

Her bucket full, Rodriguez set it on the ground for her. She stood there for a moment, a finger against her lips, then shrugging she thanked him as usual and picked up the bucket and headed back to the saloon. Rodriguez, briskly rubbing his icy hands, watched her go.

'I think about what you say,' he said to her the next morning at the well. 'And I say to myself, maybe I can do this. Maybe I can be in Mrs. Jonson's play.'

'Rodriguez!' Abigail exclaimed, clutching his hands. 'That's a wonderful idea. Why didn't I think of that?'

She glanced aside, thinking.

'Yes,' she said. 'You would make a fine actor. And I know exactly which part you would play.' Then, suddenly frowning, she said, 'Oh, but I already told Hobbs he could have the part.'

Wringing her hands she studied the ground as if it alone were the root of her quandary.

'There are no more parts?' Rodriguez asked.

'Well...' Abigail said, pondering, wondering. 'There is one more part, but I don't know if you'd be right for it.' She thought some more then said, 'I'll tell you what. Can you do something for me?'

That afternoon Abigail crossed Avon with a volume of Shakespeare in her hands and stepped into the lobby of the Stratford. Rodriguez's shoes were shinier, his bow tie crisper than usual. They sat down in opposing armchairs across a low table, Stovall every now and then eyeing them suspiciously from the counter.

'Why don't you read from here,' Abigail said, scooting the open volume across the table, her finger marking the line.

Rodriguez pulled the volume toward him. He peered intently at the page, his eyes roving back and forth over the words.

'Aloud,' Abigail said after a while.

Rodriguez picked up the volume and set it on his knees. He sat there for a long time, staring down, succumbing, it appeared, to a general paralysis. Finally he set the volume back on the table and said in a professional manner: 'I'm sorry, Mrs. Jonson, but I cannot do it.'

'But why?' Abigail said. 'You were so excited this morning.'

Rodriguez made no answer. Noticing Stovall's watchful gaze it occurred to Abigail that Rodriguez might be uncomfortable doing certain things in front of his employer. He would probably relax, she thought, in her parlor. She was about to express as much when Stovall said: 'I don't mean to pry, Mrs. Jonson, but he doesn't read.'

Abigail looked at Stovall then looked at Rodriguez, who was looking at the floor.

'Well, I don't read Spanish, do I?' Abigail said. 'Repeat after me,' she said, picking up the volume. '*O my poor Rosalind, whither wilt thou go?*'

Rodriguez, uncertain of this tack, hesitated, as if waiting for Stovall to make some remark, then repeated the line. In this way Abigail read to Rodriguez half a page of lines, Rodriguez repeating them from memory at her prompting.

'Now,' Abigail said, 'I'll read the part of Rosalind and when I nod my head you say your lines.'

In a deep, proud voice welling up through his storied blood, resounding father by father back in time, Rodriguez delivered his lines with gusto and verve, until, midway down the page, Abigail nodded and he said nothing.

She nodded again.

'*So shall we pass along, and never stir assailants,*' she said.

'Why does she call him a maid?' Rodriguez asked.

'But Rodriguez,' Abigail said, 'what ever gave you the idea you were playing a man?'

Rodriguez, otherwise still, blinked a few times.

'I don't play a man?'

'Celia is a woman,' Abigail said.

Rodriguez slumped back in his chair and turned his face aside, suddenly quiet and moody. Abigail returned Stovall's stare until he too looked aside. She closed the volume and set it beside her on the chair.

'I don't know why you're so upset,' she said. 'Hobbs and Andy didn't have any problems with it. I expected more from you.'

Rodriguez stood up and, tugging the lapels of his coat, said: 'I no play a woman.'

Andy, his suit visibly looser since his last appearance in the Ore, stepped in and calmly approached the bar.

Henry went around and set up a glass.

'Well, well, back from the grave.'

'Give me a whiskey,' Andy said.

One foot on the beam he gulped down the whiskey and set the glass back on the bar.

'Better make it another,' he said.

After his third he straightened his bent leg and stood

there half looking at the bottles on the shelf behind the bar, warmth glazing his eyes.

Someone meowed. Snorts and sniggers from the gallery. Constricted little gasps and wheezes.

'Might I have a word with you, Mr. Jonson?'

Henry leaned over and propped his hand on the bottle.

'Well, sure,' he said. 'What's on your mind?'

Andy drummed his fingers on the bar.

'Could we step outside a minute?'

The conversations of the miners, sham as they were, tapered away to silence. Henry's eyes combed Andy's face for some hint of the nature of this request. He took his hand from the bottle and straightened up.

'After you,' he gestured gentlemanly toward the door.

Andy turned and shuffled away limp as a marionette, the handle of the slingshot bossing his back pocket below the hem of his coat. Henry followed.

Scarcely had the door closed behind them than could be heard from within the sound of scooting chairs. Andy walked a little way down the face of the Ore then stopped and turned around.

'Look here, kid,' Henry said before Andy could speak. 'I don't know much about you but anyone can tell just by lookin you're a good kid, got a good head on your shoulders. Shoot, when I was your age all I wanted to do was kill someone. Now if you aim to tell me about you and Mrs. Jonson you needn't bother; she's already done told me herself. Hell, I said to her, "The boy aint done weanin yet, what'd I be mad for? He's the only friend you got."'

Andy, not quite sure what Mr. Jonson was talking about but sensing an improvement in his circumstance, began to amend the preamble of his speech.

'Course you're allowed to come visitin whenever you like. Boy like you needs the influence of a good woman. You don't have to sneak around afraid of me. Anyone starts talkin I'll set em straight.'

Henry put a hand on Andy's shoulder, worried his lower lip some as he glanced groundward, then looking Andy square in the eye said: 'Truth is, she feels bad about tellin you not to come around anymore. Said she was afraid of me gettin jealous or somethin. This very mornin she said to me, "If you see Andy today could you ask him if he might stop by this evenin?" I think she's a little lonesome, to tell you the truth. Caint hardly blame her for that.'

'She asked me to come over tonight?' Andy said, hope slowly brightening his face.

'That's what she said.'

Andy's Adam's apple bobbed once and settled.

'Did she say what for?'

Henry shrugged. 'Sure is crisp out here.'

Andy could not keep from smiling now.

'So,' Henry said, 'what is it you wanted to talk about?'

FIVE

It was still light out when the kid came strutting down Avon in his cheviot suit, his brown wool crusher planted squarely on his head. He strode past the Ore without looking in and disappeared from sight. Henry set a glass on the bar and poured a little whiskey into it.

'How can you all drink this stuff?' he offered, sipping, to whomsoever cared to listen.

A few minutes went by before he asked Blaine if he wouldn't mind watching the till for a spell.

It was going on evening but the air was growing warmer, as if the lowering sun were towing behind it the first days of spring, the western sky the color of peach flesh, shreds of cloud in the watery blue glowing pink around their tattered fringes.

The smell of the shed, of juniper and whiskey and dirt, took him back to all those summer afternoons, the rage and jealousy mellowed now to something like the dull ache of nostalgia. Fingertips around the edges of the brick he paused to consider with almost tranquil resignation the likely outcome of its extraction. Then, afraid he might already be missing something, he fixed his grip and eased the crumbling adobe brick from its niche.

They were standing close, neither seeming much at ease,

talking, her arms crossed in front of her in a guarded way. The kid kept plunging his hands into his coat pockets and taking them back out again. The only thing he had taken off was his hat. He tried to kiss her, but she turned away, the look on the kid's face expressing well Henry's own perplexity. She said something that made the kid step back, defiance stealing into his eyes, then she turned aside and shrugged, as if to say, *Suit yourself.*

At this the kid took off his jacket and began to unbutton his shirt, as if undressing for bed, so passionless was it, Abigail watching all the while.

Stark naked but for his socks the kid opened his hands as if to say, *Satisfied?*

Only when she began to unbutton her shirt did some dim memory of arousal stir Henry's blood. He shifted his weight to his other leg and pulled the blood-warmed pistol from his pocket.

Winter had plumpened her somewhat, her months in the saloon putting flesh on her bones, and Henry couldn't help but observe with a surge of pride when she handed her shirt and skirt to the kid that she was more solid than him. And remembering those wonderful few moments with her in the hotel in Bird, how young he had felt, his whole life ahead of him, Henry felt the first throb of rage.

Seeming uncertain of what he was expected to do with them, the kid handed her clothes back to Abigail. They began to argue, every exchange punctuated by the migrating shirt and skirt, the kid shaking his head in refusal, Abigail firmly insistent. Finally, her face red with exasperation, she yanked the contentious garments out of the kid's hands and flung them to the floor.

The fight gone out of him, the kid sank down, picked up the clothes and began to put them on.

223

'Judas Priest,' Henry mumbled.

Standing there in the skirt and shirt, arms hanging limp as a ragdoll's, the kid looked like Abigail's laundry hung out to dry.

Abigail stepped back and, two fingers pressed to her lips, looked at the kid and shook her head. She unfastened the hooks of her corset and handed it and her bust pads to him, making him undress and dress again in order to amend his wanting figure. Then, taking him by the hand, she led him to her dressing table and sat him down before her looking glass and proceeded to paint his face.

Henry straightened up. The slits between the boards had gone dark, the chill night air breathing softly through them now. He stood there in the dark, two holes of light illuminating the sides of the brickhole, wondering how it was he had come to this. He couldn't decide if it was him or the kid or both that she was trying to make a fool of. He rubbed the back of his neck, shifted the pistol to his other hand, then lowered his face back to the hole.

Her enhancements complete, Abigail helped the kid up and turned him around, as one might a portrait toward its patron.

A strange, vertiginous sensation feathered Henry's joints and nearly made him lose his balance at the sight of the kid's red, red lips, his blistered brows and rouged cheeks. He looked like some wigless whorechild brought down from the cathouse attic on busy nights.

Henry's left forefinger, as if possessed of a sentience wholly its own, slowly traced the cool keel of the trigger.

Now Abigail snatched the kid's trousers up from the ground and put them on. She armed into and buttoned up and tucked in his shirt. She set his brown wool crusher on her head at a jaunty angle. Then, like a general leading his troops into battle, she pointed at the mattress with her entire arm, her other hand planted squarely on her hip — a charade which struck Henry as downright grotesque. Nor did seeing her swaggering about in the kid's suit, the same suit the kid had insulted him in on more than one occasion, sit particularly well with him.

Alas the kid went down onto the mattress, the poor rendition of fear in his eyes moving Henry almost to pity. Playing coy, the kid looked up at Abigail and shook his head, *No, No*, and clutched his knees. Abigail, not to be dissuaded, unbuttoned her pants and stepped out of them, the meat of her backside flashing briefly as the laced ruffle of her underskirt slid down from its high gather, down around her smooth bare legs. For some reason not at all clear to him this peeling away the rind of a man to reveal beneath it the fruit of a woman gave Henry a jolt, his debility in an instant overcome by a surge of almost nauseating lust.

Taking hold of the kid's ankles Abigail spread his legs, hiking his skirt up over his knees, exposing to Henry's view the kid's own hardening wares, and this too, trappings of a man under semblance of a woman, increased tenfold the force of Henry's now pummeling heartbeat.

Before going down onto the kid she stole a glance toward the still life, only a glance, but with such generosity in it, as if to say, *This is all for you, my love*, that Henry felt himself welling up. Then, tossing aside the hat, she raised her underskirt, her naked haunches in the lamplight the most beautiful thing Henry had ever seen, and like some predator lowering to its kill she went down onto the kid.

'Sweet Mother of Jesus,' Henry gasped and reaching into his trousers yanked out into the chilly air his aching old pecker and clutched it with a great in-suck of breath that shed thirty years off his life.

With a piggish little snort he dug his heels into the dirt and shoved his face deeper into the brickhole.

The next day Henry had a word with Abigail.

'That thing, that that, what you did last night with the kid, all that dressin and undressin, wearin his clothes, I don't like it.'

Henry took a little walk around the room and picked up a bottle.

'I want you to cut that out, you hear me.'

'You sure seemed to like it last night,' Abigail said with a wry little smile.

Henry set the bottle down.

'What I did or didn't like last night's got nothin to do with it. I'm tellin you today I don't like it, and I don't want you doin it again. You wear your own clothes and he wears his.'

Abigail pulled the needle through the fabric and pulled the thread tight.

'I thought you'd like it, that's all.'

'Well, that's mighty thoughtful of you, Abigail, thinkin of me and all, but I'd kindly prefer you didn't do so much thinkin and get it done with nice and normal, and get him out of there. I caint stand out there all night in the freezin cold waitin for you and him to finish playin your little games.'

'All right, Henry.'

Henry nodded. He shook his head. He seemed on the verge of saying something more. He shook his head again and went back to the saloon.

Abigail carried on with the dress, smiling inwardly, the

soft afternoon light almost as warm as her pleasant frame of mind.

Three days later, after failing twice to rise to the occasion, Henry said to Abigail: 'You best go on and put him back in the dress.'

And when that failed to produce the desired result: 'I'll leave some things of my own out for you.'

V

ONE

Young Brian Frost, second adjutant surveyor for the T.S. Bain R.R., acknowledged with a cordial smile the obsequious good morning of the porter at parade rest at the foot of the staircase and stepped outside to roll his first cigarette of the day.

Deserted as he set about sprinkling a ragged file of Old Tip Top onto the paper, Avon Avenue was transformed into a bustling boomtown thoroughfare by the time he swiped the edge across the tip of his tongue. Groups of shabbily garbed men were gathering all along the storefronts to trade on the day's prospects, men on horse and muleback dismounting here and there to add their own lusty voices to the rising clamor. Sullen burros stood by stiff-legged and balloon-bellied while onto their backs men strapped small mountains of gear. Buggies bearing men in top hats stirred up powdery swirls of dust.

Frost, yawning, watched his lazy stream of smoke rise through the golden sunlight.

'Ah, Mr. Frost!'

Frost turned. 'Oh, hello, Mr. Crawford.'

'I trust you had a pleasant night's rest?' Crawford asked gaily, releasing Frost's sturdy hand.

'Apart from the midnight performance by the dogs, very pleasant, thank you.'

Crawford, tsk-tsking, sighed.

'We really must do something about them. Chinamen perhaps. Fond of dog, they say. Ah yes, before I forget — I meant to ask you last night — what sort of name is Frost anyhow? German?'

'Scandinavian,' Frost replied. 'Norwegian nobility, or so goes the family legend. I doubt it's true. By the way, I read your little treatise on the True Fissure District.'

'Did you?'

'There was a copy in the top drawer of the bureau.'

'Fancy that.'

'It was your idea then,' Frost said, 'I mean to name the town Shakespeare, the main street Avon and so forth?'

Crawford crossed his arms and rocked momentarily forward on the balls of his feet.

'Actually, I named the mines first. Tragedies as it turned out. Unintentional of course.'

'Then you just...'

'Yes, precisely. The mines gave birth to the town, as the plays to the Bard. I think it has a nice ring, don't you? *All aboard for Shakespeare!* Trippingly on the tongue.'

Frost, nearing the end of his cigarette, dropped it to the ground and tapped it once with the toe of his boot.

A man on a piebald horse, who earlier had passed heading north, passed again riding south.

'Come,' Crawford said, 'let's give you the tour.'

Side by side up busy Avon they strolled, the sun warm against the right sides of their faces, every man they passed greeting them with an exuberant good morning. Crawford pointed out the bank, the assay office, Progress & Improvement, extolling at length their respective virtues.

232

'Am I mistaken,' Frost asked in an interlude between volleys of booms emanating from the west, 'that Shakespeare has no marshal? No law enforcement of any kind?'

Crawford smiled sagely.

'You're an observant man, Mr. Frost. Apart from our local vigilance committee, whose principal purpose is to guard us from external threats, you're quite right, we have no law enforcement per se. The fact of the matter, extraordinary as it sounds, is not a single serious crime has been committed within the town limits since its inception, a fact which no other community in the Territory can honestly boast of.'

Six cowboys riding abreast, spurs jingling, made their regal way down Avon to halt before the saloon, where, one by one, they swung down from their saddles with the easy grace native to souls of the open country and, removing their hats, humbly ducked inside.

'If I were to hazard a guess,' Crawford replied to Frost's next question, 'I'd say that in the prelude to Mrs. Jonson's arrival, when we were in every sense of the word alone in the wilderness, a spirit of mutual accord was born amongst us, all of us struggling as it were against a common foe. Many of us feared in those early days that the curtain would fall on this uncommon reign of peace the moment women entered the scene, the passions of man never so enflamed as when vying for the attention of a woman. And yet, having advanced to the status of a one-woman town, with the prospect of many more to come, we have yet to witness even the slightest increase in the level of crime. Quite the contrary. I believe I can speak for all of us when I say that the salutary effect of Mrs. Jonson's presence has been established beyond cavil.'

They walked.

233

'How long has it been? Over a year, hasn't it?'

'I don't think it's been that long,' Crawford replied. 'It was a cold winter for sure, but otherwise...'

Entering the shade of an ore wagon, three of which, with partial teams, had just pulled up on the west side of the street, Crawford begged Frost's pardon and stepped aside to consult with one of the drivers.

Again the man on the piebald rode by. Peculiar town, Frost thought. The absence of women, which he had been well availed of by his superiors, as well as by every individual he encountered in the Territory who learned that Shakespeare was on his itinerary, he hadn't given much thought to; he would only be there a day before his assistants arrived. But the more he saw of Shakespeare the more he discerned in its benighted men a kind of malady of the spirit, its mark unmistakable to unafflicted eyes. A kind of disingenuous alacrity barely masking their withered pride.

'Never fails,' Crawford said, rejoining Frost. 'They overestimate the capacity of the wagons and we're forced to leave several tons of high-grade ore piled on the hillside. Shall we?'

'But just for the sake of argument,' Frost asked as they resumed the tour, 'what if say this very night there was a murder, right here on Avon Avenue? Who would bring the culprit to justice?'

Crawford, hands behind his back, eyes cast downward, nodded thoughtfully.

'Oh, I've no doubt the man would be apprehended by one or more of our hardy citizens and justice swiftly served.'

'That is my question,' Frost said. 'How would justice be served? You have no jail, no courts.'

'Shakespeare itself may not,' Crawford explained, 'but we are served by all the legal institutions of Watt County. We would simply detain the criminal by force until he could be removed to Bird.'

'But in the case of murder,' Frost persisted, 'wouldn't it send a clearer message to capitalists and other interested parties if justice, as you say, were swiftly served?'

Crawford smiled.

'I'm sure, Mr. Frost, that you will have no trouble finding men in the Territory who hold that belief, but personally I don't advocate lynchings without due process, whatever the incentive. In any case, I don't think we have anything to fear on that score. We Shakespeareans crave truth and fairness above all else. Come.'

Near the boarding house they came upon two dusty dogs that, judging by the idle attachment of their hindquarters, were savoring the afterglow of a morning tryst. Crawford shook a disgusted leg at them, and the two-backed beast scurried crabwise away.

'Parting is such sweet sorrow,' Frost remarked dryly.

Crossing to the other side of the street, they strolled past the barbershop (half a dozen smiles and waves) and carried on up the shady side of Avon.

It was standing room only in the drug store, every man clamoring for the attention of Muldoon, who, indifferent to the rush, was calmly filling orders and penciling totals on his notepad.

'You sure this'll help me drill better?' a miner holding a box of Dr. Barker's Blood Builder was asking.

'That it will,' Muldoon replied.

'And this will help me see better down in the mine?' asked another, a bottle of Dr. Walter's Celebrated Eye Water in hand.

235

'Word of honor,' Muldoon guaranteed.

'Whooee!' a chorus of miners exclaimed. 'We caint wait to get back down into that mine!'

'I can see you're busy,' Crawford said, raising his voice above the rabble. 'I just wanted you to meet Mr. Frost, surveyor-general for T.S. Bain.'

'Adjutant surveyor,' Frost corrected.

'And modest too,' Crawford, chuckling, patted Frost on the shoulder. 'Mr. Muldoon, Mr. Frost. Mr. Frost, Mr. Muldoon, Shakespeare's Hippocrates.'

'A slight exaggeration,' Muldoon said, shaking Frost's hand and gifting him a small bottle of Silver Cachous. 'Sweetens the breath.'

Their next stop was Blaine's, busier yet than Muldoon's, stacks of tools and canned goods at the feet of every anxious customer. Blaine, sleep in his eyes, was busy behind the counter.

'Perhaps we'd better come back after lunch,' Crawford whispered in Frost's ear, leading him by the arm back outside.

The man on the piebald rode by at a canter, touching the brim of his railroad hat in passing.

'Do you know that man?' Frost asked.

'I can't say as I do,' Crawford said. 'We get so many drifters coming and going. Here one day, gone the next.'

'He's been riding up and down the street all morning.'

'Has he? Must be exercising his horse.'

'I could use a drink,' Frost said.

Passing the alleyway between Blaine's and the saloon, Frost stopped abruptly and, peering east, said: 'What in the world are those people doing?'

'Ah yes,' Crawford said. 'I forgot today was their rehearsal. Let's have a peek, shall we?'

They walked down and stood at the end of the alleyway, hands visored against the sun. A hundred yards or so in the distance, tiny as midges against the vastness of their backdrop, five little figures, one of them in a dress, could be seen cavorting on a stage.

'Is that Mrs. Jonson?' Frost asked.

'Yes, and her troupe. My nephew is one of them. They're a dedicated lot, I'll give them that much, out there whenever she can round them all up. A real taskmaster, I hear. I suppose you have to be with the Bard.'

'Shakespeare?'

'Uh-mm.'

'Which play?'

'I forget,' Crawford said. 'One of those tedious comedies. Begins with an A.'

Frost, intrigued, watched the players.

'Mr. Jonson built the stage for her from the scrap of my boarding house,' Crawford said.

'Surely they don't intend to perform it out there,' Frost said.

'Oh, no. In the saloon, I believe,' Crawford said. 'Until the opera house is built, of course.'

They watched, a warm, dusty breeze gentle at their backs.

'I can never remember which lines are from which plays,' Frost said. 'I suppose it doesn't matter with Shakespeare. It's all sort of one big play, isn't it?'

'Funny you should say that,' Crawford said. 'For the longest time I've had a notion of constructing entirely from existing lines in Shakespeare's plays a new play altogether. A play within the plays you might call it.'

'The point being?' Frost asked.

'The point? Well... I suppose the point would be the joy

of resurrecting Shakespeare, wouldn't it. Of stealing from the master thief. Of hearing him in his own language — a line from Antony's great funeral speech in *Julius Caesar*, say, set down beside some inconsequential line from one of the histories — hear him say something he never actually said, in his own words. To be guided, through a glass darkly as it were, by the hand of Shakespeare himself to an apotheosis impossible to foresee. An entirely new, as yet undiscovered, Shakespeare play.'

Two of the figures on the stage appeared to be wrestling.

'When is the performance?' Frost asked.

'I don't think they know themselves.'

Frost and Crawford, hands visored against the sun, silently watched the five little figures gambol across the stage, hearing all the more in this desert dumb show the heavenly music of Shakespeare.

'How about that drink?' Crawford said.

Dusk. The clock atop the gem case softly ticking. Bulge of a tallow moon breaching the roof of the saloon. Sweet-scented heliotrope perfuming the warm twilight air.

On the desk between them, aground on rocks and tools and papers, a boxwood chessboard lay, opposing men carved of English bone, Staunton pattern. Battle *en train*.

The chair creaked as Hobbs nudged his rook forward a square, ignoring the threat to his queen.

'I see it,' he said to Kelly's gesture.

Kelly paused to reconsider then took the white queen with his rook.

'You'd think the way they was carryin on in them top hats they'd never worked a day in their life,' Hobbs said. '*Kindly hand me that there implement, Harris. Certainly, Talbot, old chap. Tally-ho! Tally-ho!*'

238

Kelly, studying the board, nodded vaguely.

'Tween them and them singin cowboys,' Hobbs said. 'I'd a been singin too. Three dollars apiece. Hell, free shaves is all he paid them boys at the barbershop.'

'And a day's wages for doing nothing,' Kelly reminded him.

The chair creaked.

'Set him back a good couple hunnerd I'd figure, that little show. Sure was a nice feelin, though, wadn't it. All kinda people in the street, hustle and bustle, like a real town. Almost made you wonder.'

Kelly, glancing out the window, noticed Andy walk by in his suit and crusher and pause to admire the pale yellow blossoms of a honey mesquite nearby before rounding the north corner of the saloon.

Kelly watched him. The moon, parting with the saloon, slid up into the deepening blue.

'Course he'll have to do it all over again when the poor fella comes back through,' Hobbs said. 'Bet he didn't think of that. Check.'

'Hmm?' Kelly said.

Hobbs pointed.

'Oh.'

Weighing his options Kelly moved his king.

'Maybe I'll be a investor next time round,' Hobbs mused. 'Yessir. Top hat and tails, that's my bag. I'll hike my nose to the moon, strut about frog-assed with a cane, spout a little Shakespeare.'

Hobbs moved his knight. Faint laughter from without.

'Poor old Jaques,' Hobbs said. 'Stuck with the likes of me. You know I been doin some thinkin on him, and I'm thinkin it aint so much he's gloomy as he's the only one sees how things really is, all the rest of em's fools. The man aint got no one to commiserate with, not a one, so he thinks when Orlando comes along maybe he's finally found someone, but Orlando's as much a fool as the rest of em. Lovedrunk. That's what I figure. And my other man, Touchstone, he's kinda like the other side a Jaques. Happy but dumber. Yessir, I've come round to thinkin old Mrs. Jonson knew what she was up to givin me the both of em, seein as how they're two sides a the same coin. She's a sharp one, that woman.'

Kelly gazed long at the old adobe absorbing nightfall, its door open, dark within.

'I'd like to have another look at that map of yours,' he said after a while.

Hobbs moved his knight.

'What fer?'

'No reason in particular.'

'Good, cuz I aint got it. Check.'

Kelly pushed the pawn.

'Where is it?'

'Aint so much anywhere as it is nowhere.'

'What does that mean?'

'Means the boys pinched it off me and burnt it up.'

Kelly sat up startled. He looked out the window, looked back at Hobbs with dismay.

'Burnt it?'

'Uh-hm.'

'Why didn't you tell me?'

Hobbs shrugged.

'Didn't see no reason to. Glad to be quit of it to tell you the truth.'

Kelly sank back in his chair. He was a long time in making his next move, an inexplicable ache of loss squeezing his heart. It was getting dark, harder to tell his king from his queen. Out in the cooling air the dogs began to bark, high sharp yipfire answered in kind from one end of town to the other.

'Who was it?' Kelly said.

Hobbs shrugged and moved.

'Check. There wadn't nothin there, anyhow, was there?'

Kelly didn't answer.

'Hard to imagine her and Henry, you know,' Hobbs said.

'Please,' Kelly said. 'I'd rather not.'

'What I figgered,' Hobbs said.

'Figured what?'

'The way you look at her and all.'

'It's called acting.'

'Oh, I'd say there's more than Orlando in there. Specially when Orlando aint nowheres around. You two was sure out there for a spell.'

'There isn't a man in this town who hasn't had a thought or two about Mrs. Jonson,' Kelly said. 'That doesn't mean I'm in love with her.'

Hobbs grinned.

'Well, you were implying it,' Kelly said.

'Was I? Huh. Funny, didn't know I was. Checkmate.'

Two

All day it blew, fierce scolding winds out of the west, raining oceans of stinging sand over the parched world, a dull bronze sun smoldering somewhere deep within. Shrubs reeled in the gales like herds of bewildered brutes, the wind raking from their meshes the excreta collected there. Molted feathers. Wasps' tails. The coiled skins of snakes. Yuccas bowed and gyred east, their meaty white petals scattering like confetti. But for the dogs shuffling blindly around Avon, their shaggy coats lashed to hackles, Shakespeare to a wandering soul seeking refuge would have seemed a ghost town long forgotten, two rows of abandoned dreams lost in a sepia haze.

Night fell, and still it blew. As if building strength for some final crushing blast, the wind eased only to blow harder yet, sweeping Avon clear of all but the weightiest rubble, hurling into oblivion empty bottles and broken tubs, toothless combs, fingerless gloves, empty tins of everything, soleless boots and bootless soles, warped saws, splintered spokes. Only in the hours before dawn did the wind relent, the eerie stillness startling awake those who slept by night. Then, with deceptively tranquil whistling, it began again.

The leaves of the calendar fluttered as Mrs. Jonson, her hair blown to a frazzle, hurried in and fought the

242

door shut behind her. A scuffed reef of sand fanned out across the floor. But for the wind all was quiet in the store, tobacco-tinted light seeping through the windows, staining brown the sparse inventory ranged without pretense over shelves and floor and ceiling. Harness and tinware pendulous in their low rigging. Off in a corner a miner standing on one leg held the clean sole of a new boot against his own weathered sole.

'Afternoon, Mrs. Jonson,' Blaine said, lowering his paper. The miner turned from his deliberations and greeted her likewise.

She took a moment to compose herself, obliging them with a small smile, then walked over to the shelves where Blaine kept a small stock of women's things on her behalf. Spools of thread. Needles. Dress materials. Hairpins. Hosiery.

'I've stopped tryin to dig it outa my ears till it blows over,' Blaine was saying to the miner. 'One grain gets to the brain it can kill ya, they say.'

'Frank Martin seen a bugle flyin through the air,' the miner said.

'That's Frank Martin for ya,' Blaine said.

'Are these all you have?' Abigail asked, holding up a few papers of sewing needles.

Blaine raised his chin the better to see in that murky light what she was holding.

'Yes'm, them's it,' he said. 'Tell me what all ya need and I'll put in a order.'

The miner, requirements met, carried the boots up to the counter.

'That be all for ya, sir?' Blaine asked.

'Less'n you got one a them in stock,' the miner said with a wry twist of his head.

Blaine grinned.

'That make's a little hard to come by these days. Should be some in next season.'

'Hope to God they're still makin em,' the miner said, and paid.

A squall of sand strafed the counter as the miner, wishing Blaine and Mrs. Jonson a good afternoon, turtled out into the wind.

Swiping it once across the counter, Blaine spread his month-old *Eagle* with a crisp thrust and feigned absorption as he watched her. She strolled around the store, pausing every so often to consider some item, the planks creaking under her measured step. In her hands a clutch of hickory buggy spokes and two balls of twine.

Blaine sighed slowly through his nose and turned the page. The wind moaning, soughing.

She browsed, picking up an item here, an item there until, her arms full, she carried what she had to the counter, each trip adding something else to the growing stack. Iron washers. Hinges. Pulleys. A length of three-inch rubber belting. A paintbrush. Bed sheets. Burlap sacking. A dozen spools of thread. Handkerchiefs. Screw eyes. A watch chain. Three pairs of long johns.

'I don't suppose you'd have any ladies' shoes, would you?' Abigail asked.

Blaine lowered the paper, winking.

'Now them I'm plumb out of.'

She handled some silver-plated whiffletree tips and put them back.

'You know, Mrs. Jonson,' Blaine said, 'I think it's mighty big of you, what you're doin and all. Awful lot of work, I expect, puttin on a show.'

Abigail browsed.

'You weren't ever in the theatre yourself, were you?' Blaine asked.

'No,' Abigail answered.

'Been ages since I been to one myself.'

He watched her. Sharp curve of hipbone. Smooth, slender neck. Visions of her in various states of undress flickering across his mind's eye.

'Mighty big of the others too,' he said. 'Takes some courage, don't it. The costume and all's one thing, but the rest of it too. The voice and all. Manners. I sure as heck couldn't do it. No, sir. Not by a long stretch.'

Abigail, inspecting seam and selvedge of a flannel shirt, nodded.

'Must make a man see the world a little different,' Blaine said. 'Give him a little more understandin.'

'That will do for now,' Abigail said, setting a coil of galvanized wire on the stack.

Blaine stood up and set about loading the rest of her goods into one of the burlap sacks.

'If there's anything I aint got,' he said, stealing glances at her hands, her bust, her lips, 'you let me know. I'll get Buddy to fetch it from Bird.'

Abigail, facing the windows, her forearm on the counter, thanked him.

'How much do I owe you?' she asked.

'Ah hell, consider it a donation to the arts.'

'Well,' Abigail said, facing him with a lukewarm smile, 'that's between you and Henry. He doesn't look favorably on charity.'

'I'll have a word with him,' Blaine said. 'Here, let me help you back.'

'Thank you,' Abigail said, 'but I can manage.'

'It's no trouble at all,' Blaine said, coming around

245

the counter and hoisting the misshapen sack onto his shoulder. He opened the door and they leaned out into the wind, disappearing from sight.

A few minutes later Blaine returned, hair in shocks, sand in every crease of his being. He locked the door and made his way to the back of the store, into the storeroom, past sacks of flour, canteens, rolled tents. Unlocking the small storage room where he kept some personal effects he stepped in and lit the candle on the stand beside the door.

'Well, fancy that, Mrs. Jonson,' he said, addressing a contraption bearing little affinity in form or feature to its namesake: an old pigskin saddle with a hole through the middle of it laid sidewise across two seat springs straddling a pail of lard.

'I don't mind if I do.

'Why, thank you, Mr. Blaine. Oh... Mr. Blaine...'

Six days on and still the wind, endless wail of a world bereft, never to be consoled. The whole air filled with a tempest of driving sand.

Through the shafts and valves of the Lear, keyed to her hollowed chambers, the wind tolled, a half-step lower in tone than it had been the previous spring.

'So tell us about it, master Hobbs. It true she got y'all playin women?'

Hobbs, eyeing the group with suspicion, turned his head and spat a thin dark cord of tobacco juice to the ground.

'Some of us.'

'Give us a little,' they said.

'Come on, Hobbs, show us some of your actin.'

'Give us a sneak.'

'Free advertisin.'

So Hobbs under the pressure of his peers set down his toolbox and affecting a somewhat pompous pose, feet turned to a T, body in profile, hand outthrust as if clutching the substance of his transports, proclaimed: '*All the world's a stage...*'

And the words as he spoke them called forth memories long since forgotten, of baby brother in Mama's arms devouring all her love; the schoolhouse in the woods where the crooked old crone rapped his knuckles and mice scrabbled over the floor in the cold dead of winter; men in gray marching off to battle, him among them, cannon fire and carnage, piles of severed limbs, his brother somewhere on the other side; Louise pressed against his back, her dog trailing below. Above the moaning wind his voice rose, ringing through the chambers of the mine, and he saw in the glimmering eyes of his fellow man that they were moved, sad lot of womenless men, hanging upon his every word, and he felt in these dressed-up words the strange wonderful nothingness that is life, some lived, some yet to be, his own and theirs alike, until it seemed that all he was was words and words alone.

'*Last scene of all*,' he lowered his voice to a whisper, '*that ends this strange eventful history, is second childishness and mere oblivion, sans teeth, sans eyes, sans taste, sans everything.*'

Silence, then an eruption of cheers and yeehaws, effete bravos, mannered clappings, boisterous cries of encore.

Hobbs, folding an arm across his waist, bowed and picked up his toolbox.

He came in from the parlor, country wench in bodice and skirt of burlap sacking, sleeves turned up the better

247

for clawing crops from the soil, white apron around his waist, linen bonnet fringing the curls of his auburn wig.

She studied him with vague discontent.

'Let me see you walk a little,' she said.

She was in hose and doublet herself, a narrow ruff around her neck, her hair tucked into a dome-shaped cap.

He walked across the room, past the drying flats and backdrops (palace grounds, garden bower, woods), turned around and walked back.

'What, pray tell, was that?' she wanted to know.

'You told me to walk.'

She stared at him, blinking, hands on her waist.

He walked again, heel to toe, hips swaying.

'Don't swing your arms so much,' she said. 'You look like a monkey.'

He came back and took his place, and they began the scene. But there was little life between them, their delivery hesitant and stilted, the gilded words dropping from their mouths like so many leaden balls.

They rehearsed it again.

'Enough,' she said, turning away from him. 'This is futile.'

'Is something the matter?' Andy asked.

'You'd think sitting bored all day in a bank you'd have time enough to memorize your lines.'

'How am I supposed to remember anything with you shouting at me?'

Abigail paced the room, rubbing her chin. She stopped before the still life and stood there brooding. It was getting dark outside.

'Maybe you were right,' she said after a while. 'Maybe you would have made a better Orlando.'

'I'll try harder,' Andy promised.

She took a deep breath and sighed.

'It's not you I'm worried about.'

Andy came over and hesitantly placed his arm around her shoulders.

'Kelly?'

'The man has no passion. It's like he's talking about his sister, or his aunt, not the love of his life.'

'They're going to love it,' he assured her, sounding relieved to know the fault wasn't his. 'You'll see.'

'He's as cold as iron.'

'He's not so bad,' Andy said. 'A little proud maybe, but so is Orlando. You'll see.'

She moped.

'They're going to love it,' he said again, tugging tenderly at her shoulder.

He gave her neck a peck.

'That's funny,' he said. 'There's two little holes in that picture.'

Abigail spun around and gave Andy a passionate kiss, slowly moving him back toward the middle of the room. She untied the strings of his bodice and reached under his chemise and caressed one of his nipples and kissed him.

'Hello,' Andy said, smiling.

'You're a dirty wench,' Abigail whispered. 'Aren't you, Audrey?'

Andy shook his head and with fumbling fingers opened her doublet and unbuttoned her shirt.

'I know what you country wenches are like,' Abigail said roguishly. 'Every dirty man in the village plowing your fields.'

Andy, palming her breast, mimed denial.

'Touchstone told me all about you,' Abigail said. 'What

you did with him and William. Don't play the virgin with me, you filthy country wench.'

'Oh God, Abigail,' Andy said, lowering his lips to her nipple.

Abigail pushed him away.

'*Abigail? Who is this Abigail? Down on your knees and thank heaven, fasting, for a good man's love; for I must tell you friendly in your ear, sell when you can: you are not for all markets.*'

Andy, suitably crushed, knelt down onto the mattress.

'*Would you not have me honest?*'

Abigail flashed him a wicked smile.

'*To cast away honesty upon a foul slut were to put good meat into an unclean dish.*'

'Oh, Ganymede!' Andy quivered.

Off came the skirt, the hose, and down they went in a tangle of frantic limbs.

Afterwards, staring up at the ceiling, sighing, a gleam of rapture in his eyes, Andy quietly said: 'I love you so much.'

'*I pray you,*' Abigail said, '*do not fall in love with me, for I am falser than vows made in wine.*'

'I'm serious,' Andy said, pulling her hand to his lips and kissing it. 'I've never...'

He swallowed.

Abigail looked at him and felt Henry's impatience emanating from behind the still life.

'You should probably be going,' she said.

'Why do I always have to rush off? You said yourself you told him we weren't to be interrupted.'

'Andy, please,' she said. 'I'm tired.'

'It's always something,' he said. 'Just one whole night with you all to myself. What I wouldn't give for that. To wake up with the sun in my face and you there beside me...'

'Andy.'

'You didn't let me finish. I was going to say, *But that's just a dream, isn't it?*'

'After the play, I promise. We'll talk about it. Now get up and get dressed. I've got things to do.'

'I thought the line was, *I'm tired*,' Andy said, and began to dress.

'How much longer she gonna keep us waitin? I'll be dead fore too long.'

'Seems that way, don't it?' Henry said.

'Which ones is playin women?' the balding one asked.

'Don't know myself,' Henry said.

The short one spat a stream of tobacco doubtfully onto the floor.

'And my name is Jesus H. Christ the third,' he said.

'It's the truth,' Henry said. 'She aint dumb. She knows what kinda hell you all'd give em.'

'All I aim to do is tip my hat when they pass and say, Mornin ma'am. Where's the harm in that?'

'We oughta do one ourself,' the balding one said.

'What, put on a show?'

'Sure. Variety act. I know a whole heap a card tricks. Butler here can show em where he got bit on the arm by a goat. Old Laird has a singin voice can fell two birds with one note. And you, why you can do that trick where you spit up like a fountain and slurp it back down without spillin a drop.'

The short one, considering this compelling vision, spat contemplatively.

'There's a whole lot more to puttin on a play than you'd think,' Henry said. 'Mrs. Jonson when she aint in here its nothin but work on the play. Back there makin costumes

251

all hours of the night. Paintin scenes. Makin trees. I go back there and she's standin there makin speeches to the walls like they's the citizens of Rome. That box that came Tuesday on the stage, you know what was in it?'

'What?'

'Wigs,' Henry said. 'Nice ones too. A couple redheads, a blonde, a brunette, some blacks. A dozen in all.'

'Shee-it. That musta set you back some.'

'Not a groat. They came from the Salon.'

'The Bird Salon? The whorehouse?'

'You mean they's whores' wigs in Shakespeare as we speak?'

'Not fifty feet from where you're sittin,' Henry said proudly.

The miners exchanged wanton glances.

'Wrote to the Madam sayin she needed some wigs for her play,' Henry said, 'would she care to make a donation. A week later there they are. Week before that a hatbox fulla buttons came in from back East. A friend of hers from that button factory she used to work at.'

'She don't do a thing halfway,' the short one said.

'And to think,' Henry said, 'it's only gonna cost you a dollar to see it.'

'Come on, Henry. Tell us when it is.'

'Who knows,' Henry said. 'Could be another month, could be tomorrow. She's the only one knows and I don't know as she knows herself.'

'And this is sposed to get some women out here, is it?'

'If Shakespeare caint do it I reckon no one can.'

'We've been Shakespeare all along.'

'There's Shakespeare and there's Shakespeare.'

'Well, I sure as hell hope they know the difference.'

They all took a drink and nodded solemnly.

THREE

Wearing a black clay worsted double-breasted Prince Albert suit lined with fine imported Italian cloth, satin piped throughout, fancy velvet arm shields under the sleeves, every pocket stayed; a laundered white linen dress shirt with full leated bosom and hand-barred button holes; collar and cuffs of extra fine Irish linen, double-stitched; a pure white China silk bow tie; black patent leather calf bals, opera toe; seamless all wool cashmere half-hose with spliced heel and toes; a tall black stiff fur Danbury, banded and bound in black silk ribbon; and holding in his right hand the sterling silver handle of an ebonized hickory cane, its steel-tipped ferrule gently thumping the dust, the Director stepped from the doorway of the Stratford Hotel and with an air of profound impatience proceeded to stand and wait.

Outside the saloon, in a chair beside the doorway, Henry sat holding a coffee tin against his right leg. The air was neither warm nor cool, the western sky grading from absinthe green to pale rose, every cloud mirroring the sky.

Another group of miners approached. Boots polished, beards groomed, shirts buttoned to collars.

'Step right in, step right in. Get a seat while you can.'

Into the tin went their dollars.

'Thank you, sir. Step right in.'

The shopkeepers locked up and made their way down to the Ore and put their dollars in the tin. In rode Taggart and his boys, the creases in their starched shirts still warm from the sad-iron. They hitched their horses to the rails and put their dollars in the tin. Prospectors down from the mountains, word passed along from those heading up, wandered in, burros in tow, and passing mutely into the saloon put their dollars in the tin. The reporter, a pudgy young man who yesterday evening had gloomily paced Avon as if his every apprehension had been thoroughly confirmed, crossed over from the hotel and put his dollar in the tin.

Henry, whistling, gave the tin a little swirl, stirring the pooled coins.

The color was fading fast from the sky when three riders raising plumes of dust appeared off to the south. Henry narrowed his eyes and watched them come, recognizing them in time by the spare mule carrying their instruments as the surveyor and his assistants.

Reaching the stables they left their mounts and ended their pilgrimage walking.

'I was afraid...' the surveyor, peering through the doorway, panted, 'we'd missed the beginning.'

His lips were dry and cracked, his clothes thick with dust.

The assistants, two sullen youths who might as well have spat in Frost's eye for the looks they were giving him, poked their heads into the saloon and withdrew them none the happier.

'Rode a long way, did ya?' Henry said.

'Twenty-three and a quarter miles,' one of the assistants said bitterly.

Henry nodded.

'Few more minutes, I expect,' he said, kicking dust at a tarantula creeping near.

Frost withdrew a handkerchief from his back pocket and, turning to survey the quiet town, wiped his face.

'Who is that?' he asked, lowering his voice.

Henry glanced up.

'The Director.'

'I was under the impression Mrs. Jonson was the director.'

'There's directors and there's Directors,' Henry said.

Frost's eyes discreetly passed over again the dark, dour figure.

'Why is he just standing there?'

'Waitin, looks like.'

Frost wiped the back of his neck and stuffed the handkerchief into his pocket. He slapped the dirt from his coat and trousers. He was about to reach for his billfold when Crawford pulled up in his buggy with two chairs stacked on the seat beside him.

'Grand of you to make it, Mr. Frost,' he hailed gaily from his seat.

Frost put his hands in his trouser pockets. 'How's the undiscovered play coming along?'

'If only I had the time,' Crawford said, and said it again. 'Here, grab the chairs. I'll meet you inside.'

Frost dropped three dollars into the tin, and the assistants, grumbling, fetched the chairs and followed him in.

Henry gave the tin a swirl.

In the rooms behind the saloon the restless rumble of the audience disquieted the nervous actors.

'Where the hell is Kelly?' Abigail asked, cinching

255

Rodriguez's lacy bodice with a sharp tug that made him wince.

No one answered.

Off in a corner Andy in an old man's shabby tunic, his hair powdered white, mumbled and paced. Hobbs, in doublet and hose, a bejeweled dagger tucked behind his wide black belt, a neat ruff at his neck, stood aloof making strange birdlike movements.

Abigail straightened Rodriguez's wig, then, leaving him to his own devices, walked over to the window. It was starting to get dark, the mountains on the horizon fading into the sky. The remnants of a smoke signal were hovering above the summit of Prince's Peak.

Excusing himself, Rodriguez stepped outside and, hitching up his skirt, hurried through the brush out to the jakes.

Abigail took a deep breath and exhaled slowly.

Out of the corner of her eye she noticed something moving across the ground near the shed. She looked down to see what looked like a giant black scorpion, fierce pincers raised, a cluster of colorless grubs squirming over its thick, curled tail.

'What a horrible-looking creature,' she said.

Hobbs came over to the window.

'Shoot, that's just a little old vinegarone,' he said. 'She aint poisonous. Just stinky.'

Andy put his forehead to the window.

'I'll kill it for you,' he said, starting for the door.

'No,' Abigail said, staying him. 'Let it be.'

The air was beginning to cool, the braver crickets to chirp. Gnatcatchers flitted dipping and banking through the air. The dogs began their nightly barkfest.

Back from parking the buggy, Crawford extricated a folded piece of paper from his watch pocket and, slowly circling the same spot of ground beside the doorway, muttered under his breath the words written on it in his tidy hand.

It had been fifteen minutes since anyone else had appeared when down from the stables rolled a shiny black Concord, the driver, an Indian in a black suit with a red scarf around his neck, rubbing sleep or drink from his eyes. Stopping in front of the Stratford the carriage picked up the Director, drove to the end of Avon, turned around, came back up the other side of the street and stopped in front of the saloon.

The Director, huffing, alighted.

'Good evening, sir,' Crawford said with ever so slight a bow.

The Director dropped a silver dollar into the tin and labored across the threshold, into the smoky dark. The driver chucked the reins, and the carriage pulled away.

Crawford looked down at his shoes.

'Looks like about it,' Henry said, standing up and shaking the stiffness from his legs. 'I'll go round and tell em.'

All the tables had been taken out, replaced by an incongruous assemblage of chairs and other vessels comparable. Trunks. Barrels. Wagon wheel hubs. One of the velvet armchairs from the Stratford lobby throned the far end of the bar, affording the Director the privacy of what in that improvised theater could only approximate an opera box. The rest of the saloon was standing room only and of that scant was left. Shoulder to shoulder they milled, packed in like convicts in the hull of a prison ship, the whole mass of them seething, ebbing, the short trying to squeeze past the tall, others quartering for the respite of a wall, still others angling for the bar, glasses of whiskey migrating hand to hand over heads from one end of the saloon to the other. The din of them all like a passing freight train.

'Dear me,' Crawford declared, wiping his brow as he sank with a sigh of relief onto the chair beside Frost. 'I haven't seen it like this since the wedding.'

They were sitting about twenty feet from the stage, the plain canvas drop curtain hanging from a crossbeam. The side panels of the proscenium — the low ceiling forbade an arch — extended flush to the sidewalls and were papered in imitation of blue satin quilting.

Frost lowered his cigarette and sucked two tusks of smoke up through his nostrils.

'It almost restores my faith in mankind,' Crawford said.

'Don't even think about it!' someone railed nearby.

The air was close and getting warmer by the minute.

'So,' Crawford said, petting his mustache, 'I trust your researches proved fruitful?'

'I was just telling Mr. Nelson I've never been so terrified in all my life,' Frost said.

Crawford leaned forward. 'Oh, pardon me, Mr. Nelson. I didn't notice you sitting there.'

The reporter's pencil paused, rose with the waving hand and fell back scribbling to the pad atop his leg, the words in that failing light illegible even to Crawford's keen eyes.

'And how is Mr. Butler?' Crawford asked.

'He sends his regards,' the reporter said.

'Tell him I should have something for him in the next few weeks,' Crawford said.

The reporter, writing, half nodded.

Crawford sat back and, turning to Frost, said, 'You were saying?'

The relief she felt when Kelly walked by the window only fueled her mounting anger when it was Henry who stepped through the door.

'Well, wouldya look at you,' he said to Abigail, the wonder of a child gleaming in his eyes.

Standing there in her frilly white skirt billowed by a farthingale, a tight, long-waisted bodice decorated with ribbon bows and buttons, a puff-sleeved shirt, a ruff, and a regal blonde wig, she might have been a fairytale princess awaiting rescue.

Glancing around the room, Henry took in Andy and Hobbs and all the paraphernalia. The changes of costume laid out along the wall. The props on the table. Neck chain. Small bag of gold. Love poems. Bloody handkerchief. Sword.

'The cattle are restless,' Henry said. 'You want me to send Crawford on?'

The question lingered unanswered in the air.

At the request of the miner behind him, Crawford removed his hat and, empathy still firmly intact, turned back to Frost.

'I'm sure it was just a pack of coyotes,' he said.

'I frankly doubt that,' Frost said. 'We'd been seeing their smoke for several days.'

'Still,' Crawford assured him, 'if it had been Indians you wouldn't be sitting here tonight about to enjoy a drama.'

'That's comforting,' Frost said.

259

'Yes,' Crawford said, missing entirely the note of sarcasm in Frost's voice. 'I do believe the Territory has seen her final days of barbarism. This corner of it at least. I can't speak for the rest of it.'

Crawford pulled his polished timepiece from his watch pocket and studied it with mild apprehension.

'Keep the audience waiting,' he said. 'That's my motto. Gets them in the spirit.'

He leaned forward, looking left.

'Tell me,' he said, 'do you often cover the arts?'

'Mining news mostly,' the reporter said upon completing a thought. 'The occasional parade.'

'But you are an aficionado of Shakespeare, I take it?'

'I'd rather watch bears fight.'

A tap landed on Crawford's shoulder.

'You're on,' Henry said.

Crawford's face went pale.

Kelly, but a Kelly without a beard and so not the Kelly any of them knew, stepped in and looked around defiantly, as if affronted to find himself in such doubtful company.

'Nice of you to join us,' Abigail said, pivoting from the window, hands on hips.

'It took longer than I expected,' Kelly said without apology.

'I'll say it did,' Hobbs said. 'Sheared off half your face along with it.'

'It's bleeding,' Rodriguez said.

Kelly wiped his neck with his hand and studied his palm.

'Here, use this,' Andy said, tossing him the bloody handkerchief.

'Are we done discussing Mr. Kelly's neck?' Abigail asked.

'No one's said how white it is,' Hobbs noted.

Abigail tossed a doublet and hose to Kelly.

'Go get changed.'

Stepping onto the stage, Crawford turned to face the audience and raised his hands. The lamps were alight, the mellow glow of their flames washing warmly over the gulf of anxious eyes.

Gradually the noise subsided to a manageable volume, marred only by the jeers of men already too drunk to comport themselves as the occasion demanded.

'Good evening,' Crawford began. 'It is my privilege and my honor to welcome you, good citizens of Shakespeare and beyond, to tonight's performance of *As You Like It* by our very own Shakespeare Players.'

Again, hands raised, he waited patiently for the noise to subside.

He continued.

'Some of you may recall the night when not so long ago, in this very saloon, the idea of Shakespeare in Shakespeare was first aired. At that time, certain tragic events conspiring with certain misperceptions about our town, hiring a famous troupe to do our bidding seemed the surest course of action. Well, the surest course, I have since discovered...'

Faces and necks powdered white, cheek bones and chins lightly touched with rouge, fine black lines around their terror-stricken eyes, the actors huddled around their fearless director.

'Before we go on,' Abigail said, 'I have something to say.'

261

She looked in turn into each of their eyes.

'...men who facing obstacles shine brightest even as they surmount them,' Crawford proclaimed, 'and men who inured by the balmy light of easy good fortune shrink with eyes averted from the dazzling motes of uncertainty.'

'I know there were times when I was hard on you,' Abigail said, 'times when you may have wondered why you were even doing this. I often wondered the same myself. Yes, there is the money, but you know in your hearts that isn't the reason you joined me.'

'...but to those men who, hearts forged with courage, blaze like comets their own celestial trails, who in the name of Progress, of Improvement, fashion out of nothing resplendent worlds to come, whose wills freight through soulless wastes as if over steel rails the precious cargo of Civilization, to them may we grant their labors' due, that it not...'

'I ask you to put those thoughts aside,' Abigail said, 'and go out there tonight and have fun. This is a comedy. We're here to make those men out there laugh. Any of you afraid of laughter, you are free to go now. You'll be paid all the same, and we'll find a way to go on without you.'

'...these are the men who tonight will grace the stage of this our humble Globe.'

'Those miners out there, in their old age,' Abigail said, 'telling their grandchildren tales of the old days in Shakespeare, will smile and say, *And one night they gave a play, and the men played women, and I never laughed so hard in all my life, and all those nights of loneliness and longing were forgotten.*'

Crawford, allowing a little time for his lofty words to soak into besotted minds, extricated the folded piece of paper from his watch pocket.

'If I may,' he said with due modesty, 'I would like to take this opportunity to share with you a poem of my own creation.'

Folding his free arm across his midsection, he gravely intoned: '*Blush not for me, O Deciduous Tree...*'

'So, tonight I want you to forget who you are, forget your worries, forget the past, forget everything but your lines.'

In the middle of the fifth verse Crawford's voice foundered on the shoals of the vision before him. Absolute silence fell over the saloon.

'What is that?' Rodriguez quivered.

The actors looked at one another, the fear dispelled by Abigail's speech creeping back into their brows.

'Wait here,' Abigail said, and headed for the door of the saloon.

It was dark backstage, the canvas curtain softly aglow but shedding no light. Everything deathly still. As if the entire audience had simply vanished.

She crossed the stage tiptoeing to the curtain and, drawing back the edge, peered out with one eye to see every head in the saloon facing the front door. The subject of their distraction being five ugly women gathered there in a loose group. Their motley dresses dowdy and ill fitting. Faces garishly painted. Bonnets tight against their skulls.

'Good God Almighty, Davis, is that you?' someone croaked, and Davis pinched the frill of his dress and, tugging, dipped, saying in a gruff squeak: 'It's Miss Dahlia to you, thank you very much.'

The saloon erupted.

The other four ladies, curtsying in turn, chimed in after: Daisy, Rose, Iris, Lily.

'There's a man or two in that outfit sacrificin his manhood for us tonight,' Miss Dahlia bellowed, cupping her outlandish bosom with clawed fingers. 'Least we could do is show em a little *support*.'

Again the saloon roared.

'Get them broads a whiskey on me!' someone hollered, and the delicate spring blossoms were given escort to the bar and there heartily toasted and mauled.

Abigail, smiling, crept back across the stage and through the door.

Crawford discreetly tucked his sonnet back into his watch pocket and with a glint of reprieve in his eyes stepped down from the stage and proceeded to light the footlights.

From their half-tin reflectors the magnesium flares burned without flicker, two tiny suns blazing the stage with silvery light, their fumes hovering heavy and low in the breezeless saloon. Pulleys squeaking, the curtain pleated up, revealing as it rose a palace grounds, courtly buildings in the near distance, the columns of the palace stage left, a garden bower stage right.

A hush descended over the audience.

Two men, a young gentleman with a rash on his neck, and an old, hunched man with a boy's face, entered stage left.

'*As I remember, Adam,*' the young gentleman declared, '*it was upon this fashion bequeath'd me by will but poor a thousand crowns, and, as thou say'st, charg'd my brother, on his blessing, to breed me well; and there begins my sadness...*'

Outside, the dogs of Shakespeare roved Avon free for a night from the torments of man, every window dark save the Ore's, and that brighter than the moon, sphinx moths

264

new from their pupae swirling like snowflakes against the glass. From every corner of town, if only by mice and shrews stealing in under cover of darkness, the sounds of men laughing could be heard, deep salvos of joy rolling out on the cooling, cricketed air.

The Director, sitting upright in bed, applauded lightly as Abigail stepped in and closed the door behind her. The lamps unlit, the room was dim in the evening blue, a smell of tinned cherries thick in the air.

'So we meet again, Mrs. Jonson,' the Director said.

He gestured, smiling, toward the chair beside the bed and watched her come around and sit.

Into a short glass the Director poured an inch of brandy. He set the glass on the table and poured another and, sipping, sighed contentedly.

'You have been a very busy lady, Mrs. Jonson. Very busy indeed. As have I. Every godforsaken town from Zephyr Flat in the north to Antelope Wells in the south, every one of them convinced despite my words of cautious pessimism that theirs will be the one. What can you say to such people?'

The Director looked at Abigail with the same perplexed admiration he had evinced during the play. Smiling to himself, he adjusted his blanket the better to cover his legs.

'Oh, how pleasant it is to speak with you again, Mrs. Jonson. I can't tell you how many hours I've squandered in idle conversation with railroad barons' wives. Ghastly lot. Always feel it incumbent upon themselves to ask, under the guise of keeping me entertained in the absence of their husbands, about the Territory. Always the subject reverting to you, Mrs. Jonson, always this, how shall I

265

put it, derailment, in the general course of the interrogation, about various physical privations, the sole purpose of which is to afford them the opportunity to express as we sit in their parlors sipping tea, the Negro help buzzing beelike about us, their thankgodfulness for being spared a fate such as yours.

'In due course the true intent of their queries arises when in hushed tones they set their cups back in their saucers and folding their gloved hands one atop the other ask in hushed tones, What — as if it were a matter of national import — What about this town called Shakespeare? This *woman*? Still there? The only one? Depending on my frame of mind, this being as you will appreciate a matter of some personal embarrassment, I answer in the affirmative while assuring them that there is every indication that the situation is a temporary one. But what is she like, this *woman*? She must be such a fascinating creature? Always at the heart of their palpitations the matter of, shall we say, your virtue. I mean no offense. Oh, never referred to directly of course, always in a roundabout fashion, something to the effect that they admire your courage but wouldn't want to be you, at which point we move on to other matters, the point being, Mrs. Jonson, insomuch as the fate of your mattress has ceased to be the axis around which their scandalized worlds revolve, you still remain a subject of boundless fascination in the eyes of the East. In short anything out of the ordinary involving your — how shall I put it? — plight, for lack of a better word, in Shakespeare, any new twist in the plot, is news more than willingly received.'

The Director took a sip and stared pensively into his glass, saying nothing. Somewhere far away dogs were faintly barking.

266

Abigail uncrossed her legs and sat up.

'To be quite honest, Mrs. Jonson,' the Director said after a while, 'I've been avoiding Shakespeare. Yes, it is true, I'm afraid. It has kept me awake many a night, always in the back of my mind the nagging sensation that I must go back, but my own sense of impotence, if you take my meaning. Afraid even to mention it to the others lest I see that look steal across their faces. Shakespeare. What to do? The Achilles' heel of the Territory. Granted, there was a time when we were under the impression that any publicity was good publicity, and perhaps in those days that was an accurate assumption, for the imperative was simply to people it, get bodies out here, of whatever ilk, the dregs of civilization if need be, we could reform them later, but to wrest it from the savages a certain threshold required.

'This was our policy in the early days, and for the most part we can claim it as one of our signal achievements, for the population of the Territory has not diminished by even one person since our efforts began. Quite the contrary, the census will bear me out. But alas there comes a point at which the quality of the immigrants supersedes the indiscriminate demand for bodies, and one begins to seek talent, men of standing, honor, integrity, vision — women too for that matter, provided they don't appear to be supplanting men from — well, provided their talents be in their own spheres of expertise, universal suffrage a nice idea on paper but hardly viable in a functioning plutocracy.

'Suffice it to say the disastrous consequences of the town meeting were not a source of great pride for us, certainly not an event we had any intention of publicizing. And as regards the vicious rumor that certain men of a desperate

267

nature were hired by certain powers that be to sabotage the mail, making it appear the work of Indians, in order that a certain dispatch should never reach the editor of a certain newspaper known to be read by the lower functionaries of certain powerful entities of the East, I can only sigh and proclaim that if imagination paid half as much as our precious metals there would be a mother lode under every pebble in the Territory.'

Night was falling fast, the features of their faces growing indistinct.

'Would you like me to light the lamp?' Abigail offered.

'That's kind of you, but no. I so love to sit and talk in the dark. Memories of my mother, her sweet voice in the gloaming. Somehow the truth better emerges in the dark, wouldn't you agree? The first time you came I had to restrain myself from extinguishing the lamp. A matter of propriety. I feel I know you better now, Mrs. Jonson.'

The Director stared at her for a while as if in fond remembrance. Abigail, feeling uncomfortable, fixed her eyes on the pattern of his blanket.

'An island of civilization in a sea of philistines,' the Director began again. 'Shakespeare in Shakespeare. Ah yes, bring out the Bard, the glorious peerless Bard, he shall solve our troubles, he has all the answers, the pinnacle of human achievement, the Bard, and yet if the scholars are to be believed he lived in a time of filth nonpareil, raw sewage in the streets, diseases, backwards superstitions, the loosest morals imaginable, this the compost from which flowered the heavenly Bard. The name alone, Shakespeare, something magic in it. Surely something of this behind Crawford's choice. Could have named it Napoleon or Jesus, but no, Shakespeare, measure of his hubris, as if the name alone portended greatness. And yet, so earnest was I in my belief that you were on to something, Mrs. Jonson, that I traveled halfway across the continent to hold, in a hotel wanting in even the most basic amenities, a personal meeting with Mr. Gidding himself.

'In the interval between my proposition and his polite refusal of it, a period surpassing several months, I was detained in a protracted bout of political wrangling in the capital and, I must confess, gladly forgot all about Shakespeare until the day I received a rather grandiose invitation to an evening of Shakespeare in Shakespeare, appended to which was a proud declaration that the performance would be attended by no less a personage than the surveyor-general of the T.S. Bain R.R. Suffice it to say I was intrigued and left the very next morning with a stabbing sensation in my left kidney.'

The Director, as if expecting from his guest some inquiry into the present state of his health, cleared his throat self-consciously, then, nothing forthcoming, forged on.

'Charming man, Mr. Frost. Unfortunate name, he really is a warm fellow. We had a most illuminating conversation last night after the performance. Here in the dark, like you and I now. When I asked him, after a few drinks, if he had enjoyed the drama, he gave the question considerable thought before confessing that he had laughed a great deal and was pleasantly surprised by the quality of the acting but, now that a little time had passed, he was left with a rather queer feeling which he couldn't quite put into words, something unsettling about the whole affair. When I asked him if he could elaborate he shifted about and said, Well, and he admitted that it had been somewhat of a shock to see men in a boomtown like Shakespeare — boomtown! — gallivanting about as women but, he said, that wasn't quite it, for he'd soon acclimated to it and had come to accept that they were what they purported to be, namely women. No, he said. It was something else. Turning to the subject of Rosalind — that is you, Mrs. Jonson — he paused such that I understood it to be some aspect of, well, I don't mean to. Let me put it this way. He hadn't realized that you weren't in fact a man yourself until I told him so. It seems he was under the impression that you were directing the play; it never occurred to him you might be in it as well. Oh yes, I said, she was Rosalind. Why this should be the source of his unease I cannot say. In any case, I'm positive I heard or read somewhere that in Elizabethan times women's roles were played by boys. Beside the point, but alas, the heart of the matter, I'm afraid.'

It was now pitch black in the room.

'To come or not to come?' the Director mused. 'That is surely the question facing the T.S. Bain R.R., isn't it? If I may be candid, Mrs. Jonson, it would be unfortunate, in my opinion, if just when the misconceptions about Shakespeare which have so doggedly plagued it since your arrival are beginning to wane, they were to be replaced by yet another episode which makes Shakespeare something of the laughing stock of the Territory. Too late, I'm afraid, to do much about the reporter. Perhaps I miscalculated, but I couldn't speak to both at once, not my style, had to choose: surveyor or journalist? I would have liked nothing better than to bribe them both, but we don't have the resources even for one significant bribe, let alone two, some discussion in fact of downgrading my carriage to a lesser model to conserve funds. None of this your concern. I'm only trying to impress upon you

270

the gravity of the situation. Not only is Shakespeare a one-woman town but the men dress as women to amuse themselves.'

The Director paused to gather his thoughts.

'Don't misunderstand me, Mrs. Jonson, these aren't my own appraisals. I very much loved the performance. A tremendous amount of work you and your players must have put into it. A truly unique performance. Shakespeare would have been proud, the Mexican particularly endearing, and the young man who played the country wench, there is some real talent as a woman. Whatever you have done to instruct them in the arts of feminine wiles has been most effective, my own wife could use some lessons of this sort.'

Again the Director paused.

'Where was I? I lost my train of thought.'

'Gravity of the situation,' Abigail said.

'Yes, right. I don't believe my fears are unfounded when I say that this could very well be the death knell of Shakespeare. I have recently come to believe, and the other Directors are inclined to concur, that we were wholly mistaken in assuming that the problem with Shakespeare was its dearth of women. In fact it seems our strategy had the unintended effect of casting into a negative light Shakespeare's men, for strange as it may seem the blame was placed entirely on them for not being men enough to attract mates. And so, we no longer endeavor to lure women to Shakespeare, nature will take its course, but only to assure that the men already here are perceived as such. As Men, that is. A small but important shift of perspective.

'I'm sure you will appreciate the irony, Mrs. Jonson, when I say that your play is precisely the inverse of our

271

new position, not that we have any idea how to go about fulfilling it, our capacity not so much creative as critical. We ask ourselves, what is it that men do? What makes a man a man? And one of the first things that comes to mind is murder. Men kill each other, women seldom do. Am I wrong? Oh, we certainly have no intention of promoting murder, attracting outlaws and the like, but this record of lawfulness in Shakespeare, we have come to see, must be at the very heart of its troubles.

'If the Territory is ever to have a proper name, to become in the eyes of the East worthy of being subsumed into the bosom of the Union, sharing measure for measure her powers and her glories alike, then we must demonstrate to her our manliness. She is watching us, like a female bird watching impassively the colorful male of the species dancing and singing about her, watching to see if we are worthy of her attentions. In short the eagle eyes of the East are upon us, Mrs. Jonson, unforgiving of even our slightest weakness, for in judging us they are in truth judging themselves. That which they cannot abide in themselves they castigate in us. They mock our every ambition, condemn our every illusion, seeing in them only lies when in truth without the promise of outrageous fortune we would be ignored altogether. And so our hand is forced. They demand on the one hand that we believe in our illusions and on the other punish us for doing so. This the final stage before admission. What the Union needs to see, in short, is the Territory turn away from her, provoke her disapproval, a gesture which emphatically proves our independence, for only when it fears it might lose us will the Union admit us into her fold.

'I believe what we need, Mrs. Jonson, is boldness, acts that demonstrate our strength and independence, in short acts of violence one against another. It's all well and good to kill Indians, but when we begin killing ourselves the Union sits up and takes notice, for here, she discerns, there is something worth fighting for.'

The door opened briefly, as if by mistake, then quickly closed.

'We should be grateful, I suppose, that the East has finally lost interest in your mattress, the election having distracted them long enough to forget. But we haven't much time, Mrs. Jonson. The Indians will soon be on the rampage again, if not already, the first massacres of the season upon us, and once again Capital's window will slowly close. And so, Mrs. Jonson, in the interest of the progress and improvement of Shakespeare, of the Territory as a whole, of the Union itself, it might behoove us all if your play was not performed again.'

A long period of silence followed these remarks.

'Mrs. Jonson?'

The room was dark and quiet. The Director sat blinking his eyes, straining to see his guest.

'Mrs. Jonson?'

Stovall tapped a button of ash from the tip of his cigar and read on: '*As an example, a group of men who call themselves the Knights of Shakespeare, the town's sometime militia, dubbing themselves flowers, arrived for the performance in dresses...* — That was very funny. I wish you had seen them. — *Stranger yet was the eager, one is tempted to say voracious, manner in which the audience embraced them, giving an outsider the impression that in the absence of real women the men of Shakespeare have learned to make do with the resources at hand.*'

273

'What does it say about me?' Rodriguez, leaning over the counter, asked.

'I'm looking,' Stovall said, scanning the column. '*A. W. Crawford...* Blah blah... *Mr. Selgren...*'

Reading to himself he chuckled softly.

'What?' Rodriguez asked.

'Nothing, nothing.' Stovall puffed on his cigar. 'Here is something. *Mr. Rodriguez.*'

Stovall read to himself, nodding, smiling.

'What does it say?' Rodriguez demanded to know.

Stovall, setting his cigar on the rim of the ashtray, took up the paper and read with authority: '*Mr. Rodriguez, the actor playing "Celia" has a kind of quaint nobility reminiscent of old Spanish princesses. He has beauty and sincerity, but his vocation has not been judiciously trained, and his earnest desire to excel impels him a little to excess, equally of action and utterance.*'

'Is this good?'

Stovall smiled.

'Yes. Very good.'

Yellowed by the candle flame the pages between the driller's hands might have been news from another century.

'*Mr. Hobbes' denotement of that condition — in the pale and ravaged countenance, the harsh, incisive voice, the splenetic movements of the tyrannical usurper — was exceedingly subtle and sharply effective.*'

'You sure he's talkin about me?' Hobbs said.

'Jest let him read it, why don't ya?' the driver said.

'Says here, *Mr. Hobbes.* That's your name aint it?'

'I spose so, but I aint ever heard that kinda talk around it.'

'There's more. *Mr. Hobbes also acted the melancholy*

274

"Jaques", and gave the speech of the Seven Ages so as to bring tears to many eyes.'

'Amen,' the driver said.

'The versatility Mr. Hobbes showed in all his parts, especially as "Touchstone", the merry fool, bespeaks an actor of a most auspicious order.'

'Well, well,' the driller gibed. 'Looks like Master Hobbs has found himself a callin.'

'Too good fer us common folk,' the driver agreed.

'Hell,' Hobbs said, trying hard not to smile, 'them aint nothin but words on a page.'

Reading backwards bottom to top, Andy followed the words as his uncle read them from the other side of the desk.

'The performance went with dash and vim and never a halt with the exception of the mechanism of the curtain, which interfered with the climax of the—'

'What does he say about me?'

'Hold on, for Christ's sake,' Crawford chided. 'I'm looking... Here we are. *The evening began with a recitation of a limerick* — Limerick! Bloody fool — *a limerick by Mr. A.W. Crawford, who during a conversation before the performance asserted with the confidence of the Delphic Oracle that Shakespeare in a few years' time would be the center of the greatest mining district of the world.'*

Andy leaned forward, his eyes roving the columns for capital As and Ss.

'What!' Crawford cried, snatching up the paper.

Andy, fearing the worst, pulled himself erect.

'What is it?'

'The gall!'

'What? Tell me,' Andy repeated, trying without success to see what Crawford was reading.

275

Crawford, beside himself, read with sneering contempt: '*During my stay in Shakespeare I was besieged by dogs of every size and color. On the night of the performance, and after I had retired for the night, in the neighborhood of forty dogs —* Forty dogs! *— congregated in front of the Stratford Hotel, where I was stopping, and kept up a most abominable noise for several hours...*'

Andy exhaled.

'I can't bear any more,' Crawford said, tossing the paper onto the desk and turning away in disgust.

Andy, finding his name at last, steeled himself and read silently, a smile slowly blooming across his lips.

'Do you want to hear what he says?' he asked eagerly.

'The man can't write,' Crawford said. 'What place does a dissertation on dogs have in a drama review? *Rather watch bears fight!*'

'*The demeanor and speeches of "Adam", as played by young Mr. Selgren, seemed particularly notable because of their apt denotement of a character matured and saddened by hard experience. It is not always that a little part is played so well. Better still, his embodiment of "Audrey" showed exuberant animal spirits and caused much merriment, making that agricultural peasant comical without vulgarity, and investing her with a fresh animal beauty, quite explanatory of the whimsical "Touchstone's" ardor.*'

Andy lowered the paper, smiling.

'*Matured and saddened by hard experience,*' Crawford sneered. 'That's amusing.'

Henry, raising his voice, leaned closer to the paper and read on.

'*...but it was Mrs. Jonson, as "Rosalind", who was the hit of the evening with her sparkling acting. At*

each appearance she was applauded in a hearty and
— Blaine?'

Blaine, leaning over the bar with head craned, studied the word.

'*Vociferous*,' he pronounced.

'*...vociferous manner. Mrs. Jonson's ideal of "Rosalind" rejected, at the outset, the old theory that this character is made of gossamer and moonshine.* — Lord Almighty, he can shovel it — *"Rosalind" is born for conquest. She sweeps away every obstacle; she triumphs because of a personality...*'

'Hell, I caint make head or tail of this. Someone else read it.'

Spinning the paper around, Blaine found the line and carried on.

'*...a personality intrinsically victorious; and therefore the character exacts from its representation an incessant impartment of physical charm and mental vivacity.*'

'Hey now, he caint talk about our bartender like at!' someone barked.

'*To see Mrs. Jonson, who has already achieved a measure of notoriety through no effort of her own, commanding the stage is to think of an imperial woman. Her face is lovely, her figure lithe, her step elastic, her demeanor buoyant, her articulation delicious, and even in her boy's dress she cuts a graceful figure. One is compelled to wonder if being the only woman in Shakespeare hasn't in fact burnished Mrs. Jonson's natural luster.*'

Henry, standing tall, nodded proudly.

'*The idea of staging this show was hers, and she went into it with heart and soul, superintending all the rehearsals and assuming the entire charge of the artistic portion of the entertainment. It was an arduous task for*

277

a woman, but one so well executed that the success of the performance is almost entirely due to her efforts.'

Three cheers went up and all fell to drinking.

'Alas, the ungracious part of critical duty...' Blaine proceeded somberly.

Abigail, summoned by three angry knocks, opened the back door.

'That's it!' Kelly fumed, a newspaper clenched in his fist. 'I won't be made a fool of again.'

He stepped in, reading spitefully: *'Mr. Joseph Kelly, M.E., who appeared as "Orlando", possesses several of the qualifications that are essential for that character — the fine figure, the pleasing voice, the manly bearing; but, on this occasion, he did not display much passion at all. Perhaps the part does not, as yet, fully awaken the actor's sympathy. "Orlando" must be made sensitive, alert, impetuous and ardent. He must not seem inert. He must not flag. Mr. Kelly's "Orlando", however, was a rustic Hamlet, mooning about in the woods, listless as idleness, and lymphatic to the verge of sleep. Mr. Kelly's performance, if fine at all, is fine only in practical execution; and to summarize it as highly tedious is not unjust.'*

Kelly, eyes red, lowered the paper.

'You wouldn't listen. You had to have me as Orlando. Well, you got me, didn't you. Now I'm through. You can keep your lousy ten dollars. I refuse to be made a fool of again.'

'Fine,' Abigail said.

'I mean it,' Kelly said. 'Give Orlando to your little friend. You can get someone else to do his parts.'

'Fine.'

Kelly, apparently expecting more of a struggle, went

quiet for a moment, then said rather rudely: 'You are doing it again, aren't you?'

Abigail leveled her somewhat amused gaze on him.

'What do you care?'

'I don't,' he said unconvincingly. 'It just seems strange to put all that work into something for only one performance.'

'It does, doesn't it?'

Kelly looked down at the paper and shook his head, the red slowly fading from his face.

Henry and Abigail set out walking due east from the back of the saloon. Though the nights were still cold, the days were inching toward summer, the plants, ever wary of some looming cataclysm, tentatively testing their greens. Walking close behind him through the brush, Abigail, uncertain as to where he was taking her, or why the need for this air of secrecy, found herself sifting through a list of possible infractions, compiling one of her own on him. A few hundred yards out Henry stopped and, spreading his arms, said: 'Well, what do you think?'

'Think?' Abigail said. 'About what?'

'It's ours. Five acres thataway and five thataway.'

Abigail looked in the directions he was pointing and saw nothing but the same barren scrub she saw in every other direction. It had been so long since they had spoken of the plot that she had forgotten about it entirely. She didn't know what to say.

'Ah, hell,' Henry said, putting his arm around her shoulders. 'I never coulda done it without you. Every inch of it's as much yours as mine.'

Taking a thrice-folded deed from his trouser pocket, Henry unfolded it and showed her the language.

'I expect we'll be able to start buildin in another month or so. Course we'll have to figure out what all you want in it. How many bedrooms and whatnot. We put a tank in you can have your own toilet inside. I aint too particular myself.'

Henry went on in this manner, building for her his vision of their home, a greenhouse for fresh vegetables in the winter, a real parlor with a working piano, a kitchen with everything she needed in it. Abigail had never heard Henry so excited. So much so that it seemed she was listening to Andy. Henry's arm around her, so happy in his vision of their future, Abigail couldn't bring herself to ask him if there would be in this house a shed with a hole in the wall.

'Does this mean I don't have to work in the saloon anymore?' she said, half joking.

'Well,' Henry replied, 'I was about to get to that.'

Walking back to the saloon Henry explained that getting the land had cost them nearly every cent of their savings, including what they had made from the play, and a small loan on top of that. To his way of thinking, what with the cost of lumber and labor and everything else, even if she did the play a few more times they wouldn't be able to get started next month unless she stayed on working in the saloon a little longer.

'I don't know what I'd do with myself mornings not working in the saloon,' Abigail said not quite seriously.

'You'd find something,' Henry said.

They walked in silence. Shakespeare from that distance and direction seemed to Abigail like some other town entirely, she and Henry wanderers off the desert seeking human society, and she tried to imagine what it would feel like to her, a woman, discovering that she was the only one around, but it had been too long now. She couldn't remember anymore what it must have felt like.

'I want you to know,' Henry said. 'I'm real proud of what you've done. With your play, I mean. Real proud.'

He glanced at her.

Abigail, unaware until he said them how much these words meant to her, took Henry's hand in hers, and though nothing in his expression suggested it, she felt for the first time what agony it was for him to touch her. She moved to take her hand away but he closed his fingers around it and didn't let go until they were back in the saloon.

FOUR

'It must have just been nerves the first night,' he said. 'He was a completely different Orlando tonight.'

'Yes, he was, wasn't he?' she said.

Andy walked over and checked the lock on the door to the saloon, doing so, Abigail noted with satisfaction, with a casual authority wholly new to him. There being nowhere else to sit, Abigail planted herself on the edge of the mattress, legs outstretched, arms propping her up behind.

'Too bad the reporter wasn't here,' Andy said, squatting down and falling back. 'You could really feel the love between you two.'

'Yes,' she said.

'And you were so worried he wasn't right for the part. I told you he was right, didn't I?'

He turned onto his side.

'You know what I think?' he said. 'I think we could go on tour. The Shakespeare Players. Travel all over the Territory. There's money to be made. What do you think?'

Abigail smiled but made no reply.

'I'm serious,' Andy said. 'We're good. You read the review. He thought we were better than a lot of professionals. I say we do it. Just go.'

'Andy,' Abigail said.

'What? What's so crazy about it?'

Andy sat up and looked at her.

'Kelly didn't think it was a bad idea,' he said. 'I asked him not five minutes ago.'

'Is that right?'

'Those were his exact words. "That's not a bad idea." Why don't we talk to the others?'

She sighed boredly.

'Is this what you came back to talk about?'

Andy fiddled with the tongue of his shoe.

'Stop that,' she said.

'What's wrong?'

'Nothing.'

'You haven't been yourself for days. Why don't you tell me what's wrong?'

She sat silent, staring at the oranges in the still life. He tried to kiss her but she turned her face away.

'Now you're starting to annoy me,' she said.

'Fine,' he said, standing up in a huff.

He walked over to the table and picked up Duke Frederick's bejeweled dagger. Gazing abstractedly at the bits of colored glass, he nodded to himself as if savoring some little irony.

'I should have told him when I set out to the first time,' he said.

'Told who what?' Abigail said.

'I should have told Henry. I was this close. But he said you wanted to see me, and I lost my courage.'

'Well, I'm glad you didn't,' Abigail said. 'That would have been foolish.'

'Why?'

'What do you mean why? Did you think he'd shake your hand and thank you for being a good honest boy?'

Andy set the dagger back on the table and squared up defiantly.

'I'm as much a man as anyone in this town. As much as Henry.'

'I know you are, Andy.'

'I refuse to live my life in fear.'

'And that's what I love about you. Now come here and give me a kiss goodnight and let me get some rest.'

Andy, still sulking if slightly less so, knelt down at the foot of the mattress and gave Abigail a long, manly kiss. He reached around behind her and pulled her arms in and lowered her to the mattress.

'Just wanted to talk, is it?' Abigail said playfully.

'There's more than one way to talk,' Andy said, trailing kisses down her neck.

At that moment, as if from somewhere inside the room, there came a brittle crunching sound followed by a kind of startled grunt.

Andy spun around and stared uneasily at the wall, the window, the door.

'Did you hear that?' he whispered.

'Hear what?' Abigail said, nonchalantly smoothing her skirt.

Andy got up and walked over to the stretch of bare wall between the still life and the window and, head cocked, listened.

'What are you doing?'

Andy pressed a finger to his lips.

A soft rustling sound, as of cloth, seemed to be emanating from within the wall. Andy, eyes widening, gave Abigail a look of vindication.

'It's probably just an animal,' she said dismissively, adding, 'You know, I was thinking the other day, I haven't seen Theodore in a long time? Why is that?'

Quietly, stealthily, Andy stole over to the table and picked up the dagger and pulled the dull steel blade from its sheath.

'Andy,' Abigail said with an incredulous little laugh. 'Don't be ridiculous.'

Dagger in hand Andy sidled over to the back door and slowly opened it a foot or so, his free hand pleading silence behind him. The strident chiming of the crickets, hardly noticeable before, now seemed almost visible it was so loud. Abigail, pointing at Andy, made emphatic faces at the still life. Andy opened the door a little wider. Faintly through the pulsing shimmer came the dry squeak of a hinge slowly pivoting. Andy opened the door still wider and stepped outside.

Abigail leapt up from the mattress and hurried across the room to the still life and peered anxiously into its holes but they were dark.

'Who's there!' Andy shouted.

A loud smack followed quick upon this query, then sounds of scuffling. Shoes and boots skidding wildly in the dirt. Low animal grunts. Heavy breathing. A yelp atop a dull thud. Fabric ripping. Labored hissing through clenched teeth. More scuffling and grunting. Then a long quiet moment filled with panting. The very air charged with recognition.

Abigail stepped toward the door then stopped, warned off by a blood-curdling yowl that silenced the crickets. A moment later she was jolted to the bones by the concussion of a gunshot, and hard upon the hanging stillness something hit the dirt with a heavy *whump*. Then absolute silence.

She stood, as if rooted to the floor, the bang ringing in

her ears. She waited and waited for someone to appear, but no one came. At some point chairs began to scoot across the floor of the saloon, boot heels thumping into the stillness.

Then he was there in the doorway, a small splatter of blood on the front of his torn shirt. There was in his eyes a look of peace, of a man come home from a lifetime wandering the lonely earth to find his love as he left her. Young and strong and more beautiful even than he remembered. In his right hand the pistol hung limply, wisps of gray smoke still curling from the barrel. He looked down almost apologetically at the blood on his shirt then looked up again and opened his mouth.

They stared at one another in the silence, the tang of gun smoke and vinegar lacing the air between them. She went to take a step but her body didn't move.

Something fled flapping through some unseen breach when they opened the door to bring him in, a high gamey stink wafting over them, subsequent investigation revealing at the back of the room a veneer of hardened scat scattered over an ossuary of diminutive bones, leathered rinds of fur, feathers.

'Puts me in mind of the time my old man hoisted me up to the attic to try to get a old barn owl out,' Davis, sentried with a rifle at the front door, was saying. 'Lord Almighty what a stink. You'll never believe what was up there.'

Apart from the year-old calendar — PREPARED UNDER THE AUSPICES OF THE TERRITORIAL BUREAU OF IMMIGRATION — highlighting the resources of the Territory with bold ads and a wealth of statistics, the walls were bare. A flat oak desk and a swiveling chair, in which the prisoner presently sat, were the only pieces of furniture in the long dusty room narrow as a train carriage. Against the right-hand wall, halfway back, the body lay covered by a wagonsheet, a wine-dark stain beginning to bleed through the canvas.

'It was chock fulla dead skunks,' Davis said.

'That a fact?' Brown said from the back of the room.

'There I was crawlin along, lookin for a nest, when what do you know but I come face to face with her,' Davis said. 'You ever been two inches from a owl's face and it starin you in the eyes not even blinkin, just starin, like if you was a little smaller it'd eat you too?'

'Can't say I have,' Brown said.

'Liked to have scared the livin bejesus outa me,' Davis said. 'I hate owls. Birds aint sposed to be that smart.'

'They aint no smarter than any other bird,' Brown said.

'Says who?' Davis said.

'It's a fact a Science. They only look smarter on account of their eyes bein stuck on the front of their faces like us. Aint that right, Henry?'

Henry nodded noncommittally.

A nervous knuckle loudly rapped the glass of the front door. Davis stepped around the partition, the clamor of the aspiring lynchers surging briefly before the door banged shut.

'Show me,' Crawford said, taking only passing notice of Henry.

Davis, picking up the lamp, escorted Crawford back to the body, their footfalls echoing hollowly through the room.

Kneeling down on one knee, Crawford slowly folded back the edge of the canvas. All at once his breath squeezed out of him. Setting the lamp on the floor, Davis left Crawford to his grief.

Crawford lingered there quietly sobbing for several minutes. Then, tenderly resettling the sheet, he labored up and shuffled across the room to Henry, a world of incomprehension in each watery eye.

'Is that everything you remember?'

They were side by side a foot apart on the sofa. Her color was beginning to return but her face was still pale, her eyes deep in their own livid shadows. In her hands she held the small vial of smelling salts Muldoon had given her.

She nodded weakly.

Kelly, sighing, ran his fingers through his hair, his hand lingering a long time at the back of his head. All was quiet but for the plangent refrain of the crickets.

'Poor Andy,' he said. 'Only a few hours ago he was...'

He stared morosely at the wall, visions in his mind of Audrey on the other side, capering across the stage.

'So full of life.' He shook his head in disbelief. 'So eager. And I was always so mean to him.'

Abigail rubbed his shoulder sympathetically.

'I was,' he said. 'He never had anything but kind words for me. That time I clobbered him during rehearsal, over nothing.'

He swallowed and looked down at his hands.

They gazed sorrow-struck for a long time at nothing in particular. Then, taking her hand from his shoulder and holding it, Kelly turned and looked into Abigail's eyes.

'You don't think he thought you and Andy...?'

'No,' Abigail said, looking away.

She rubbed her nose with the back of her hand.

From the saloon came the steadily increasing volume of men gathering to hear and be heard.

'They're going to hang him,' Abigail said flatly.

'They can't hang him,' Kelly assured her. 'You said Andy came at him with a knife. You can't hang a man for defending his life.'

Abigail stood up and, taking a sniff of the salts, walked around to the back of the sofa and stayed there facing the bath screen.

'You had better get back,' she said. 'They'll be waiting for you.'

Kelly picked up his hat from the seat of the sofa and, like some commercial traveler, business concluded, restored it to his head. He came around and stood before her. If ever there was a moment when he wanted nothing more than to take her into his arms and kiss her and tell her that she was the only woman he had ever truly loved, it was now, when he could not. He set his hand gently on her shoulder and looked into her eyes.

'Don't worry,' he said. 'They are reasonable men.'

'With all due respect, Arthur,' Muldoon politely disagreed, 'I don't see that we have any choice at all but to put Mr. Jonson on the next stage to Bird. This isn't a court of law. We don't know anything about the circumstances behind this killing.'

It was true then, Rodriguez thought, there on his stool in the dark. The kid was dead. Not two hours ago he was alive and happy, bowing to the audience. Now dead. Killed by Mr. Jonson. Shot in the heart. Rodriguez made the sign of the cross, forehead-lip-breastbone.

'This is a sad night for all of us,' Stovall said. 'We have lost a friend. Mr. Crawford has lost a loved one. The man who killed him is also our friend. We all know Henry Jonson to be a good and decent man. I do not think he had the intention of killing Andy tonight. If it is true the kid went at him with a knife, then Henry did what any of us would have done.'

'My nephew is dead,' Crawford gravely reminded them. 'Andy is dead. He never hurt anyone in his life. He was a happy, loving boy.'

Rodriguez, hearing the pain in Crawford's voice, felt himself choking up.

'He went at Henry with a knife,' Stovall repeated.

'He was only playing, surely,' Crawford said pleadingly. 'It was a mere prop. A blunt dagger.'

'We don't know that he was only playing,' Muldoon said. 'As you well know, and I mean no disrespect, Andy was known to suffer from bouts of melancholy. His blood ran hot. He was entirely capable, given the right conditions, of acting rashly.'

'He didn't have to die!' Crawford shouted. 'Henry didn't have to shoot him in the heart. Are we going to let lawyers set our murderers free so they can murder again and become famous for their misdeeds, or are we going to send a strong message to the world that Shakespeare has no tolerance for killing?'

'I really don't understand you,' Muldoon said. 'All this talk about sending messages to the world. What good has it done us? The world doesn't know we exist. They don't care.'

'Gentlemen,' Stovall intervened. 'We should not fight.'

'I always said the theatre aint nothin but a den of iniquity,' Blaine confided generally. 'Thought it was a bad idea from the start. All this, men lollygaggin around in dresses. It aint natural. Somethin like this was bound to happen sooner or later. How do we know

290

she and the kid weren't doin somethin they shouldn't of?'

'I resent that,' Crawford retorted. 'My nephew was a poet, a man whose thoughts ranged on a plane higher than ours. You have no right to cast aspersions without evidence on either his or Mrs. Jonson's character. I pity the man who can't imagine a beautiful friendship between a man and a woman.'

'Maybe we have no right pretending we're a jury,' Muldoon maintained. 'I for one want no part in any lynching party.'

'Has anyone given a thought to Mrs. Jonson?' Stovall asked. 'She would be left a widow.'

'And we are to coddle murderers because they happen to have wives?' Crawford replied.

'We don't know anything about the circumstances behind this tragedy,' Muldoon said. 'At the very least we need to interview Mrs. Jonson. I want to question her myself.'

'Yes,' Stovall agreed. 'We should speak with her.'

'I'll go get her,' Kelly said.

Rodriguez, starting to perspire, heard Kelly leave the hotel. In the interim the others made no further comments, the steady drone of the crickets the only sound penetrating the closet under the stairs.

In time two pairs of footsteps, one quieter than the other, came walking across the floor.

'Please have a seat, Mrs. Jonson,' Muldoon said.

'I'd rather stand.'

'Mrs. Jonson, I know this must be very hard for you, Andy was quite fond of you, but it's important that you tell us everything you know about what happened. Spare no detail. Your husband's life may depend on what you say.'

'I told Mr. Kelly everything I know,' she said.

'What was the kid doin there in the first place?' Blaine blurted out.

'Please, Mr. Blaine,' Muldoon implored.

'He came back to tell me an idea he'd got when he was walking home. He was impulsive that way. No sooner would he get an idea than he would have to share it with someone.'

'Could you share with us that idea?' Crawford asked, his voice wavering under the strain of emotion.

'He wanted us, the whole troupe, to go on the road with the play.'

'And what did you say?' Muldoon asked.

'I didn't think it was a good idea.'

'Did he seem upset by this?'

'Mr. Muldoon,' Crawford broke in. 'What is the point of this?'

'I'm merely trying to ascertain your nephew's state of mind before the incident.'

'It's irrelevant,' Crawford said.

'It is absolutely relevant,' Muldoon insisted. 'If the boy was made distraught by the rejection of his idea, he may have been plunged into a condition of nervous excitability, which would go a long way toward explaining why an otherwise peaceable young man would suddenly attack someone with a knife.'

'Isn't the real question,' Crawford countered, 'why was Henry Jonson, a known murderer, prowling around outside his own back door with a pistol?'

A weighty silence followed this remark.

'I'm sorry,' Crawford said. 'We all must share the blame for not telling you sooner, Mrs. Jonson.'

'I have ears, Mr. Crawford,' she said.

'Then you know what they say about Henry?' Stovall said. 'That he once was an outlaw.'

'*They say the best men are molded out of faults,*' she said, '*and, for the most part, become much more the better for being a little bad.*'

'There's words and there's life,' Blaine said.

'We appreciate your thespian talents, Mrs. Jonson,' Muldoon said. 'Apart from what you have already told us is there anything else you know that could shed light on this tragedy?'

'Mrs. Jonson,' Crawford cut in. 'A pillar of our community, my nephew, is dead. Justice must be served.'

'This isn't a court of law,' she said. 'Hanging Henry won't make a bit of difference to your precious railroad.'

'Your opinion has been duly noted, Mrs. Jonson,' Crawford replied with overweening solicitude. 'If you have nothing further to add you are free to go.'

Back across the floor and out the door the quiet footsteps went. Rodriguez, sweat dripping down his face, wiped his forehead with his sleeve.

'Kelly, you're quiet,' Crawford said. 'Do you have anything to say?'

There was a long pause.

'She's told us everything she knows,' Kelly said quietly.

'There's a crowd out there demanding justice,' Crawford said.

'They could care less about justice,' Muldoon said. 'They just want to see a man hung. They respect Henry Jonson as much as we do. They don't want to see him die. They just want to see someone hung. Anyone. It doesn't matter who. I suspect there's some part of all of us at this point, a year gone and still only one woman, that just wants to see a man hang.'

'This has nothing to do with women,' Crawford argued, his voice rising. 'They want revenge for the murder of my nephew. A Henry for an Andy. An eye for an eye.'

'*Judge not lest ye be judged*,' Muldoon said. 'That's what the Bible says.'

'*He who strikes a man so that he dies*,' Blaine fired back, '*shall surely be put to death*. Exodus 21:12.'

'Maybe we should talk to Henry,' Kelly suggested.

'Yes,' Stovall said, endorsing the suggestion. 'I will go get him.'

'He has nothing to say,' Crawford said. 'I already tried.'

'We'll be the judge of that,' Muldoon said. 'Go ahead, Mr. Stovall.'

Across the floor and out the door plodded the footsteps Rodriguez knew better than his own. A short while later, accompanied by the slow, sinister footsteps of a killer and his escort, they returned.

'Whatever she said on my behalf,' Henry said, dispensing with procedure, 'you can forget it. She's a good woman. Best wife a man ever had. I killed him because I wanted to and that's the truth, so you can all quit your deliberatin and get on with it. And when you hang me it won't be for just the kid but for the sixteen other people I sent to an early grave.'

'Take him away!' Crawford roared.

And the prisoner was escorted from the premises.

'I rest my case,' Crawford said with smug finality. 'He should have been hung long ago.'

'This is absurd,' Muldoon said. 'Sixteen people. I no more believe that than I believe pigs have wings.'

'Justice must be served!' Crawford railed, stomping his foot. 'Justice, justice, justice, justice!'

'Clearly we have a disagreement here, gentlemen,' Stovall observed. 'This being a Territory of a democratic country, I suggest we take a vote. There are five of us.'

The wisdom of this remark was acknowledged only by the solemn silence that followed it.

'Those in favor of hanging Henry Jonson for the murder of Andrew Selgren,' Crawford said, 'raise your hands. All others abstain.'

A long, heavy silence.

'So be it,' Crawford said.

She crossed Avon holding one of Henry's shirts folded under her right arm. At her approach the dozen or so men still loitering outside Progress & Improvement dispersed into the surrounding dark.

'Evenin, Mrs. Jonson,' Davis said, opening the door and looking past her in search of the crowd.

She stepped in.

Rounding the partition she took in with disconcerted eyes and nose the deadness of the place, a wave of nausea rolling through her at the sight of the lumpy, bloodstained wagonsheet on the floor, Henry at the desk, the other guard dark in the shadows at the back. She closed her eyes briefly, allowing her insides to settle, then went to Henry.

Henry looked at the shirt, back at her. He took the shirt and, holding it up by the shoulders, appraised it as one might a potential purchase.

'Not my best,' he said, 'but it'll do.'

Abigail cast disapproving glances around the room.

'Aren't they going to give you anywhere to sleep?'

'Floor's down there if I want it,' he said.

Davis, caught staring, averted his eyes.

'Could we have a moment alone, please?' Abigail asked.

Davis nodded to Brown and they opened their respective doors and stepped outside.

The lamp, resting on the floor near the partition, dimly spilled its warm yellow light over the lower third of the room, leaving the upper reaches in darkness.

Abigail walked slowly across the room to the body. Kneeling down she folded back the wagonsheet. His face was gray as ash, his eyelashes still smudged with umber. Flecks of crimson clung here and there to his slightly parted lips. Speaking to some part of him no longer of this world she told him that she was sorry and that if there was cause for blame much of it was hers and that come the day of judgment she would be called to account, reaping what she sowed. These silent confidences yielded neither comfort nor absolution.

Henry, the torn and bloodied shirt replaced by the clean one, stood up as she neared.

'Some husband I turned out to be,' Henry said.

'Listen, Henry.'

'No speeches. What's done's done.'

He caressed her cheek with his fingertips. She closed her eyes, tears pooling in them when she opened them again.

'Come on now,' Henry said.

Turning away she walked over to the left-hand wall and stood before a calendar tacked there. *December. O.E. Snyder Dental Office. The Most Complete Apparatus and Appliances for Operative and Mechanical Dentistry in the Territory. Teeth Extracted Without Pain by Use of Nitrous Oxide Gas.*

'Whatever's in the bank's yours,' Henry said. 'And the land. I expect you'll be movin on to greener pastures.'

Abigail flipped the page back to November. *Academy of Our Lady of Light. Under the Management of the Sisters of Loretto. Specially Adapted to the Education of Young Ladies. Instruction Given in English, Spanish, Music, Painting, Drawing and Fancy Work.*

'If you run into any trouble there's a man in Pecan named Ray Carlson owes me some favors,' Henry said, adding, 'Not that I don't think you can take care of yourself.'

October. W.W. Stecker & Son. Cabinet Makers & Undertakers. Prompt Attention Given to All Orders Sent by Mail.

She looked through the preceding months, reading the ads as if by perusing the past she might postpone the future. Then she let the pages fall and walked back to Henry.

He was standing with his hands braced on the back of the chair. Not looking at her he said: 'You should get on back. I have some things to settle with myself.'

'I'm staying with you tonight,' Abigail said.

'No,' Henry said. 'The times we done spent together been some of the most confusin in my life. Now I want you to go on back so I can think back on things on my own.'

She placed her left hand on his, smooth over coarse. He looked at it, looked at her.

'Just get on back and start forgettin you ever met me. I mean it,' he said. 'Go on. I'll call them guards back in to take you out.'

He turned away.

She squeezed his hand and said quietly, 'Goodbye, Henry.'

Henry remained standing behind the chair, listening to her footsteps.

Davis, returning, whistled loud, and Brown came back in.

'One of you get me a piece of paper and a pen,' Henry said.

The rider rode in fast off the desert to the north and in a burst of dust arrested his blowing steed short of the well.

'What's the rush, friend?' the miner asked, letting his feminized ladle sink back into the bucket.

'I heard they's hangin Henry Jonson today,' the rider said. The horse, smelling water, whinnied wildly and tossed its head. 'I couldn't believe my ears. Come in to see for myself.'

'I'll save you the trouble. You done missed it.'

The rider glanced regretfully toward the saloon then swung down slow from the saddle.

'Were you there?' he said.

'Me and everyone else.'

'What happened?'

'You can figure that one out.'

Placing his hands on the low adobe surround, the rider peered sadly down into the water.

'Did he do it? Kill the kid?'

'That's what he was hung for.'

'I'm sorry to hear it.'

'We all are.'

They stared into the water.

'Well,' the rider said after a while, 'was it a good hangin at least?'

'As good a hangin as ever I saw. Ever man in town out there round Crawford's tree. The leaves just comin in. Sun shinin. Birds singin. The missus there by his side, tears runnin down her cheeks. Crawford gave a perty speech.'

'How did Henry take it?'

'I aint sure I ever seen a happier man at his own hangin than Henry Jonson. Not a mote a fear in his eye. A man through and through. That was Henry Jonson. Went on bein a man too, long after they brung him down. I reckon it was fixin to bust right through the front of his trousers, jest kep on growin and growin. Standin right up like a revival tent.'

'I'll be,' the rider said, amazed. 'It's true then, what they say happens to a man gets hung.'

'Yessir, old Henry Jonson's Johnson done him proud. And if I aint mistaken I thought I saw behind them tears a little smile a pride on the missus' lips.'

They stared down into the mirror of water far below, two proud faces on a plate of sky. A third, equine, nudged in, flared nostrils black as empty eyes.

FIVE

They carried the furniture out of the hotel and loaded it into the ore wagons, Stovall, cigar migrating from mouth to hand and back, berating the miners for their clumsiness. Out came the armchairs, settees, tables, lamps, chucked from man to man up into the wagons. Leaning against the front of the building, the Duchess of Gurovoc in her heavy drapery seemed unhappy to be exposed to such bright light. Down from the upper story came all the mattresses, headboards, bureaus, toilet sets. Armoires yet to hold a lady's apparel. Fat rolled rugs. Looking glasses. Board by board, baluster by baluster, the great mahogany staircase was dismantled and hauled out and stacked in the wagons. Rodriguez carried the chandelier himself, climbing up into the wagon to secure it for travel. Then they stripped all the decorative elements from the outside of the building — lintels, cornice, the cast-iron lower facade — leaving the once grand Stratford all but a crude wooden shell of itself.

Most of the miners were already gone, left the day following the news that Chloride had won the railroad, those that stayed out of loyalty or lack of funds or simple indecision hiring themselves out as jobbers to the merchants closing up and moving on. Muldoon was gone, all his drugs and sundries stowed aboard the prairie schooner that brought him from the East, carrying him back none the richer. Blaine was gone, a few dusty tins of beans all that remained on the General Store's shelves. Henderson and Duncan and Miles, gone.

By sundown everything of value had been gutted from the Stratford, stacked into three ore wagons hitched together, ready for an early morning departure.

'Drink up,' Abigail said to the group of sweaty men just starting to relax along the bar. 'I'll be closing soon.'

'Aint Hobbs workin tonight?' one of them asked.

'No,' Abigail said.

Noticing Rodriguez crossing the street with an air of farewell about him, Abigail stepped outside to afford him a little privacy.

'I came to say goodbye, Mrs. Jonson,' he said.

He stood beside her, both of them facing the denuded hotel.

'Back to your wife and son?' Abigail asked.

Rodriguez, looking down, scuffed the ground idly with his shoe. They stared at the hotel. High above, a formation of Canada geese heading north flew by honking. 'Where will you go?' Rodriguez asked her.

'Somewhere with some women,' she said.

Rodriguez, eyes getting misty, turned and offered her his hand.

'Come to Bird and see the new Stratford,' he said. 'It will be even more beautiful.'

'I will,' Abigail promised, holding his hand.

It seemed he wanted to say more but didn't quite know how. He lingered there, looking at her face. Then with an awkward smile he released her hand and made his way back across the street.

'Out,' she said to the men, and as they left, grumbling, she gave them a full bottle, which seemed to make them happy.

She locked up and went out back, the eastern sky a sharp beryl blue softened here and there by graying stratus clouds touched with pink. Meandering roughly east she walked through the brush, pausing every so often to pick another flower, the bouquet in her hand growing bigger and more colorful as she went. Last week there had been poppies and marigolds, but already the desert was getting stingy of show, husbanding its resources for the scorching to come. She made do with an ensemble of daisies, feather dalea, chicory and peppergrass.

She walked on, every step she took sending some little creature scurrying for cover, lizard or kangaroo rat or silky pocket mice. Farther out bevies of quail pranced in file from bush to bush, jackrabbits zigzagged in great gangly bounds across the land.

A few green weeds were starting to sprout in the otherwise barren patch of ground two hundred yards east of town, a granite headstone and an unpainted wooden cross staking the claims of the dead.

Crawford had taken Andy's epitaph from Shakespeare:

Fear no more the heat o' the sun,
Nor the furious winter's rages;
Thou thy world task hast done,
Home art gone and ta'en thy wages.

Henry had written his own:

Here lies the bones of Henry Jonson
Who would have done things different.

Bending down, Abigail pulled the dry and shriveled blooms from the bottles, and splitting her bouquet in two, garnished the humble graves with fresh ones. Again she felt their presence, a silent yearning voice tuned to the same fever pitch, their faces in her memory melding into one, neither old nor young, leaving behind no clear impression.

A hawk's cry startled her from her thoughts. She stood up and watched it for some time, circling high in the darkening sky, then she made her way slowly back to the saloon.

It had not been dark long when an unfamiliar volley of knocks landed on the back door.

Abigail set the stereoscope on the sofa and, taking the lamp with her, went into the bedroom. She took the pistol from the top drawer of Henry's dresser, on which his personal effects still sat untouched, and pointing it at the door she asked in a threatening voice who was there.

'Just me, Mrs. Jonson,' the voice of Hobbs said.

Abigail returned the gun to the drawer and opened the door.

'Hate to bother you,' Hobbs said, 'but I'm shovin off in the mornin and figured I'd best collect my pay.'

'Come in,' Abigail said. She was happy to have a little company.

Hobbs thanked her and meekly stepped in. Pardoning herself, Abigail returned to the parlor to get the money.

'The Indians killed some settlers out Aguja Bend way,' Hobbs said from the other room. 'It'll be better if we all go together.'

'Yes,' Abigail said, opening the keepsake box.

From a stack of bills representing the now defunct account of the late Mr. Henry Albert Jonson, all moneys therein withdrawn on demand by the deceased's lawful wife, a balance of $162.50, less the sum of fifty dollars rent for the month of April, she took twenty dollars and returned to the bedroom.

'There you are,' she said, handing him the money. 'I appreciate your helping me as long as you did.'

'Shoot,' Hobbs said. 'A month stayin up all night jawin in a saloon. Best job I ever had.'

He glanced around the room, the only remnant of the play a scrap of blue-and-white paper from the proscenium lying in a corner. He stared at it nostalgically.

'I guess you know Kelly's leavin tomorrow too,' he said.

'So I heard,' she said.

'I think he's crazy goin back to that woman after what she put him through. First she's marryin someone else then she aint. Not that I'm anyone to talk.'

This was news to Abigail and she received it with more unhappiness than she knew she had any right to.

'What about you?' Hobbs said. 'What's your next stop?'

'Hm?' Abigail said, her mind elsewhere.

'I said, where you headed?'

'Oh,' she said. 'I don't know. Oliver Gidding wrote asking if I would be interested in joining the Overland Players. It seems he read the review and thinks I would add some notoriety to his troupe.'

'Hot damn,' Hobbs exclaimed. 'You're gonna be famous, and I'll say I knew her when she wadn't nothin but a whiskey peddler.'

Abigail smiled faintly.

'You better start packin,' Hobbs said, heading for the door. 'They're sayin it's Buddy's last run tomorrow.'

'Yes,' Abigail said. 'I'd better.'

'I'll sure miss you, Mrs. Jonson,' Hobbs said, holding out his hand. 'There aint another like you.'

'There are plenty like me,' Abigail said, shaking his hand.

She saw him out and bidding him farewell gently closed the door behind him. Back in the parlor she watched for a long time the ebbing gradations of light and shadow softly wavering on the wall opposite the sofa. Never had she known such silence, such dreadful calm, never understood so well the allure of the cloister.

Unread for many months she took her Bible down from the shelf and opened it to the beginning and read in language that rivaled Shakespeare's how God created the heavens and the earth and all the beasts of the fields, and how from a rib of noble man He created sin, which he called woman. She read a few chapters, then, as always, lost interest in the story and went to bed.

Deep in the night she thought she heard a knock on the door, but it was only the wind.

Crawford was the first to come knocking in the morning.

'You can't stay here alone, Mrs. Jonson,' he said through the locked door. 'I won't allow it.'

'Go away,' she said, and after a few more attempts to talk some sense into her he did.

Rodriguez came next, confessing that Crawford had asked him to.

'You should come,' he said. 'We are all waiting.'

'I'll leave when I decide to,' Abigail said.

Next came Hobbs.

'They're right,' he said. 'It don't make no sense. I thought we had a understandin you was takin the stage. Now come on, Buddy's out there waitin on you. We're all waitin. We caint go without you.'

'Then I guess you won't be going,' Abigail said. 'And

305

tell Crawford I'll shoot any man that tries to come in here and get me.'

Nearly an hour passed before Kelly came knocking. She was sitting in a chair facing the back door, the pistol in her lap.

'I came to tell you we're leaving,' he said. 'I wanted to say goodbye.'

'Goodbye,' she said.

'May I come in,' Kelly said after a while.

'You've said your goodbye,' Abigail said. 'What more is there to say?'

'I do have some things I'd like to say,' he said, 'and I'd rather not say them to a door.'

'There's a window over there,' Abigail said, and when nothing was forthcoming from without, she added, 'Why so talkative all of a sudden? You haven't so much as looked at me for a month.'

'I didn't know how to.'

Neither said anything more for a while.

Setting the pistol on the chair, Abigail got up and went to the door, and, knowing things would be easier if she didn't, she unlocked and opened it.

His beard was almost full again and he had about him the look of a man only recently recovered from some usually mortal ailment.

'May I come in?' he said, taking off his hat.

Peering past him, as if for signs of ambush, she stepped aside. He came in. She closed and locked the door.

'I see you mean business,' he said in reference to the pistol.

He glanced around the room then back at her and said: 'You can't stay here alone. How will you leave?'

'On Henry's horse. What do you care anyway? You're going back to your faithful little sweetheart.'

Kelly made no attempt to deny this, his whole being seeming to absorb guiltily the sting of these words. He nodded, glancing briefly at the floor, then said: 'I had some things to say but now that I'm here I seem to have forgotten what they were.'

Somewhere in the room a fly was buzzing. Kelly looked at her, his eyes filling with emotion. He looked aside. Then he stepped forward and took her into his arms and kissed her with the force of a desire too long withheld, his hands clutching her back so hard she had to struggle to break free.

She stepped back, leveling her eyes on his with a cold look of contempt.

'That might have meant something when you had something to lose.'

The tenderness quickly faded from Kelly's eyes.

'You don't know how I longed for you, Abigail,' he said, as if it were some fault of hers.

'Yes, I do.'

Kelly turned his head a little to the side but went on looking at her. The fly had stopped buzzing and now it was only the sound of Kelly's breathing that tempered the silence.

'Abigail,' he said in a sort of pleading whisper.

He took a step toward her.

'If you have nothing more to say,' Abigail said, 'I will kindly ask you to leave, Mr. Kelly.'

Kelly seemed not to hear. He took another step toward her.

'I said I would like you to leave,' Abigail repeated more sternly.

She glanced briefly toward the pistol, Kelly's eyes following hers. He was a good two feet closer than she was. Her eyes turned back to his hands, the one nearer the pistol holding his hat. She looked into his eyes. He smiled almost sadly.

'That won't be necessary,' he said.

He put his hat back on, gave her one last yearning look, then turned to leave.

'I was against the hanging,' he said, pausing at the door. 'I voted against it.'

'That was noble of you,' Abigail said.

Kelly touched the brim of his hat, said thank you, then left.

It was a long time after the sounds of men had ceased before she raised the pistol and fired it at the door. There was little in her life preceding to compare to the feeling of that explosion in her hands. As if suddenly the future had no horizon, the past reduced to a single drop of light shining through the door. She fired again. She fired until the hammer clicked on the empty chamber.

Carrying the pistol with her, she went into the saloon and walked out the front door. There was no one on Avon. No signs of life at all, even the dogs gone. She walked out into the middle of the street and stood there looking toward the Little Bullocks, half expecting to see the dust plume of the stagecoach still hanging in the air, but there was nothing there. It was hot, only a few clouds in the sky and those far away. She stood perfectly still, listening to the silence, savoring the thought that there wasn't a single man in Shakespeare. Not a man around for miles.